Love Works Wonders
A Novel

by

Charlotte M. Brame

Double 9
BOOKS

Love Works Wonders
A Novel
by Charlotte M. Brame

Copyright © 2024

All Rights reserved.

ISBN: 978-93-64280-36-5

Published by

DOUBLE 9 BOOKS

2/13-B, Ansari Road
Daryaganj, New Delhi – 110002
info@double9books.com
www.double9books.com
Tel. 011-40042856

ABOUT THE AUTHOR

Charlotte M. Brame was a prolific and diverse Victorian author who wrote novels, short stories, and serialized fiction throughout her career. Among her outstanding works is "A Fair Mystery: The Story of a Coquette," a riveting story that exemplifies Brame's ability to weave intricate plots and engaging characters. In "A Fair Mystery," Brame expertly builds a story centered on the intriguing character of the coquette, a beguiling yet elusive creature whose actions and reasons propel the plot along. Set against the backdrop of Victorian society, the novel delves into themes of love, betrayal, and atonement as the coquette navigates the complexities of romance and mystery. Brame's literary style is distinguished by vivid descriptions, emotional depth, and subtle character development. She vividly describes the vibrant world of the Victorian era, engaging readers in a compelling narrative of love, passion, and deception. "A Fair Mystery" demonstrates Brame's storytelling prowess and ability to attract audiences with intriguing narratives. With its sophisticated narrative twists, compelling characters, and wonderfully drawn landscapes, the novel is a timeless masterpiece that continues to captivate readers today.

CONTENTS

"O you, that have the charge of Love,
Keep him in rosy bondage bound,
As in the Fields of Bliss above
He sits with flowerets fetter'd round;
Loose not a tie that round him clings,
Nor ever let him use his wings;
For even an hour, a minute's flight
Will rob the plumes of half their light."

Moore.

His grand old face flushed, and his stately head was bowed, as though some of the memories that swept over him were not free from shame; and then, with a little gesture of his white hand, on which shone a large diamond ring, he said:

"There is no need for me to tell you, Miss Hastings, that the Darrells are one of the oldest families in England—ancient, honorable, and, I must confess, proud—very proud. My father, the late Sir Hildebert Darrell, was, I should say, one of the proudest and most reserved of men. He had but two children, myself and a daughter twelve years younger—my sister Felicia. I was educated abroad. It was one of my father's fancies that I should see many lands, that I should study men and women before settling down to my right position in the world; so that I knew but little of my sister Felicia. She was a child when I left home—the tragedy of her life had happened before I returned."

Again a great rush of color came over the pale, aristocratic face.

"I must apologize, Miss Hastings, for troubling you with these details, but unless you understand them you will not understand my niece. I cannot tell you how it happened, but it did so happen that while I was away my sister disgraced herself; she left home with a French artist, whom Sir Hildebert had engaged to renovate some choice and costly pictures at Darrell Court. How it came about I cannot say—perhaps there were excuses for her. She may have found home very dull—my father was harsh and cold, and her mother was dead. It may be that when the young artist told her of warm love in sunny lands she was tempted, poor child, to leave the paternal roof.

"My father's wrath was terrible; he pursued Julian L'Estrange with unrelenting fury. I believe the man would have been a successful artist but for my father, who had vowed to ruin him, and who never rested until he had done so—until he had reduced him to direst poverty—and then my sister appealed for help, and my father refused to grant it. He would not allow her name to be mentioned among us; her portrait was destroyed; everything belonging to her was sent away from Darrell Court.

"When I returned—in an interview that I shall never forget—my father threatened me not only with disinheritance, but with his curse, if I made any attempt to hold the least communication with my sister. I do not know that I should have obeyed him if I could have found her, but I did not even know what part of the world she was in. She died, poor girl, and I have no doubt that her death was greatly hastened by privation. My father told me of her death, also that she had left one daughter; he did more—he wrote to Julian

L'Estrange, and offered to adopt his daughter on the one condition that he would consent never to see her or hold the least communication with her.

"The reply was, as you may imagine, a firm refusal and a fierce denunciation. In the same letter came a note, written in a large, childish hand:

"'I love my papa, and I do not love you. I will not come to live with you. You are a cruel man, and you helped to kill my dear mamma.'

"It was a characteristic little note, and was signed 'Pauline L'Estrange.' My father's anger on receiving it was very great. I confess that I was more amused than angry.

"My father, Miss Hastings, lived to a good old age. I was not a young man when I succeeded him. He left me all his property. You must understand the Darrell and Audleigh Royal estates are not entailed. He made no mention in his will of the only grandchild he had; but, after I had arranged all my affairs, I resolved to find her. For ten years I have been doing all I could—sending to France, Italy, Spain, and every country where I thought it possible the artist might have sought refuge.

"Three months since I received a letter from him, written on his death-bed, asking me to do something for Pauline, who had grown up into a beautiful girl of seventeen. I found then that he had been living for some years in the Rue d'Orme, Paris. I buried him, brought his daughter to England, and made arrangements whereby she should assume the name of Darrell. But I little knew what a task I had undertaken. Pauline ought to be my heiress, Miss Hastings. She ought to succeed me at Darrell Court. I have no other relatives. But—well, I will not despair; you will see what can be done with her."

"What are her deficiencies?" asked Miss Hastings.

Sir Oswald raised his white hands with a gesture of despair.

"I will tell you briefly. She has lived among artists. She does not seem to have ever known any of her own sex. She is—I am sorry to use the word—a perfect Bohemian. Whether she can be transformed into anything faintly resembling a lady, I cannot tell. Will you undertake the task, Miss Hastings?"

She looked very thoughtful for some minutes, and then answered:

"I will do my best, Sir Oswald."

"I thank you very much. You must permit me to name liberal terms, for your task will be no light one."

And the interview ended, to their mutual satisfaction.

CHAPTER II
"DARRELL COURT IS A PRISON TO ME!"

It was a beautiful May day, bright with fresh spring loveliness. The leaves were springing fresh and green from the trees; the hedges were all abloom with pink hawthorn; the chestnut trees were all in flower; the gold of the laburnum, the purple of the lilac, the white of the fair acacia trees, and the delicate green of the stately elms and limes gave a beautiful variety of color. The grass was dotted with a hundred wild-flowers; great clusters of yellow buttercups looked in the distance like the upspreading of a sea of gold; the violets perfumed the air, the bluebells stirred in the sweet spring breeze, and the birds sang out loudly and jubilantly.

If one spot looked more lovely than another on this bright May day, it was Darrell Court, for it stood where the sun shone brightest, in one of the most romantic and picturesque nooks of England—the part of Woodshire bordering on the sea.

The mansion and estates stood on gently rising ground; a chain of purple hills stretched away into the far distance; then came the pretty town of Audleigh Royal, the Audleigh Woods, and the broad, deep river Darte. The bank of the river formed the boundary of the Darrell estates, a rich and magnificent heritage, wherein every beauty of meadow and wood seemed to meet. The park was rich in its stately trees and herds of deer; and not far from the house was a fir-wood—an aromatic, odorous fir-wood, which led to the very shores of the smiling southern sea.

By night and by day the grand music of nature was heard in perfection at Darrell Court. Sometimes it was the roll of the wind across the hills, or the beat of angry waves on the shore, or the wild melody of the storm among the pine trees, or the full chorus of a thousand feathered songsters. The court itself was one of the most picturesque of mansions. It did not belong to any one order or style of architecture—there was nothing stiff or formal about it—but it looked in that bright May sunshine a noble edifice, with its square towers covered with clinging ivy, gray turrets, and large arched windows.

Did the sun ever shine upon such a combination of colors? The spray of the fountains glittered in the air, the numerous balconies were filled with flowers; wherever it was possible for a flower to take root, one had been placed to grow—purple wistarias, sad, solemn passion-flowers, roses of every hue. The star-like jessamine and scarlet creepers gave to the walls of the old mansion a vivid glow of color; gold and purple enriched the gardens, heavy white lilies breathed faintest perfume. The spot looked a very Eden.

The grand front entrance consisted of a large gothic porch, which was reached by a broad flight of steps, adorned with white marble vases filled with flowers; the first terrace was immediately below, and terrace led from terrace down to the grand old gardens, where sweetest blossoms grew.

There was an old-world air about the place—something patrician, quiet, reserved. It was no vulgar haunt for vulgar crowds; it was not a show place; and the master of it, Sir Oswald Darrell, as he stood upon the terrace, looked in keeping with the surroundings.

There was a *distingue* air about Sir Oswald, an old-fashioned courtly dignity, which never for one moment left him. He was thoroughly well bred; he had not two sets of manners—one for the world, and one for private life; he was always the same, measured in speech, noble in his grave condescension. No man ever more thoroughly deserved the name of aristocrat; he was delicate and fastidious, with profound and deeply-rooted dislike for all that was ill-bred, vulgar, or mean.

Even in his dress Sir Oswald was remarkable; the superfine white linen, the diamond studs and sleeve links, the rare jewels that gleamed on his fingers—all struck the attention; and, as he took from his pocket a richly engraved golden snuff-box and tapped it with the ends of his delicate white fingers, there stood revealed a thorough aristocrat—the ideal of an English patrician gentleman.

Sir Oswald walked round the stately terraces and gardens.

"I do not see her," he said to himself; "yet most certainly Frampton told me she was here."

Then, with his gold-headed cane in hand, Sir Oswald descended to the gardens. He was evidently in search of some one. Meeting one of the gardeners, who stood, hat in hand, as he passed by, Sir Oswald asked:

"Have you seen Miss Darrell in the gardens?"

"I saw Miss Darrell in the fernery some five minutes since, Sir Oswald," was the reply.

Sir Oswald drew from his pocket a very fine white handkerchief and diffused an agreeable odor of millefleurs around him; the gardener had been near the stables, and Sir Oswald was fastidious.

A short walk brought him to the fernery, an exquisite combination of rock and rustic work, arched by a dainty green roof, and made musical by the ripple of a little waterfall. Sir Oswald looked in cautiously, evidently rather in dread of what he might find there; then his eyes fell upon something, and he said:

"Pauline, are you there?"

A rich, clear, musical voice answered:

"Yes, I am here, uncle."

"My dear," continued Sir Oswald, half timidly, not advancing a step farther into the grotto, "may I ask what you are doing?"

"Certainly, uncle," was the cheerful reply; "you may ask by all means. The difficulty is to answer; for I am really doing nothing, and I do not know how to describe 'nothing.'"

"Why did you come hither?" he asked.

"To dream," replied the musical voice. "I think the sound of falling water is the sweetest music in the world. I came here to enjoy it, and to dream over it."

Sir Oswald looked very uncomfortable.

"Considering, Pauline, how much you have been neglected, do you not think you might spend your time more profitably—in educating yourself, for example?"

"This is educating myself. I am teaching myself beautiful thoughts, and nature just now is my singing mistress." And then the speaker's voice suddenly changed, and a ring of passion came into it. "Who says that I have been neglected? When you say that, you speak ill of my dear dead father, and no one shall do that in my presence. You speak slander, and slander ill becomes an English gentleman. If I was neglected when my father was alive, I wish to goodness such neglect were my portion now!"

Sir Oswald shrugged his shoulders.

"Each one to his or her taste, Pauline. With very little more of such neglect you would have been a——"

He paused; perhaps some instinct of prudence warned him.

"A what?" she demanded, scornfully. "Pray finish the sentence, Sir Oswald."

"My dear, you are too impulsive, too hasty. You want more quietness of manner, more dignity."

Her voice deepened in its tones as she asked:

"I should have been a what, Sir Oswald? I never begin a sentence and leave it half finished. You surely are not afraid to finish it?"

"No, my dear," was the calm reply; "there never yet was a Darrell afraid of anything on earth. If you particularly wish me to do so, I will finish what I was about to say. You would have been a confirmed Bohemian, and nothing could have made you a lady."

"I love what you call Bohemians, and I detest what you call ladies, Sir Oswald," was the angry retort.

"Most probably; but then, you see, Pauline, the ladies of the house of Darrell have always been ladies—high-bred, elegant women. I doubt if any of them ever knew what the word 'Bohemian' meant."

She laughed a little scornful laugh, which yet was sweet and clear as the sound of silver bells.

"I had almost forgotten," said Sir Oswald. "I came to speak to you about something, Pauline; will you come into the house with me?"

They walked on together in silence for some minutes, and then Sir Oswald began:

"I went to London, as you know, last week, Pauline, and my errand was on your behalf."

She raised her eyebrows, but did not deign to ask any questions.

"I have engaged a lady to live with us here at Darrell Court, whose duties will be to finish your education, or, rather, I may truthfully say, to begin it, to train you in the habits of refined society, to—to—make you presentable, in fact, Pauline, which I am sorry, really sorry to say, you are not at present."

She made him a low bow—a bow full of defiance and rebellion.

"I am indeed indebted to you, Sir Oswald."

"No trifling," said the stately baronet, "no sarcasm, Pauline, but listen to me! You are not without sense or reason—pray attend. Look around you," he continued; "remember that the broad fair lands of Darrell Court form one of the grandest domains in England. It is an inheritance almost royal in its extent and magnificence. Whoso reigns here is king or queen of half a county, is looked up to, respected, honored, admired, and imitated. The owner of Darrell Court is a power even in this powerful land of ours; men and women look up to such a one for guidance and example. Judge then what the owner of the inheritance should be."

The baronet's grand old face was flushed with emotion.

"He must be pure, or he would make immorality the fashion; honorable, because men will take their notions of honor from him; just, that justice may abound; upright, stainless. You see all that, Pauline?"

"Yes," she assented, quickly.

"No men have so much to answer for," continued Sir Oswald, "as the great ones of the land—men in whose hands power is vested—men to whom others look for example, on whose lives other lives are modeled—men who, as it were, carry the minds, if not the souls, of their fellow men in the hollows of their hands."

Pauline looked more impressed, and insensibly drew nearer to him.

"Such men, I thank Heaven," he said, standing bareheaded as he uttered the words, "have the Darrells been—loyal, upright, honest, honorable, of stainless repute, of stainless life, fitted to rule their fellow men—grand men, sprung from a grand old race. And at times women have reigned here—women whose names have lived in the annals of the land—who have been as shining lights from the purity, the refinement, the grandeur of their lives."

He spoke with a passion of eloquence not lost on the girl by his side.

"I," he continued, humbly, "am one of the least worthy of my race. I have done nothing for its advancement; but at the same time I have done nothing to disgrace it. I have carried on the honors passively. The time is coming when Darrell Court must pass into other hands. Now, Pauline, you have heard, you know what the ruler of Darrell Court should be. Tell me, are you fitted to take your place here?"

"I am very young," she murmured.

"It is not a question of youth. Dame Sibella Darrell reigned here when she was only eighteen; and the sons she trained to succeed her were among the greatest statesmen England has ever known. She improved and enlarged the property; she died, after living here sixty years, beloved, honored, and revered. It is not a question of age."

"I am a Darrell!" said the girl, proudly.

"Yes, you have the face and figure of a Darrell; you bear the name, too; but you have not the grace and manner of a Darrell."

"Those are mere outward matters of polish and veneer," she said, impatiently.

"Nay, not so. You would not think it right to see an unformed, untrained, uneducated, ignorant girl at the head of such a house as this. What did you do yesterday? A maid displeased you. You boxed her ears. Just imagine it. Such a proceeding on the part of the mistress of Darrell Court would fill one with horror."

A slight smile rippled over the full crimson lips.

"Queen Elizabeth boxed her courtiers' ears," said the girl, "and it seemed right to her."

"A queen, Pauline, is hedged in by her own royalty; she may do what she will. The very fact that you are capable of defending an action so violent, so unlady-like, so opposed to all one's ideas of feminine delicacy, proves that you are unfit for the position you ought to occupy."

"I am honest, at least. I make no pretensions to be what I am not."

"So is my butler honest, but that does not fit him to be master of Darrell Court. Honesty is but one quality—a good one, sturdy and strong; it requires not one, but many qualities to hold such a position as I would fain have you occupy."

Miss Darrell's patience was evidently at an end.

"And the upshot of all this, Sir Oswald, is— —"

"Exactly so—that I am anxious to give you every chance in my power— that I have found an estimable, refined, elegant woman, who will devote her time and talents to train you and fit you for society."

A low, musical laugh broke from the perfect lips.

"Have you any idea," she asked, "what I shall be like when I am trained?"

"Like a lady, I trust—a well-bred lady. I can imagine nothing more beautiful than that."

"When is she coming, this model of yours, Sir Oswald?"

"Nay, your model, niece, not mine. She is here now, and I wish to introduce her to you. I should like you, if possible," he concluded, meekly, "to make a favorable impression on her."

There was another impatient murmur.

"I wish you to understand, Pauline," he resumed, after a short pause, "that I shall expect you to render the most implicit obedience to Miss Hastings—to follow whatever rules she may lay down for you, to attend to your studies as she directs them, to pay the greatest heed to all her corrections, to copy her style, to imitate her manners, to— —"

"I hate her!" was the impetuous outburst. "I would sooner be a beggar all my life than submit to such restraint."

"Very well," returned Sir Oswald, calmly. "I know that arguing with you is time lost. The choice lies with yourself. If you decide to do as I wish— to study to become a lady in the truest sense of the word—if you will fit yourself for the position, you shall be heiress of Darrell Court; if not—if you persist in your present unlady-like, unrefined, Bohemian manner, I shall leave the whole property to some one else. I tell you the plain truth without any disguise."

"I do not want Darrell Court!" she cried, passionately; "it is a prison to me!"

"I excuse you," rejoined Sir Oswald, coldly; "you are excited, and so not answerable for what you say."

"Uncle," said the girl, "do you see that beautiful singing bird there, giving voice to such glorious melody? Do you think you could catch it and put it in a cage?"

"I have no doubt that I could," replied Sir Oswald.

"But, if you did," she persisted; "even suppose you could make it forget its own wild melodies, could you teach it to sing formally by note and at your will?"

"I have never supposed anything of the kind," said Sir Oswald. "You are possessed of far too much of that kind of nonsense. The young ladies of the present day—properly educated girls—do not talk in that way."

"I can easily believe it," she returned, bitterly.

"Miss Hastings is in the library," said Sir Oswald, as they entered the house. "I hope to see you receive her kindly. Put away that frown, Pauline, and smile if you can. Remember, it is characteristic of the Darrells to be gracious to strangers."

With these words Sir Oswald opened the library door, and holding his niece's hand, entered the room. Miss Hastings rose to receive them. He led Pauline to her, and in the kindest manner possible introduced them to each other.

"I will leave you together," he said. "Pauline will show you your rooms, Miss Hastings; and I hope that you will soon feel happy, and quite at home with us."

Sir Oswald quitted the library, leaving the two ladies looking in silence at each other.

CHAPTER III
"YOUR GOOD SOCIETY IS ALL DECEIT"

Miss Hastings had been prepared to see a hoiden, an awkward, unfledged schoolgirl, one who, never having seen much of good society, had none of the little graces and charms that distinguish young ladies. She had expected to see a tall, gaunt girl, with red hands, and a general air of not knowing what to do with herself—that was the idea she had formed. She gazed in wonder at the reality—a magnificent figure—a girl whose grand, pale, statuesque beauty was something that could never be forgotten. There was nothing of the boarding-school young lady about her; no acquired graces. She was simply magnificent—no other word could describe her. Miss Hastings, as she looked at her, thought involuntarily of the graceful lines, the beautiful curves, the grand, free grace of the world-renowned Diana of the Louvre; there was the same arched, graceful neck, the same royal symmetry, the same harmony of outline.

In one of the most celebrated art galleries of Rome Miss Hastings remembered to have seen a superb bust of Juno; as she looked at her new pupil, she could almost fancy that its head had been modeled from hers. Pauline's head was royal in its queenly contour; the brow low, white, and rounded at the temples; the hair, waving in lines of inexpressible beauty, was loosely gathered together and fastened behind with a gleaming silver arrow. The eyes were perhaps the most wonderful feature in that wonderful face; they were dark as night itself, somewhat in hue like a purple heartsease, rich, soft, dreamy, yet at times all fire, all brightness, filled with passion more intense than any words, and shining then with a strange half-golden light. The brows were straight, dark, and beautiful; the lips crimson, full, and exquisitely shaped; the mouth looked like one that could persuade or contemn—that could express tenderness or scorn, love or pride, with the slightest play of the lips.

Every attitude the girl assumed was full of unconscious grace. She did not appear to be in the least conscious of her wonderful beauty. She had walked to the window, and stood leaning carelessly against the frame, one beautiful arm thrown above her head, as though she were weary, and would fain rest—an attitude that could not have been surpassed had she studied it for years.

"You are not at all what I expected to see," said Miss Hastings, at last. "You are, indeed, so different that I am taken by surprise."

"Am I better or worse than you had imagined me?" she asked, with careless scorn.

"You are different—better, perhaps, in some things. You are taller. You are so tall that it will be difficult to remember you are a pupil."

"The Darrells are a tall race," she said, quietly. "Miss Hastings, what have you come here to teach me?"

The elder lady rose from her seat and looked lovingly into the face of the girl; she placed her hand caressingly on the slender shoulders.

"I know what I should like to teach you, Miss Darrell, if you will let me. I should like to teach you your duty to Heaven, your fellow-creatures, and yourself."

"That would be dry learning, I fear," she returned. "What does my uncle wish me to learn?"

"To be in all respects a perfectly refined, graceful lady."

Her face flushed with a great crimson wave that rose to the white brow and the delicate shell-like ears.

"I shall never be that," she cried, passionately. "I may just as well give up all hopes of Darrell Court. I have seen some ladies since I have been here. I could not be like them. They seem to speak by rule; they all say the same kind of things, with the same smiles, in the same tone of voice; they follow each other like sheep; they seem frightened to advance an opinion of their own, or even give utterance to an original thought. They look upon me as something horrible, because I dare to say what I think, and have read every book I could find."

"It is not always best to put our thoughts in speech; and the chances are, Miss Darrell, that, if you have read every book you could find, you have read many that would have been better left alone. You are giving a very one-sided, prejudiced view after all."

She raised her beautiful head with a gesture of superb disdain.

"There is the same difference between them and myself as between a mechanical singing bird made to sing three tunes and a wild, sweet bird of the woods. I like my own self best."

"There is not the least doubt of that," observed Miss Hastings, with a smile; "but the question is not so much what we like ourselves as what others like in us. However, we will discuss that at another time, Miss Darrell."

"Has my uncle told you that if I please him—if I can be molded into the right form—I am to be heiress of Darrell Court?" she asked, quickly.

"Yes; and now that I have seen you I am persuaded that you can be anything you wish."

"Do you think, then, that I am clever?" she asked, eagerly.

"I should imagine so," replied Miss Hastings. "Pauline—I need not call you Miss Darrell—I hope we shall be friends; I trust we shall be happy together."

"It is not very likely," she said, slowly, "that I can like you, Miss Hastings."

"Why not?" asked the governess, astonished at her frankness.

"Because you are to correct me; continual correction will be a great annoyance, and will prevent my really liking you."

Miss Hastings looked astounded.

"That may be, Pauline," she said; "but do you know that it is not polite of you to say so? In good society one does not tell such unpleasant truths."

"That is just it," was the eager retort; "that is why I do not like good society, and shall never be fit for it. I am truthful by nature. In my father's house and among his friends there was never any need to conceal the truth; we always spoke it frankly. If we did not like each other, we said so. But here, it seems to me, the first lesson learned to fit one for society is to speak falsely."

"Not so, Pauline; but, when the truth is likely to hurt another's feelings, to wound susceptibility or pride, why speak it, unless it is called for?"

Pauline moved her white arms with a superb gesture of scorn.

"I would rather any day hear the truth and have my mind hurt," she said, energetically, "than feel that people were smiling at me and deceiving me. Lady Hampton visits Sir Oswald. I do not like her, and she does not like me; but she always asks Sir Oswald how his 'dear niece' is, and she calls me a 'sweet creature—original, but very sweet' You can see for yourself, Miss Hastings, that I am not that."

"Indeed, you are not sweet," returned the governess, smiling; "but, Pauline, you are a mimic, and mimicry is a dangerous gift."

She had imitated Lady Hampton's languid tones and affected accent to perfection.

"Sir Oswald bows and smiles all the time Lady Hampton is talking to him; he stands first upon one foot, and then upon the other. You would think, to listen to him, that he was so charmed with her ladyship that he could not exist out of her presence. Yet I have seen him quite delighted at her departure, and twice I heard him say 'Thank Heaven'—it was for the relief. Your good society is all deceit, Miss Hastings."

"I will not have you say that, Pauline. Amiability, and the desire always to be kind and considerate, may carry one to extremes at times; but I am inclined to prefer the amiability that spares to the truth that wounds."

"I am not," was the blunt rejoinder. "Will you come to your rooms, Miss Hastings? Sir Oswald has ordered a suite to be prepared entirely for our use. I have three rooms, you have four; and there is a study that we can use together."

They went through the broad stately corridors, where the warm sun shone in at the windows, and the flowers breathed sweetest perfume. The rooms that had been prepared for them were bright and pleasant with a beautiful view from the windows, well furnished, and supplied with every comfort. A sigh came from Miss Hastings as she gazed—it was all so pleasant. But it seemed very doubtful to her whether she would remain or not—very doubtful whether she would be able to make what Sir Oswald desired out of that frank, free-spoken girl, who had not one conventional idea.

"Sir Oswald is very kind," she said, at length, looking around her; "these rooms are exceedingly nice."

"They are nice," said Pauline; "but I was happier with my father in the Rue d'Orme. Ah me, what liberty we had there! In this stately life I feel as though I were bound with cords, or shackled with chains—as though I longed to stretch out my arms and fly away."

Again Miss Hastings sighed, for it seemed to her that the time of her residence at Darrell Court would in all probability be very short.

CHAPTER IV
"YOU ARE GOING TO SPOIL MY LIFE"

Two days had passed since Miss Hastings' arrival. On a beautiful morning, when the sun was shining and the birds were singing in the trees, she sat in the study, with an expression of deepest anxiety, of deepest thought on her face. Pauline, with a smile on her lips, sat opposite to her, and there was profound silence. Miss Darrell was the first to break it.

"Well," she asked, laughingly, "what is your verdict, Miss Hastings?"

The elder lady looked up with a long, deep-drawn sigh.

"I have never been so completely puzzled in all my life," she replied. "My dear Pauline, you are the strangest mixture of ignorance and knowledge that I have ever met. You know a great deal, but it is all of the wrong kind; you ought to unlearn all that you have learned."

"You admit then that I know something."

"Yes; but it would be almost better, perhaps, if you did not. I will tell you how I feel, Pauline. I know nothing of building, but I feel as though I had been placed before a heap of marble, porphyry, and granite, of wood, glass, and iron, and then told from those materials to shape a magnificent palace. I am at a loss what to do."

Miss Darrell laughed with the glee of a child. Her governess, repressing her surprise, continued:

"You know more in some respects than most educated women; in other and equally essential matters you know less than a child. You speak French fluently, perfectly; you have read a large number of books in the French language—good, bad, and indifferent, it appears to me; yet you have no more idea of French grammar or of the idiom or construction of the language than a child."

"That, indeed, I have not; I consider grammar the most stupid of all human inventions."

Miss Hastings offered no comment.

"Again," she continued, "you speak good English, but your spelling is bad, and your writing worse. You are better acquainted with English literature than I am—that is, you have read more. You have read indiscriminately; even the titles of some of the books you have read are not admissible."

The dark eyes flashed, and the pale, grand face was stirred as though by some sudden emotion.

"There was a large library in the house where we lived," she explained, hurriedly, "and I read every book in it. I read from early morning until late at night, and sometimes from night until morning; there was no one to tell me what was right and what was wrong, Miss Hastings."

"Then," continued the governess, "you have written a spirited poem on Anne Boleyn, but you know nothing of English history—neither the dates nor the incidents of a single reign. You have written the half of a story, the scene of which is laid in the tropics, yet of geography you have not the faintest notion. Of matters such as every girl has some idea of—of biography, of botany, of astronomy—you have not even a glimmer. The chances are, that if you engaged in conversation with any sensible person, you would equally astonish, first by the clever things you would utter, and then by the utter ignorance you would display."

"I cannot be flattered, Miss Hastings," Pauline put in, "because you humiliate me; nor can I be humiliated, because you flatter me."

But Miss Hastings pursued her criticisms steadily.

"You have not the slightest knowledge of arithmetic. As for knowledge of a higher class, you have none. You are dreadfully deficient. You say that you have read Auguste Comte, but you do not know the answer to the first question in your church catechism. Your education requires beginning all over again. You have never had any settled plan of study, I should imagine."

"No. I learned drawing from Jules Lacroix. Talk of talent, Miss Hastings. You should have known him—he was the handsomest artist I ever saw. There was something so picturesque about him."

"Doubtless," was the dry response; "but I think 'picturesque' is not the word to use in such a case. Music, I presume, you taught yourself?"

The girl's whole face brightened—her manner changed.

"Yes, I taught myself; poor papa could not afford to pay for my lessons. Shall I play to you, Miss Hastings?"

There was a piano in the study, a beautiful and valuable instrument, which Sir Oswald had ordered for his niece.

"I shall be much pleased to hear you," said Miss Hastings.

Pauline Darrell rose and went to the piano. Her face then was as the face of one inspired. She sat down and played a few chords, full, beautiful, and harmonious.

"I will sing to you," she said. "We often went to the opera—papa, Jules, Louis, and myself. I used to sing everything I heard. This is from 'Il Puritani.'"

And she sang one of the most beautiful solos in the opera.

Her voice was magnificent, full, ringing, vibrating with passion—a voice that, like her face, could hardly be forgotten; but she played and sang entirely after a fashion of her own.

"Now, Miss Hastings," she said, "I will imitate Adelina Patti."

Face, voice, manner, all changed; she began one of the far-famed prima-donna's most admired songs, and Miss Hastings owned to herself that if she had closed her eyes she might have believed Madame Patti present.

"This is a la Christine Nilsson," continued Pauline; and again the imitation was brilliant and perfect.

The magnificent voice did not seem to tire, though she sang song after song, and imitated in the most marvelous manner some of the grandest singers of the day. Miss Hasting left her seat and went up to her.

"You have a splendid voice, my dear, and great musical genius. Now tell me, do you know a single note of music?"

"Not one," was the quick reply.

"You know nothing of the keys, time, or anything else?"

"Why should I trouble myself when I could play without learning anything of the kind?"

"But that kind of playing, Pauline, although it is very clever, would not do for educated people."

"Is it not good enough for them?" she asked, serenely.

"No; one cannot help admiring it, but any educated person hearing you would detect directly that you did not know your notes."

"Would they think much less of me on that account?" she asked, with the same serenity.

"Yes; every one would think it sad to see so much talent wasted. You must begin to study hard; you must learn to play by note, not by ear, and then all will be well. You love music, Pauline?"

How the beautiful face glowed and the dark eyes shone.

"I love it," she said, "because I can put my whole soul into it—there is room for one's soul in it. You will be shocked, I know, but that is why I liked Comte's theories—because they filled my mind, and gave me so much to think of."

"Were I in your place I should try to forget them, Pauline."

"You should have seen Sir Oswald's face when I told him I had read Comte and Darwin. He positively groaned aloud."

And she laughed as she remembered his misery.

"I feel very much inclined to groan myself," said Miss Hastings. "You shall have theories, or facts, higher, more beautiful, nobler, grander far than any Comte ever dreamed. And now we must begin to work in real earnest."

But Pauline Darrell did not move; her dark eyes were shadowed, her beautiful face grew sullen and determined.

"You are going to spoil my life," she said. "Hitherto it has been a glorious life—free, gladsome, and bright; now you are going to parcel it out. There will be no more sunshiny hours; you are going to reduce me to a kind of machine, to cut off all my beautiful dreams, my lofty thoughts. You want to make me a formal, precise young lady, who will laugh, speak, and think by rule."

"I want to make you a sensible woman, my dear Pauline," corrected Miss Hastings, gravely.

"Who is the better or the happier for being so sensible?" demanded Pauline.

She paused for a few minutes, and then she added, suddenly:

"Darrell Court and all the wealth of the Darrells are not worth it, Miss Hastings."

"Not worth what, Pauline?"

"Not worth the price I must pay."

"What is the price?" asked Miss Hastings, calmly.

"My independence, my freedom of action and thought, my liberty of speech."

"Do you seriously value these more highly than all that Sir Oswald could leave you?"

"I do—a thousand times more highly," she replied.

Miss Hastings was silent for some few minutes, and then said:

"We must do our best; suppose we make a compromise? I will give you all the liberty that I honestly can, in every way, and you shall give your attention to the studies I propose. I will make your task as easy as I can for you. Darrell Court is worth a struggle."

"Yes," was the half-reluctant reply, "it is worth a struggle, and I will make it."

But there was not much hope in the heart of the governess when she commenced her task.

CHAPTER V
PAULINE'S GOOD POINTS

How often Sir Oswald's simile of the untrained, unpruned, uncultivated vine returned to the mind of Miss Hastings! Pauline Darrell was by nature a genius, a girl of magnificent intellect, a grand, noble, generous being all untrained. She had in her capabilities of the greatest kind—she could be either the very empress of wickedness or angelic. She was gloriously endowed, but it was impossible to tell how she would develop; there was no moderation in her, she acted always from impulse, and her impulses were quick, warm, and irresistible. If she had been an actress, she would surely have been the very queen of the stage. Her faults were like her virtues, all grand ones. There was nothing trivial, nothing mean, nothing ungenerous about her. She was of a nature likely to be led to the highest criminality or the highest virtue; there could be no medium of mediocre virtue for her. She was full of character, charming even in her willfulness, but utterly devoid of all small affectations. There was in her the making of a magnificent woman, a great heroine; but nothing could have brought her to the level of commonplace people. Her character was almost a terrible one in view of the responsibilities attached to it.

Grand, daring, original, Pauline was all force, all fire, all passion. Whatever she loved, she loved with an intensity almost terrible to witness. There was also no "middle way" in her dislikes—she hated with a fury of hate. She had little patience, little toleration; one of her greatest delights consisted in ruthlessly tearing away the social vail which most people loved to wear. There were times when her grand, pale, passionate beauty seemed to darken and to deepen, and one felt instinctively that it was in her to be cruel even to fierceness; and again, when her heart was touched and her face softened, one imagined that she might be somewhat akin to the angels.

What was to become of such a nature? What was to develop it— what was to train it? If from her infancy Pauline had been under wise and tender guidance, if some mind that she felt to be superior to her own had influenced her, the certainty is that she would have grown up into a thoughtful, intellectual, talented woman, one whose influence would have been paramount for good, one to whom men would have looked for guidance almost unconsciously to themselves.

But her training had been terribly defective. No one had ever controlled her. She had been mistress of her father's house and queen of his little coterie; with her quiet, unerring judgment, she had made her own estimate of the strength, the mind, the intellect of each one with whom she came in contact, and the result was always favorable to herself—she saw no one superior to herself. Then the society in which her father had delighted was the worst possible for her; she reigned supreme over them all—clever, gifted artists, good-natured Bohemians, who admired and applauded her, who praised every word that fell from her lips, who honestly believed her to be one of the marvels of the world, who told her continually that she was one of the most beautiful, most talented, most charming of mortals, who applauded every daring sentiment instead of telling her plainly that what was not orthodox was seldom right—honest Bohemians, who looked upon the child as a wonder, and puzzled themselves to think what destiny was high enough for her—men whose artistic tastes were gratified by the sight of her magnificent loveliness, who had for her the deepest, truest, and highest respect, who never in her presence uttered a syllable that they would not have uttered in the presence of a child—good-natured Bohemians, who sometimes had money and sometimes had none, who were always willing to share their last *sou* with others more needy than themselves, who wore shabby, threadbare coats, but who knew how to respect the pure presence of a pure girl.

Pauline had received a kind of education. Her father's friends discussed everything—art, science, politics, and literature—in her presence; they discussed the wildest stories, they indulged in unbounded fun and satire, they were of the wittiest even as they were of the cleverest of men. They ridiculed unmercifully what they were pleased to call the "regulations of polite society;" they enjoyed unvarnished truth—as a rule, the more disagreeable the truth the more they delighted in telling it. They scorned all etiquette, they pursued all dandies and belles with terrible sarcasm; they believed in every wild or impossible theory that had ever been started; in fact, though honest as the day, honorable, and true, they were about the worst associates a young girl could have had to fit her for the world. The life she led among them had been one long romance, of which she had been queen.

The house in the Rue d'Orme had once been a grand mansion; it was filled with quaint carvings, old tapestry, and the relics of a by-gone generation. The rooms were large—most of them had been turned into studios. Some of the finest of modern pictures came from the house in the

Rue d'Orme, although, as a rule, the students who worked there were not wealthy.

It was almost amusing to see how this delicate young girl ruled over such society. By one word she commanded these great, generous, unworldly men—with one little white finger upraised she could beckon them at her will; they had a hundred pet names for her—they thought no queen or empress fit to be compared with their old comrade's daughter. She was to be excused if constant flattery and homage had made her believe that she was in some way superior to the rest of the world.

When the great change came—when she left the Rue d'Orme for Darrell Court—it was a terrible blow to Pauline to find all this superiority vanish into thin air. In place of admiration and flattery, she heard nothing but reproach and correction. She was given to understand that she was hardly presentable in polite society—she, who had ruled like a queen over scholars and artists! Instead of laughter and applause, grim silence followed her remarks. She read in the faces of those around her that she was not as they were—not of their world. Her whole soul turned longingly to the beautiful free Bohemian world she had left. The crowning blow of all was when, after studying her carefully for some time, Sir Oswald told her that he feared her manners were against her—that neither in style nor in education was she fitted to be mistress of Darrell Court. She had submitted passively to the change in her name; she was proud of being a Darrell—she was proud of the grand old race from which she had sprung. But, when Sir Oswald had uttered that last speech, she flamed out in fierce, violent passion, which showed him she had at least the true Darrell spirit.

There were points in her favor, he admitted. She was magnificently handsome—she had more courage and a higher spirit than fall even to the lot of most men. She was a fearless horse-woman; indeed it was only necessary for any pursuit to be dangerous and to require unlimited courage for her instantly to undertake it.

Would the balance at last turn in her favor? Would her beauty, her spirits, her daring, her courage, outweigh defective education, defective manner, and want of worldly knowledge?

CHAPTER VI
THE PROGRESS MADE BY THE PUPIL

It was a beautiful afternoon in June. May, with its lilac and hawthorn, had passed away; the roses were in fairest bloom, lilies looked like great white stars; the fullness and beauty, the warmth and fragrance of summer were on the face of the land, and everything living rejoiced in it.

Pauline had begged that the daily readings might take place under the great cedar tree on the lawn.

"If I must be bored by dry historical facts," she said, "let me at least have the lights and shadows on the lawn to look at. The shadow of the trees on the grass is beautiful beyond everything else. Oh, Miss Hastings, why will people write dull histories? I like to fancy all kings heroes, and all queens heroines. History leaves us no illusions."

"Still," replied the governess, "it teaches us plenty of what you love so much—truth."

The beautiful face grew very serious and thoughtful.

"Why are so many truths disagreeable and sad? If I could rule, I would have the world so bright, so fair and glad, every one so happy. I cannot understand all this under-current of sorrow."

"Comte did not explain it, then, to your satisfaction?" said Miss Hastings.

"Comte!" cried the girl, impatiently. "I am not obliged to believe all I read! Once and for all, Miss Hastings, I do not believe in Comte or his fellows. I only read what he wrote because people seemed to think it clever to have done so. You know—you must know—that I believe in our great Father. Who could look round on this lovely world and not do so?"

Miss Hastings felt more hopeful of the girl then than she had ever felt before. Such strange, wild theories had fallen at times from her lips that it was some consolation to know she had still a child's faith.

Then came an interruption in the shape of a footman, with Sir Oswald's compliments, and would the ladies go to the drawing-room? There were visitors.

"Who are they?" asked Miss Darrell, abruptly.

The man replied:

"Sir George and Lady Hampton."

"I shall not go," said Pauline, decidedly; "that woman sickens me with her false airs and silly, false graces. I have not patience to talk to her."

"Sir Oswald will not be pleased," remonstrated Miss Hastings.

"That I cannot help—it is not my fault. I shall not make myself a hypocrite to please Sir Oswald."

"Society has duties which must be discharged, and which do not depend upon our liking; we must do our duty whether we like it or not."

"I detest society," was the abrupt reply—"it is all a sham!"

"Then why not do your best to improve it? That would surely be better than to abuse it."

"There is something in that," confessed Miss Darrell, slowly.

"If we each do our little best toward making the world even ever so little better than we found it," said Miss Hastings, "we shall not have lived in vain."

There was a singular grandeur of generosity about the girl. If she saw that she was wrong in an argument or an opinion, she admitted it with the most charming candor. That admission she made now by rising at once to accompany Miss Hastings.

The drawing-room at Darrell Court was a magnificent apartment; it had been furnished under the superintendence of the late Lady Darrell, a lady of exquisite taste. It was all white and gold, the white hangings with bullion fringe and gold braids, the white damask with a delicate border of gold; the pictures, the costly statues gleamed in the midst of rich and rare flowers; graceful ornaments, tall, slender vases were filled with choicest blossoms; the large mirrors, with their golden frames, were each and all perfect in their way. There was nothing gaudy, brilliant, or dazzling; all was subdued, in perfect good taste and harmony.

In this superb room the beauty of Pauline Darrell always showed to great advantage; she was in perfect keeping with its splendor. As she entered now, with her usual half-haughty, half-listless grace, Sir Oswald looked up with admiration plainly expressed on his face.

"What a queenly mistress she would make for the Court, if she would but behave like other people!" he thought to himself, and then Lady Hampton rose to greet the girl.

"My dear Miss Darrell, I was getting quite impatient; it seems an age since I saw you—really an age."

"It is an exceedingly short one," returned Pauline; "I saw you on Tuesday, Lady Hampton."

"Did you? Ah, yes; how could I forget? Ah, my dear child, when you reach my age—when your mind is filled with a hundred different matters—you will not have such a good memory as you have now."

Lady Hampton was a little, over-dressed woman. She looked all flowers and furbelows—all ribbons and laces. She was, however, a perfect mistress of all the arts of polite society; she knew exactly what to say and how to say it; she knew when to smile, when to look sympathetic, when to sigh. She was not sincere; she never made the least pretense of being so. "Society" was her one idea—how to please it, how to win its admiration, how to secure a high position in it.

The contrast between the two was remarkable—the young girl with her noble face, her grand soul looking out of her clear dark eyes; Lady Hampton with her artificial smiles, her shifting glances, and would-be charming gestures. Sir Oswald stood by with a courtly smile on his face.

"I have some charming news for you," said Lady Hampton. "I am sure you will be pleased to hear it, Miss Darrell."

"That will quite depend on what it is like," interposed Pauline, honestly.

"You dear, droll child! You are so original; you have so much character. I always tell Sir Oswald you are quite different from any one else."

And though her ladyship spoke smilingly, she gave a keen, quiet glance at Sir Oswald's face, in all probability to watch the effect of her words.

"Ah, well," she continued, "I suppose that in your position a little singularity may be permitted," and then she paused, with a bland smile.

"To what position do you allude?" asked Miss Darrell.

Lady Hampton laughed again. She nodded with an air of great penetration.

"You are cautious, Miss Darrell. But I am forgetting my news. It is this—that my niece, Miss Elinor Rocheford, is coming to visit me."

She waited evidently for Miss Darrell to make some complimentary reply. Not a word came from the proud lips.

"And when she comes I hope, Miss Darrell, that you and she will be great friends."

"It is rather probable, if I like her," was the frank reply.

Sir Oswald looked horrified. Lady Hampton smiled still more sweetly.

"You are sure to like her. Elinor is most dearly loved wherever she goes."

"Is she a sweet creature?" asked Pauline, with such inimitable mimicry that Miss Hastings shuddered, while Sir Oswald turned pale.

"She is indeed," replied Lady Hampton, who, if she understood the sarcasm, made no sign. "With Sir Oswald's permission, I shall bring her to spend a long day with you, Miss Darrell."

"I shall be charmed," said Sir Oswald—"really delighted, Lady Hampton. You do me great honor indeed."

He looked at his niece for some little confirmation of his words, but that young lady appeared too haughty for speech; the word "honor" seemed to her strangely misapplied.

Lady Hampton relaxed none of her graciousness; her bland suavity continued the same until the end of the visit; and then, in some way, she contrived to make Miss Hastings understand that she wanted to speak with her. She asked the governess if she would go with her to the carriage, as she wished to consult her about some music. When they were alone, her air and manner changed abruptly. She turned eagerly to her, her eyes full of sharp, keen curiosity.

"Can you tell me one thing?" she asked. "Is Sir Oswald going to make that proud, stupid, illiterate girl his heiress—mistress of Darrell Court?"

"I do not know," replied Miss Hastings. "How should I be able to answer such a question?"

"Of course I ask in confidence—only in strict confidence; you understand that, Miss Hastings?"

"I understand," was the grave reply.

"All the county is crying shame on him," said her ladyship. "A French painter's daughter. He must be mad to think of such a thing. A girl brought up in the midst of Heaven knows what. He never can intend to leave Darrell Court to her."

"He must leave it to some one," said Miss Hastings; "and who has a better right to it than his own sister's child?"

"Let him marry," she suggested, hastily; "let him marry, and leave it to children of his own. Do you think the county will tolerate such a mistress for Darrell Court—so blunt, so ignorant? Miss Hastings, he must marry."

"I can only suppose," replied the governess, "that he will please himself, Lady Hampton, without any reference to the county."

CHAPTER VII
CAPTAIN LANGTON

June, with its roses and lilies, passed on, the laburnums had all fallen, the lilies had vanished, and still the state of affairs at Darrell Court remained doubtful. Pauline, in many of those respects in which her uncle would fain have seen her changed, remained unaltered—indeed it was not easy to unlearn the teachings of a life-time.

Miss Hastings, more patient and hopeful than Sir Oswald, persevered, with infinite tact and discretion. But there were certain peculiarities of which Pauline could not be broken. One was a habit of calling everything by its right name. She had no notion of using any of those polite little fictions society delights in; no matter how harsh, how ugly the word, she did not hesitate to use it. Another peculiarity was that of telling the blunt, plain, abrupt truth, no matter what the cost, no matter who was pained. She tore aside the flimsy vail of society with zest; she spared no one in her almost ruthless denunciations. Her intense scorn for all kinds of polite fiction was somewhat annoying.

"You need not say that I am engaged, James," she said, one day, when a lady called whom she disliked. "I am not engaged, but I do not care to see Mrs. Camden."

Even that bland functionary looked annoyed. Miss Hastings tried to make some compromise.

"You cannot send such a message as that, Miss Darrell. Pray listen to reason."

"Sir Oswald and yourself agreed that she was——"

"Never mind that," hastily interrupted Miss Hastings. "You must not hurt any one's feelings by such a blunt message as that; it is neither polite nor well-bred."

"I shall never cultivate either politeness or good breeding at the expense of truth; therefore you had better send the message yourself, Miss Hastings."

"I will do so," said the governess, quietly. "I will manage it in such a way as to show Mrs. Camden that she is not expected to call again, yet so as not to humiliate her before the servants; but, remember, not at any sacrifice of truth."

Such contests were of daily, almost hourly, occurrence. Whether the result would be such a degree of training as to fit the young lady for taking the position she wished to occupy, remained doubtful.

"This is really very satisfactory," said Sir Oswald, abruptly, one morning, as he entered the library, where Miss Hastings awaited him. "But," he continued, "before I explain myself, let me ask you how are you getting on—what progress are you making with your tiresome pupil?"

The gentle heart of the governess was grieved to think that she could not give a more satisfactory reply. Little real progress had been made in study; less in manner.

"There is a mass of splendid material, Sir Oswald," she said; "but the difficulty lies in putting it into shape."

"I am afraid," he observed, "people will make remarks; and I have heard more than one doubt expressed as to what kind of hands Darrell Court is likely to fall into should I make Pauline my heiress. You see she is capable of almost anything. She would turn the place into an asylum; she would transform it into a college for philosophers, a home for needy artists—in fact, anything that might occur to her—without the least hesitation."

Miss Hastings could not deny it. They were not speaking of a manageable nineteenth century young lady, but of one to whom no ordinary rules applied, whom no customary measures fitted.

"I have a letter here," continued Sir Oswald, "from Captain Aubrey Langton, the son of one of my oldest and dearest friends. He proposes to pay me a visit, and—pray, Miss Hastings, pardon me for suggesting such a thing, but I should be so glad if he would fall in love with Pauline. I have an idea that love might educate and develop her more quickly than anything else."

Miss Hastings had already thought the same thing; but she knew whoever won the love of such a girl as Pauline Darrell would be one of the cleverest of men.

"I am writing to him to tell him that I hope he will remain with us for a month; and during that time I hope, I fervently hope, he may fall in love with my niece. She is beautiful enough. Pardon me again, Miss Hastings, but has she ever spoken to you of love or lovers?"

"No. She is in that respect, as in many others, quite unlike the generality of girls. I have never heard an allusion to such matters from her lips—never once."

This fact seemed to Sir Oswald stranger than any other; he had an idea that girls devoted the greater part of their thoughts to such subjects.

"Do you think," he inquired, "that she cared for any one in Paris—any of those men, for instance, whom she used to meet at her father's?"

"No," replied Miss Hastings; "I do not think so. She is strangely backward in all such respects, although she was brought up entirely among gentlemen."

"Among—pardon me, my dear madame, not gentlemen—members, we will say, of a gentlemanly profession."

Sir Oswald took from his gold snuff-box a pinch of most delicately-flavored snuff, and looked as though he thought the very existence of such people a mistake.

"Any little influence that you may possess over my niece, Miss Hastings, will you kindly use in Captain Langton's favor? Of course, if anything should come of my plan—as I fervently hope there may—I shall stipulate that the engagement lasts two years. During that time I shall trust to the influence of love to change my niece's character."

It was only a fresh complication—one from which Miss Hastings did not expect much.

That same day, during dinner, Sir Oswald told his niece of the expected arrival of Captain Langton.

"I have seen so few English gentlemen," she remarked, "that he will be a subject of some curiosity to me."

"You will find him—that is, if he resembles his father—a high-bred, noble gentleman," said Sir Oswald, complacently.

"Is he clever?" she asked. "What does he do?"

"Do!" repeated Sir Oswald. "I do not understand you."

"Does he paint pictures or write books?"

"Heaven forbid!" cried Sir Oswald, proudly. "He is a gentleman."

Her face flushed hotly for some minutes, and then the flush died away, leaving her paler than ever.

"I consider artists and writers gentlemen," she retorted—"gentlemen of a far higher stamp than those to whom fortune has given money and nature has denied brains."

Another time a sharp argument would have resulted from the throwing down of such a gantlet. Sir Oswald had something else in view, so he allowed the speech to pass.

"It will be a great pleasure for me to see my old friend's son again," he said. "I hope, Pauline, you will help me to make his visit a pleasant one."

"What can I do?" she asked, brusquely.

"What a question!" laughed Sir Oswald. "Say, rather, what can you not do? Talk to him, sing to him. Your voice is magnificent, and would give any one the greatest pleasure. You can ride out with him."

"If he is a clever, sensible man, I can do all that you mention; if not, I shall not trouble myself about him. I never could endure either tiresome or stupid people."

"My young friend is not likely to prove either," said Sir Oswald, angrily; and Miss Hastings wondered in her heart what the result of it all would be.

That same evening Miss Darrell talked of Captain Langton, weaving many bright fancies concerning him.

"I suppose," she said, "that it is not always the most favorable specimens of the English who visit Paris. We used to see such droll caricatures. I like a good caricature above all things—do you, Miss Hastings?"

"When it is good, and pains no one," was the sensible reply.

The girl turned away with a little impatient sigh.

"Your ideas are all colorless," she said, sharply. "In England it seems to me that everybody is alike. You have no individuality, no character."

"If character means, in your sense of the word, ill-nature, so much the better," rejoined Miss Hastings. "All good-hearted people strive to save each other from pain."

"I wonder," said Pauline, thoughtfully, "if I shall like Captain Langton! We have been living here quietly enough; but I feel as though some great change were coming. You have no doubt experienced that peculiar sensation which comes over one just before a heavy thunder-storm? I have that strange, half-nervous, half-restless sensation now."

"You will try to be amiable, Pauline," put in the governess, quietly. "You see that Sir Oswald evidently thinks a great deal of this young friend of his. You will try not to shock your uncle in any way—not to violate those little conventionalities that he respects so much."

"I will do my best; but I must be myself—always myself. I cannot assume a false character."

"Then let it be your better self," said the governess, gently; and for one minute Pauline Darrell was touched.

"That sweet creature, Lady Hampton's niece, will be here next week," she remarked, after a short pause. "What changes will be brought into our lives, I wonder?"

Of all the changes possible, least of all she expected the tragedy that afterward happened.

CHAPTER VIII
THE INTRODUCTION

It was a never-to-be-forgotten evening when Captain Langton reached Darrell Court—an evening fair, bright, and calm. The sweet southern wind bore the perfume of flowers; the faint ripples of the fountains, the musical song of the birds, seemed almost to die away on the evening breeze; the sun appeared unwilling to leave the sapphire sky, the flowers unwilling to close. Pauline had lingered over her books until she could remain in-doors no longer; then, by Miss Hastings' desire, she dressed for dinner—which was delayed for an hour—and afterward went into the garden.

Most girls would have remembered, as they dressed, that a handsome young officer was coming; Miss Darrell did not make the least change in her usual toilet. The thin, fine dress of crape fell in statuesque folds round the splendid figure; the dark hair was drawn back from the beautiful brow, and negligently fastened with her favorite silver arrow; the white neck and fair rounded arms gleamed like white marble through the thin folds of crape. There was not the least attempt at ornament; yet no queen arrayed in royal robes ever looked more lovely.

Pauline was a great lover of the picturesque. With a single flower, a solitary knot of ribbon, she could produce an effect which many women would give all their jewels to achieve. Whatever she wore took a kind of royal grace from herself which no other person could impart. Though her dress might be made of the same material as that of others, it never looked the same. On her it appeared like the robes of a queen.

As Pauline was passing through the corridor, Miss Hastings met her. The governess looked scrutinizingly at the plain evening dress; it was the same that she had worn yesterday. Evidently there was no girlish desire to attract.

"Pauline, we shall have a visitor this evening," said Miss Hastings; "you might add a few flowers to your dress."

She passed on, with a smile of assent. Almost the first thing that caught her attention out of doors was a large and handsome fuchsia. She gathered a spray of the rich purple and crimson flowers, and placed it negligently in her hair. Many women would have stood before their mirror for an hour without producing the same superb effect. Then she placed another spray of the same gorgeous flowers in the bodice of her dress. It was all done without effort, and she would have been the last in the world to suspect how beautiful she looked. Then she went on to the fountain, for the beautiful, calm evening had awakened all the poet's soul within her. The grand, sensitive nature thrilled—the beautiful, poetic mind reveled in this hour of nature's most supreme loveliness. A thousand bright fancies surged through her heart and brain; a thousand poetical ideas shaped themselves into words, and rose to her lips.

So time passed, and she was unconscious of it, until a shadow falling over the great white lilies warned her that some one was near.

Looking up quickly, she saw a tall, fair, handsome young man gazing at her with mingled admiration and surprise. Beside him stood Sir Oswald, courtly, gracious, and evidently on the alert.

"Captain Langton," he said, "let me introduce you to my niece, Miss Darrell."

Not one feature of the girl's proud, beautiful face moved, but there was some little curiosity in her dark eyes. They rested for a minute on the captain's face, and then, with a dreamy look, she glanced over the heads of the white lilies behind him. He was not her ideal, not her hero, evidently. In that one keen, quick glance, she read not only the face, but the heart and soul of the man before her.

The captain felt as though he had been subjected to some wonderful microscopic examination.

"She is one of those dreadfully shrewd girls that pretend to read faces," he said to himself, while he bowed low before her, and replied with enthusiasm to the introduction.

"My niece is quite a Darrell," said Sir Oswald, proudly. "You see she has the Darrell face."

Again the gallant captain offered some flattering remark—a neatly turned compliment, which he considered ought to have brought her down, as a skillful shot does a bird—but the dark eyes saw only the lilies, not him.

"She is proud, like all the Darrells," he thought; "my father always said they were the proudest race in England."

"I hope," said Sir Oswald, courteously, "that you will enjoy your visit here, Aubrey. Your father was my dearest friend, and it gives me great delight to see you here."

"I am sure of it, Sir Oswald. I am equally happy; I cannot see how any one could be dull for one minute in this grand old place."

Sir Oswald's face flushed with pleasure, and for the first time the dark eyes slowly left the lilies and looked at the captain.

"I find not only one minute, but many hours in which to be dull," said Pauline. "Do you like the country so well?"

"I like Darrell Court," he replied, with a bow that seemed to embrace Sir Oswald, his niece, and all his possessions.

"You like it—in what way?" asked Pauline, in her terribly downright manner. "It is your first visit, and you have been here only a few minutes. How can you tell whether you like it?"

For a few moments Captain Langton looked slightly confused, and then he rallied. Surely a man of the world was not to be defied by a mere girl.

"I have seen that at Darrell Court," he said, deferentially, "which will make the place dear to me while I live."

She did not understand him. She was far too frank and haughty for a compliment so broad. But Sir Oswald smiled.

"He is losing no time," thought the stately old baronet; "he is falling in love with her, just as I guessed he would."

"I will leave you," said Sir Oswald, "to get better acquainted. Pauline, you will show Captain Langton the aviary."

"Yes," she assented, carelessly. "But will you send Miss Hastings here? She knows the various birds far better than I do."

Sir Oswald, with a pleased expression on his face, walked away.

"So you have an aviary at the Court, Miss Darrell. It seems to me there is nothing wanting here. You do not seem interested; you do not like birds?"

"Not caged ones," she replied. "I love birds almost as though they were living friends, but not bright-plumaged birds in golden cages. They should be free and wild in the woods and forests, filling the summer air with joyous song. I love them well then."

"You like unrestricted freedom?" he observed.

"I do not merely like it, I deem it an absolute necessity. I should not care for life without it."

The captain looked more attentively at her. It was the Darrell face, surely enough—features of perfect beauty, with a soul of fire shining through them.

"Yet," he said, musingly, cautiously feeling his way, "there is but little freedom—true freedom—for women. They are bound down by a thousand narrow laws and observances—caged by a thousand restraints."

"There is no power on earth," she returned, hastily, "that can control thoughts or cage souls; while they are free, it is untrue to say that there is no freedom."

A breath of fragrant wind came and stirred the great white lilies. The gallant captain saw at once that he should only lose in arguments with her.

"Shall we visit the aviary?" he asked.

And she walked slowly down the path, he following.

"She is like an empress," he thought. "It will be all the more glory for me if I can win such a wife for my own."

CHAPTER IX
THE BROKEN LILY

Pauline Darrell was a keen, shrewd observer of character. She judged more by small actions than by great ones; it was a characteristic of hers. When women have that gift, it is more to be dreaded than the cool, calm, matured judgment of men. Men err sometimes in their estimate of character, but it is very seldom that a woman makes a similar mistake.

The garden path widened where the tall white lilies grew in rich profusion, and there Pauline and Captain Langton walked side by side. The rich, sweet perfume seemed to gather round them, and the dainty flowers, with their shining leaves and golden bracts, looked like great white stars.

Captain Langton carried a small cane in his hand. He had begun to talk to Pauline with great animation. Her proud indifference piqued him. He was accustomed to something more like rapture when he devoted himself to any fair lady. He vowed to himself that he would vanquish her pride, that he would make her care for him, that the proud, dark eyes should soften and brighten for him; and he gave his whole mind to the conquest. As he walked along, one of the tall, white lilies bent over the path; with one touch of the cane he beat it down, and Pauline gave a little cry, as though the blow had pained her. She stopped, and taking the slender green stem in her hand, straightened it; but the blow had broken one of the white leaves.

"Why did you do that?" she asked, in a pained voice.

"It is only a flower," he replied, with a laugh.

"Only a flower! You have killed it. You cannot make it live again. Why need you have cut its sweet life short?"

"It will not be missed from among so many," he said.

"You might say the same thing of yourself," she retorted. "The world is full of men, and you would hardly be missed from so many; yet you would not like— —"

"There is some little difference between a man and a flower, Miss Darrell," he interrupted, stiffly.

"There is, indeed; and the flowers have the advantage," she retorted.

The captain solaced himself by twisting his mustache, and relieved his feelings by some few muttered words, which Miss Darrell did not hear. In her quick, impulsive way, she judged him at once.

"He is cruel and selfish," she thought; "he would not even stoop to save the life of the sweetest flower that blows. He shall not forget killing that lily," she continued, as she gathered the broken chalice, and placed it in her belt. "Every time he looks at me," she said, "he shall remember what he has done."

The captain evidently understood her amiable intention, and liked her accordingly. They walked on for some minutes in perfect silence; then Pauline turned to him suddenly.

"Have you been long in the army, Captain Langton?"

Flattered by a question that seemed to evince some personal interest, he hastened to reply:

"More than eight years. I joined when I was twenty."

"Have you seen any service?" she asked.

"No," he replied. "My regiment had been for many years in active service just before I joined, so that we have been at home since then."

"In inglorious ease," she said.

"We are ready for work," he returned, "when work comes."

"How do you employ your time?" she asked; and again he was flattered by the interest that the question showed. His face flushed. Here was a grand opportunity of showing this haughty girl, this "proudest Darrell of them all," that he was eagerly sought after in society such as she had not yet seen.

"You have no conception of the immense number of engagements that occupy our time," he replied; "I am fond of horses—I take a great interest in all races."

If he had added that he was one of the greatest gamblers on the turf, he would have spoken truthfully.

"Horse racing," said Miss Darrell—"that is the favorite occupation of English gentlemen, is it not?"

"I should imagine so. Then I am considered—you must pardon my boasting—one of the best billiard players in London."

"That is not much of a boast," she remarked, with such quiet contempt that the captain could only look at her in sheer wonder.

"There are balls, operas, parties, suppers—I cannot tell what; and the ladies engross a great deal of our time. We soldiers never forget our devotion and chivalry to the fair sex, Miss Darrell."

"The fair sex should be grateful that they share your attention with horses and billiards," she returned. "But what else do you do, Captain Langton? I was not thinking of such trifles as these."

"Trifles!" he repeated. "I do not call horse racing a trifle. I was within an inch of winning the Derby—I mean to say a horse of mine was. If you call that a trifle, Miss Darrell, you go near to upsetting English society altogether."

"But what great things do you do?" she repeated, her dark eyes opening wider. "You cannot mean seriously that this is all. Do you never write, paint—have you no ambition at all?"

"I do not know what you call ambition," he replied, sullenly; "as for writing and painting, in England we pay people to do that kind of thing for us. You do not think that I would paint a picture, even if I could?"

"I should think you clever if you did that," she returned; "at present I cannot see that you do anything requiring mind or intellect."

"Miss Darrell," he said, looking at her, "you are a radical, I believe."

"A radical?" she repeated, slowly. "I am not quite sure, Captain Langton, that I know what that means."

"You believe in aristocracy of intellect, and all that kind of nonsense," he continued. "Why should a man who paints a picture be any better than the man who understands the good points of a horse?"

"Why, indeed?" she asked, satirically. "We will not argue the question, for we should not agree."

"I had her there," thought the captain. "She could not answer me. Some of these women require a high hand to keep them in order."

"I do not see Miss Hastings," she said at last, "and it is quite useless going to the aviary without her. I do not remember the name of a single bird; and I am sure you will not care for them."

"But," he returned, hesitatingly, "Sir Oswald seemed to wish it."

"There is the first dinner-bell," she said, with an air of great relief; "there will only just be time to return. As you seem solicitous about Sir Oswald's wishes we had better go in, for he dearly loves punctuality."

"I believe," thought the captain, "that she is anxious to get away from me. I must say that I am not accustomed to this kind of thing."

The aspect of the dining-room, with its display of fine old plate, the brilliantly arranged tables, the mingled odor of rare wines and flowers, restored him to good humor.

"It would be worth some little trouble," he thought, "to win all this."

He took Pauline in to dinner. The grand, pale, passionate beauty of the girl had never shown to greater advantage than it did this evening, as she sat with the purple and crimson fuchsias in her hair and the broken lily in her belt. Sir Oswald did not notice the latter until dinner was half over. Then he said:

"Why, Pauline, with gardens and hothouses full of flowers, have you chosen a broken one?"

"To me it is exquisite," she replied.

The captain's face darkened for a moment, but he would not take offense. The elegantly appointed table, the seductive dinner, the rare wines, all made an impression on him. He said to himself that there was a good thing offered to him, and that a girl's haughty temper should not stand in his way. He made himself most agreeable, he was all animation, vivacity, and high spirits with Sir Oswald. He was deferential and attentive to Miss Hastings, and his manner to Pauline left no doubt in the minds of the lookers on that he was completely fascinated by her. She was too proudly indifferent, too haughtily careless, even to resent it. Sir Oswald Darrell was too true a gentleman to offer his niece to any one; but he had given the captain to understand that, if he could woo her and win her, there would be no objection raised on his part.

For once in his life Captain Langton had spoken quite truthfully.

"I have nothing," he said; "my father left me but a very moderate fortune, and I have lost the greater part of it. I have not been careful or prudent, Sir Oswald."

"Care and prudence are not the virtues of youth," Sir Oswald returned. "I may say, honestly, I should be glad if your father's son could win my niece; as for fortune, she will be richly dowered if I make her my heiress. Only yesterday I heard that coal had been found on my Scotch estates, and, if that be true, it will raise my income many thousands per annum."

"May you long live to enjoy your wealth, Sir Oswald!" said the young man, so heartily that tears stood in the old baronet's eyes.

But there was one thing the gallant captain did not confess. He did not tell Sir Oswald Darrell—what was really the truth—that he was over head and ears in debt, and that this visit to Darrell Court was the last hope left to him.

CHAPTER X
PAULINE STILL INCORRIGIBLE

Sir Oswald lingered over his wine. It was not every day that he found a companion so entirely to his taste as Captain Langton. The captain had a collection of anecdotes of the court, the aristocracy, and the mess-room, that could not be surpassed. He kept his own interest well in view the whole time, making some modest allusions to the frequency with which his society was sought, and the number of ladies who were disposed to regard him favorably. All was narrated with the greatest skill, without the least boasting, and Sir Oswald, as he listened with delight, owned to himself that, all things considered, he could not have chosen more wisely for his niece.

A second bottle of fine old port was discussed, and then Sir Oswald said:

"You will like to go to the drawing-room; the ladies will be there. I always enjoy forty winks after dinner."

The prospect of a *tete-a-tete* with Miss Darrell did not strike the captain as being a very rapturous one.

"She is," he said to himself, "a magnificently handsome girl, but almost too haughty to be bearable. I have never, in all my life, felt so small as I do when she speaks to me or looks at me, and no man likes that sort of thing."

But Darrell Court was a magnificent estate, the large annual income was a sum he had never even dreamed of, and all might be his—Sir Oswald had said so; his, if he could but win the proud heart of the proudest girl it had ever been his fortune to meet. The stake was well worth going through something disagreeable for.

"If she were only like other women," he thought, "I should know how to manage her; but she seems to live in the clouds."

The plunge had to be made, so the captain summoned all his courage, and went to the drawing-room. The picture there must have struck the least imaginative of men.

Miss Hastings, calm, elegant, lady-like, in her quiet evening dress of gray silk, was seated near a small stand on which stood a large lamp, by the light of which she was reading. The part of the room near her was brilliantly illuminated. It was a spacious apartment—unusually so even for a large mansion. It contained four large windows, two of which were closed, the gorgeous hangings of white and gold shielding them from view; the other end of the room was in semi-darkness, the brilliant light from the lamp not reaching it—the windows were thrown wide open, and the soft, pale moonlight came in. The evening came in, too, bringing with it the sweet breath of the lilies, the perfume of the roses, the fragrance of rich clover, carnations, and purple heliotropes. Faint shadows lay on the flowers, the white silvery light was very peaceful and sweet; the dewdrops shone on the grass—it was the fairest hour of nature's fair day.

Pauline had gone to the open window. Something had made her restless and unquiet; but, standing there, the spell of that beautiful moonlit scene calmed her, and held her fast. With one look at that wonderful sky and its myriad stars, one at the soft moonlight and the white lilies, the fever of life died from her, and a holy calm, sweet fancies, bright thoughts, swept over her like an angel's wing.

Then she became conscious of a stir in the perfumed air; something less agreeable mingled with the fragrance of the lilies scent of which she did not know the name, but which—some she disliked ever afterward because the captain used it. A low voice that would fain be tender murmured something in her ear; the spell of the moonlight was gone, the quickly thronging poetical fancies had all fled away, the beauty seemed to have left even the sleeping flowers. Turning round to him, she said, in a clear voice, every word sounding distinctly:

"Have the goodness, Captain Langton, not to startle me again. I do not like any one to come upon me in that unexpected manner."

"I was so happy to find you alone," he whispered.

"I do not know why that should make you happy. I always behave much better when I am with Miss Hastings than when I am alone."

"You are always charming," he said. "I want to ask you something, Miss Darrell. Be kind, be patient, and listen to me."

"I am neither kind nor patient by nature," she returned; "what have you to say?"

It was very difficult, he felt, to be sentimental with her. She had turned to the window, and was looking out again at the flowers; one little white hand played impatiently with a branch of guelder roses that came peeping in.

"I am jealous of those flowers," said the captain; "will you look at me instead of them?"

She raised her beautiful eyes, and looked at him so calmly, with so much conscious superiority in her manner, that the captain felt "smaller" than ever.

"You are talking nonsense to me," she said, loftily; "and as I do not like nonsense, will you tell me what you have to say?"

The voice was calm and cold, the tones measured and slightly contemptuous; it was very difficult under such circumstances to be an eloquent wooer, but the recollection of Darrell Court and its large rent-roll came to him and restored his fast expiring courage.

"I want to ask a favor of you," he said; and the pleading expression that he managed to throw into his face was really creditable to him. "I want to ask you if you will be a little kinder to me. I admire you so much that I should be the happiest man in all the world if you would but give me ever so little of your friendship."

She seemed to consider his words—to ponder them; and from her silence he took hope.

"I am quite unworthy, I know; but, if you knew how all my life long I have desired the friendship of a good and noble woman, you would be kinder to me—you would indeed!"

"Do you think, then, that I am good and noble?" she asked.

"I am sure of it; your face——"

"I wish," she interrupted, "that Sir Oswald were of your opinion. You have lived in what people call 'the world' all your life, Captain Langton, I suppose?"

"Yes," he replied, wondering what would follow.

"You have been in society all that time, yet I am the first 'good and noble woman' you have met! You are hardly complimentary to the sex, after all."

The captain was slightly taken aback.

"I did not say those exact words, Miss Darrell."

"But you implied them. Tell me why you wish for my friendship more than any other. Miss Hastings is ten thousand times more estimable than I am—why not make her your friend?"

"I admire you—I like you. I could say more, but I dare not. You are hard upon me, Miss Darrell."

"I have no wish to be hard," she returned. "Who am I that I should be hard upon any one? But, you see, I am unfortunately what people call very plain-spoken—very truthful."

"So much the better," said Captain Langton.

"Is it? Sir Oswald says not. If he does not make me his heiress, it will be because I have such an abrupt manner of speaking; he often tells me so."

"Truth in a beautiful woman," began the captain, sentimentally; but Miss Darrell again interrupted him—she had little patience with his platitudes.

"You say you wish for my friendship because you like me. Now, here is the difficulty—I cannot give it to you, because I do not like you."

"You do not like me?" cried the captain, hardly able to believe the evidence of his own senses. "You cannot mean it! You are the first person who ever said such a thing!"

"Perhaps I am not the first who ever thought it; but then, as I tell you, I am very apt to say what I think."

"Will you tell me why you do not like me?" asked the captain, quietly. He began to see that nothing could be gained in any other fashion.

Her beautiful face was raised quite calmly to his, her dark eyes were as proudly serene as ever, she was utterly unconscious that she was saying anything extraordinary.

"I will tell you with pleasure," she replied. "You seem to me wanting in truth and earnestness; you think people are to be pleased by flattery. You flatter Sir Oswald, you flatter Miss Hastings, you flatter me. Being agreeable is all very well, but an honest man does not need to flatter—does not think of it, in fact. Then, you are either heedless or cruel—I do not know which. Why should you kill that beautiful flower that Heaven made to enjoy the sunshine, just for one idle moment's wanton sport?"

Captain Langton's face grew perfectly white with anger.

"Upon my word of honor," he said, "I never heard anything like this!"

Miss Darrell turned carelessly away.

"You see," she said, "friendship between us would be rather difficult. But I will not judge too hastily; I will wait a few days, and then decide."

She had quitted the room before Captain Langton had sufficiently recovered from his dismay to answer.

CHAPTER XI
HOW WILL IT END?

It was some minutes before Captain Langton collected himself sufficiently to cross the room and speak to Miss Hastings. She looked up at him with a smile.

"I am afraid you have not had a very pleasant time of it at that end of the room, Captain Langton," she said; "I was just on the point of interfering."

"Your pupil is a most extraordinary young lady, Miss Hastings," he returned; "I have never met with any one more so."

Miss Hastings laughed; there was an expression of great amusement on her face.

"She is certainly very original, Captain Langton; quite different from the pattern young lady of the present day."

"She is magnificently handsome," he continued; "but her manners are simply startling."

"She has very grand qualities," said Miss Hastings; "she has a noble disposition and a generous heart, but the want of early training, the mixing entirely with one class of society, has made her very strange."

"Strange!" cried the captain. "I have never met with any one so blunt, so outspoken, so abrupt, in all my life. She has no notion of repose or polish; I have never been so surprised. I hear Sir Oswald coming, and really, Miss Hastings, I feel that I cannot see him; I am not equal to it—that extraordinary girl has quite unsettled me. You might mention that I have gone out in the grounds to smoke my cigar; I cannot talk to any one."

Miss Hastings laughed as he passed out through the open French window into the grounds. Sir Oswald came in, smiling and contented; he talked for a few minutes with Miss Hastings, and heard that the captain was smoking his cigar. He expressed to Miss Hastings his very favorable opinion of the young man, and then bade her good-night.

"How will it end?" said the governess to herself. "She will never marry him, I am sure. Those proud, clear, dark eyes of hers look through all his little airs and graces; her grand soul seems to understand all the narrowness and selfishness of his. She will never marry him. Oh, if she would but be civilized! Sir Oswald is quite capable of leaving all he has to the captain, and then what would become of Pauline?"

By this time the gentle, graceful governess had become warmly attached to the beautiful, wayward, willful girl who persisted so obstinately in refusing what she chose to call "polish."

"How will it end?" said the governess. "I would give all I have to see Pauline mistress of Darrell Court; but I fear the future."

Some of the scenes that took place between Miss Darrell and the captain were very amusing. She had the utmost contempt for his somewhat dandified airs, his graces, and affectations.

"I like a grand, rugged, noble man, with the head of a hero, and the brow of a poet, the heart of a lion, and the smile of a child," she said to him one day; "I cannot endure a coxcomb."

"I hope you may find such a man, Miss Darrell," he returned, quietly. "I have been some time in the world, but I have never met with such a character."

"I think your world has been a very limited one," she replied, and the captain looked angry.

He had certainly hoped and intended to dazzle her with his worldly knowledge, if nothing else. Yet how she despised his knowledge, and with what contempt she heard him speak of his various experiences!

Nothing seemed to jar upon her and to irritate her as did his affectations. She was looking one morning at a very beautifully veined leaf, which she passed over to Miss Hastings.

"Is it not wonderful?" she asked; and the captain, with his eye-glass, came to look at it.

"Are you short-sighted?" she asked him, abruptly.

"Not in the least," he replied.

"Is your sight defective?" she continued.

"No, not in the least degree."

"Then why do you use that eye-glass, Captain Langton?"

"I-ah-why, because everybody uses one," he replied.

"I thought it was only women who did that kind of thing—followed a fashion for fashion's sake," she said, with some little contempt.

The next morning the captain descended without his eye-glass, and Miss Hastings smiled as she noticed it.

Another of his affectations was a pretended inability to pronounce his "t's" and "r's."

"Can you really not speak plainly?" she said to him one day.

"Most decidedly I can," he replied, wondering what was coming next.

"Then, why do you call 'rove' 'wove' in that absurd fashion?"

The captain's face flushed.

"It is a habit I have fallen into, I suppose," he replied. "I must break myself of it."

"It is about the most effeminate habit a man can fall into," said Miss Darrell. "I think that, if I were a soldier, I should delight in clear, plain speaking. I cannot understand why English gentlemen seem to think it fashionable to mutilate their mother tongue."

There was no chance of their ever agreeing—they never did even for one single hour.

"What are you thinking about, Pauline?" asked Miss Hastings one day.

Her young pupil had fallen into a reverie over "The History of the Peninsular War."

"I am thinking," she replied, "that, although France boasts so much of her military glory, England has a superior army; her soldiers are very brave; her officers the truest gentlemen."

"I am glad to hear that you think so. I have often wondered if you would take our guest as a sample."

Her beautiful lips curled with unutterable contempt.

"Certainly not. I often contrast him with a Captain Lafosse, who used to visit us in the Rue d'Orme, a grand man with a brown, rugged face, and great brown hands. Captain Langton is a coxcomb—neither more nor less, Miss Hastings."

"But he is polished, refined, elegant in his manner and address, which, perhaps, your friend with the brown, rugged face was not."

"We shall not agree, Miss Hastings, we shall not agree. I do not like Captain Langton."

The governess, remembering all that Sir Oswald wished, tried in vain to represent their visitor in a more favorable light. Miss Darrell simply looked haughty and unconvinced.

"I am years younger than you," she said, at last, "and have seen nothing of what you call 'life'; but the instinct of my own heart tells me that he is false in heart, in mind, in soul; he has a false, flattering tongue, false lips, false principles—we will not speak of him."

Miss Hastings looked at her sadly.

"Do you not think that in time, perhaps, you may like him better?"

"No," was the blunt reply, "I do not. I told him that I did not like him, but that I would take some time to consider whether he was to be a friend of mine or not; and the conclusion I have arrived at is, that I could not endure his friendship."

"When did you tell him that you did not like him?" asked Miss Hastings, gravely.

"I think it was the first night he came," she replied.

Miss Hastings looked relieved.

"Did he say anything else to you, Pauline?" she asked, gently.

"No; what should he say? He seemed very much surprised, I suppose, as he says most people like him. But I do not, and never shall."

One thing was certain, the captain was falling most passionately in love with Miss Darrell. Her grand beauty, her pride, her originality, all seemed to have an irresistible charm for him.

CHAPTER XII
ELINOR ROCHEFORD

It was a morning in August, when a gray mist hung over the earth, a mist that resulted from the intense heat, and through which trees, flowers, and fountains loomed faintly like shadows. The sun showed his bright face at intervals, but, though he withheld his gracious presence, the heat and warmth were great; the air was laden with perfume, and the birds were all singing as though they knew that the sun would soon reappear.

One glance at her pupil's face showed Miss Hastings there was not much to be done in the way of study. Pauline wanted to watch the mist rise from the hills and trees. She wanted to see the sunbeams grow bright and golden.

"Let us read under the lime trees, Miss Hastings," she said, and Captain Langton smiled approval. For the time was come when he followed her like her shadow; when he could not exist out of her presence; when his passionate love mastered him, and brought him, a very slave, to her feet; when the hope of winning her was dearer to him than life itself; when he would have sacrificed even Darrell Court for the hope of calling her his wife.

If she knew of his passion, she made no sign; she never relaxed from her haughty, careless indifference; she never tried in the least to make herself agreeable to him.

Sir Oswald watched her with keen eyes, and Miss Hastings trembled lest misfortune should come upon the girl she was learning to love so dearly. She saw and understood that the baronet was slowly but surely making up his mind; if Pauline married the captain, he would make her his heiress; if not, she would never inherit Darrell Court.

On this August morning they formed a pretty group under the shadowy, graceful limes. Miss Hastings held in her hands some of the fine fancy work which delights ladies; the captain reclined on a tiger-skin rug on the grass, looking very handsome, for, whatever might be his faults of mind, he was one of the handsomest men in England. Pauline, as usual, was beautiful, graceful, and piquant, wearing a plain morning dress of some gray material—a dress which on any one else would have looked plain, but which she had made picturesque and artistic by a dash of scarlet—and a pomegranate blossom in her hair. Her lovely face looked more than usually noble under the influence of the words she was reading.

"Tennyson again!" said the captain, as she opened the book. "It is to be regretted that the poet cannot see you, Miss Darrell, and know how highly you appreciate his works."

She never smiled nor blushed at his compliments, as she had seen other girls do. She had a fashion of fixing her bright eyes on him, and after one glance he generally was overcome with confusion before his compliment was ended. .

"I should not imagine that anything I could say would flatter a poet," she replied, thoughtfully. "Indeed he is, I should say, as far above blame as praise."

Then, without noticing him further, she went on reading. Captain Langton's eyes never left her face; its pale, grand beauty glowed and changed, the dark eyes grew radiant, the beautiful lips quivered with emotion. He thought to himself that a man might lay down his life and every hope in it to win such love as hers.

Suddenly she heard the sound of voices, and looking up saw Sir Oswald escorting two ladies.

"What a tiresome thing!" grumbled the captain. "We can never be alone a single hour."

"I thought you enjoyed society so much!" she said.

"I am beginning to care for no society on earth but yours," he whispered, his face flushing, while she turned haughtily away.

"You are proud," murmured the captain to himself—"you are as haughty as you are beautiful; but I will win you yet."

Then Sir Oswald, with his visitors, advanced. It was Pauline's aversion, Lady Hampton, with her niece, Miss Rocheford.

Lady Hampton advanced in her usual grave, artificial manner.

"Sir Oswald wanted to send for you, but I said 'no.' What can be more charming than such a group under the trees? I am so anxious to introduce my niece to you, Miss Darrell—she arrived only yesterday. Elinor, let me introduce you to Miss Darrell, Miss Hastings, and Captain Langton."

Pauline's dark eyes glanced at the blushing, sweet face, and the shrinking graceful figure. Miss Hastings made her welcome; and the captain, stroking his mustache, thought himself in luck for knowing two such pretty girls.

There could not have been a greater contrast than Pauline Darrell and Elinor Rocheford. Pauline was dark, proud, beautiful, passionate, haughty, and willful, yet with a poet's soul and a grand mind above all worldliness, all meanness, all artifice. Elinor was timid, shrinking, graceful, lovely, with a delicate, fairy-like beauty, yet withal keenly alive to the main chance, and never forgetting her aunt's great maxim — to make the best of everything for herself.

On this warm August morning Miss Rocheford wore a charming gossamer costume of lilac and white, with the daintiest of Parisian hats on her golden head. Her gloves, shoes, laces, parasol, were perfection — not a fold was out of place, not a ribbon awry — contrasting most forcibly with the grand, picturesque girl near her.

Lady Hampton seated herself, and Miss Rocheford did the same. Sir Oswald suggesting how very refreshing grapes and peaches would be on so warm a morning, Captain Langton volunteered to go and order some. Lady Hampton watched him as he walked away.

"What a magnificent man, Sir Oswald! What a fine clever face! It is easy to see that he is a military man — he is so upright, so easy; there is nothing like a military training for giving a man an easy, dignified carriage. I think I understood that he was the son of a very old friend of yours?"

"The son of the dearest friend I ever had in the world," was the reply; "and I love him as though he were my own — indeed I wish he were."

Lady Hampton sighed and looked sympathetic.

"Langton," she continued, in a musing tone — "is he one of the Langtons of Orde?"

"No," replied Sir Oswald; "my dear old friend was of a good family, but not greatly blessed by fortune."

It was wonderful to see how Lady Hampton's interest in the captain at once died out; there was no more praise, no more admiration for him. If she had discovered that he was heir to an earldom, how different it would have been! Before long the captain returned, and then a rustic table was spread under the lime trees, with purple grapes, peaches, crimson and gold apricots, and ruby plums.

"It's quite picturesque," Lady Hampton declared, with a smile; "and Elinor, dear child, enjoys fruit so much."

In spite of Lady Hampton's wish, there did not appear to be much cordiality between the two girls. Occasionally Elinor would look at the captain, who was not slow to return her glances with interest. His eyes said plainly that he thought her very lovely.

Miss Rocheford was in every respect the model of a well brought up young lady. She knew that the grand end and aim of her existence was to marry well—she never forgot that. She was well-born, well-bred, beautiful, accomplished, but without fortune. From her earliest girlhood Lady Hampton had impressed upon her the duty of marrying money.

"You have everything else, Elinor," she was accustomed to say. "You must marry for title and money."

Miss Rocheford knew it. She had no objection to her fate—she was quite passive over it—but she did hope at times that the man who had the title and money would be young, handsome, and agreeable. If he were not, she could not help it, but she hoped he would be.

Lady Hampton had recently become a widow. In her youth she had felt some little hope of being mistress of Darrell Court; but that hope had soon died. Now, however, that a niece was thrown upon her hands, she took heart of grace in another respect; for Sir Oswald was not an old man. It was true his hair was white, but he was erect, dignified, and, in Lady Hampton's opinion, more interesting than a handsome young man, who would think of nothing but himself. If he would be but sensible, and, instead of adopting that proud, unformed girl, marry, how much better it would be!

She knew that her niece was precisely the style that he admired—elegant, delicate, utterly incapable of any originality, ready at any moment to yield her opinions and ideas, ready to do implicitly as she was told, to believe in the superiority of her husband—a model woman, in short, after Sir Oswald's own heart. She saw that the baronet was much struck with Elinor; she knew that in his own mind he was contrasting the two girls—the graceful timidity of the one, her perfect polish of manner, with the brusque independence and terribly plain-spoken fashion of the other.

"It would be ten thousand pities," said Lady Hampton to herself, "to see that girl mistress of Darrell Court. She would make a good queen for the Sandwich Islands. Before I go, I must open Sir Oswald's eyes, and give him a few useful hints."

CHAPTER XIII
SIR OSWALD THINKS OF MARRIAGE

Fortune favored Lady Hampton. Sir Oswald was so delighted with his visitors that he insisted upon their remaining for luncheon.

"The young ladies will have time to become friends," he said; but it was well that he did not see how contemptuously Pauline turned away at the words. "Pauline," he continued, "Miss Rocheford will like to see the grounds. This is her first visit to Darrell Court. Show her the fountains and the flower-gardens."

Elinor looked up with a well-assumed expression of rapture; Pauline's look of annoyance indicated that she obeyed greatly against her will.

Sir Oswald saw the captain looking wistfully after the two girlish figures.

"Go," he said, with a courtly smile. "Young people like to be together. I will entertain Lady Hampton."

Greatly relieved, the captain followed. He was so deeply and so desperately in love that he could not endure to see Pauline Darrell talking even to the girl by her side. He would fain have engrossed every word, every glance of hers himself; he was madly jealous when such were bestowed upon others.

The three walked down the broad cedar path together, the captain all gallant attention, Miss Rocheford all sweetness, Pauline haughty as a young barbaric queen bound by a conqueror's chains. She did not like her companions, and did not even make a feint of being civil to them.

Meanwhile the opportunity so longed for by Lady Hampton had arrived; and the lady seized it with alacrity. She turned to Sir Oswald with a smile.

"You amuse me," she said, "by giving yourself such an air of age. Why do you consider yourself so old, Sir Oswald? If it were not that I feared to flatter you, I should say that there were few young men to compare with you."

"My dear Lady Hampton," returned the baronet, in a voice that was not without pathos, "look at this."

He placed his thin white hand upon his white hair. Lady Hampton laughed again.

"What does that matter? Why, many men are gray even in their youth. I have always wondered why you seek to appear so old, Sir Oswald. I feel sure, judging from many indications, that you cannot be sixty."

"No; but I am over fifty—and my idea is that, at fifty, one is really old."

"Nothing of the kind!" she said, with great energy. "Some of the finest men I have known were only in the prime of life then. If you were seventy, you might think of speaking as you do. Sir Oswald," she asked, abruptly, looking keenly at his face, "why have you never married?"

He smiled, but a flush darkened the fine old face.

"I was in love once," he replied, simply, "and only once. The lady was young and fair. She loved me in return. But a few weeks before our marriage she was suddenly taken ill and died. I have never even thought of replacing her."

"How sad! What sort of a lady was she, Sir Oswald—this fair young love of yours?"

"Strange to say, in face, figure, and manner she somewhat resembled your lovely young niece, Lady Hampton. She had the same quiet, graceful manner, the same polished grace—so different from——"

"From Miss Darrell," supplied the lady, promptly. "How that unfortunate girl must jar upon you!"

"She does; but there are times when I have hopes of her. We are talking like old friends now, Lady Hampton. I may tell you that I think there is one and only one thing that can redeem my niece, and that is love. Love works wonders sometimes, and I have hopes that it may do so in her case. A grand master-passion such as controls the Darrells when they love at all—that would redeem her. It would soften that fierce pride and hauteur, it would bring her to the ordinary level of womanhood; it would cure her of many of the fantastic ideas that seem to have taken possession of her; it would make her—what she certainly is not now—a gentlewoman."

"Do you think so?" queried Lady Hampton, doubtfully.

"I am sure of it. When I look at that grand face of hers, often so defiant, I think to myself that she may be redeemed by love."

"And if this grand master-passion does not come to her—if she cares for some one only after the ordinary fashion of women—what then?"

He threw up his hands with a gesture indicative of despair.

"Or," continued Lady Hampton—"pray pardon me for suggesting such a thing, Sir Oswald, but people of the world, like you and myself, know what odd things are likely at any time to happen—supposing that she should marry some commonplace lover, after a commonplace fashion, and that then the master-passion should find her out, what would be the fate of Darrell Court?"

"I cannot tell," replied Sir Oswald, despairingly.

"With a person, especially a young girl, of her self-willed, original, independent nature, one is never safe. How thankful I am that my niece is so sweet and so womanly!"

Sir Oswald sat for some little time in silence. He looked on this fair ancestral home of his, with its noble woods and magnificent gardens. What indeed would become of it if it fell into the ill-disciplined hands of an ill-disciplined girl—unless, indeed, she were subject to the control of a wise husband?

Would Pauline ever submit to such control? Her pale, grand face rose before him, the haughty lips, the proud, calm eyes—the man who mastered her, who brought her mind into subjection, would indeed be a superior being. For the first time a doubt crossed Sir Oswald's mind as to whether she would ever recognize that superior being in Captain Langton. He knew that there were depths in the girl's nature beyond his own reach. It was not all pride, all defiance—there were genius, poetry, originality, grandeur of intellect, and greatness of heart before which the baronet knew that he stood in hopeless, helpless awe.

Lady Hampton laid her hand on his arm.

"Do not despond, old friend," she said. "I understand you. I should feel like you. I should dread to leave the inheritance of my fathers in such dangerous hands. But, Sir Oswald, why despond? Why not marry?"

The baronet started.

"Marry!" he repeated. "Why, I have never thought of such a thing."

"Think of it now," counseled the lady, laughingly; "you will find the advice most excellent. Instead of tormenting yourself about an ill-conditioned girl, who delights in defying you, you can have an amiable, accomplished, elegant, and gentle wife to rule your household and attend to your comfort—you might have a son of your own to succeed you, and Darrell Court might yet remain in the hands of the Darrells."

"But, my dear Lady Hampton, where should I find such a wife? I am no longer young—who would marry me?"

"Any sensible girl in England. Take my advice, Sir Oswald. Let us have a Lady Darrell, and not an ill-trained girl who will delight in setting the world at defiance. Indeed, I consider that marriage is a duty which you owe to society and to your race."

"I have never thought of it. I have always considered myself as having, so to speak, finished with life."

"You have made a great mistake, but it is one that fortunately can be remedied."

Lady Hampton rose from her seat, and walked a few steps forward.

"I have put his thoughts in the right groove," she mused; "but I ought to say a word about Elinor."

She turned to him again.

"You ask me who would marry you. Why, Sir Oswald, in England there are hundreds of girls, well-bred, elegant, graceful, gentle, like my niece, who would ask nothing better from fortune than a husband like yourself."

She saw her words take effect. She had turned his thoughts and ideas in the right direction at last.

"Shall we go and look after our truants?" she asked, suavely.

And they walked together down the path where Pauline had so indignantly gathered the broken lily. As though unconsciously, Lady Hampton began to speak of her niece.

"I have adopted Elinor entirely," she said—"indeed there was no other course for me to pursue. Her mother was my youngest sister; she has been dead many years. Elinor has been living with her father, but he has just secured a government appointment abroad, and I asked him to give his daughter to me."

"It was very kind of you," observed Sir Oswald.

"Nay, the kindness is on her part, not on mine. She is like a sunbeam in my house. Fair, gentle, a perfect lady, she has not one idea that is not in itself innately refined and delicate. I knew that if she went into society at all she would soon marry."

"Is there any probability of that?" asked Sir Oswald.

"No, for by her own desire we shall live very quietly this year. She wished to see Darrell Court and its owner—we have spoken so much of you—but with that exception we shall go nowhere."

"I hope she is pleased with Darrell Court," said Sir Oswald.

"How could she fail to be, as well as delighted with its hospitable master? I could read that much in her pretty face. Here they are, Sir Oswald—Miss Darrell alone, looking very dignified—Elinor, with your friend. Ah, she knows how to choose friends!"

They joined the group, but Miss Darrell was in one of her most dignified moods. She had been forced to listen to a fashionable conversation between Captain Langton and Miss Rocheford, and her indignation and contempt had got the better of her politeness.

They all partook of luncheon together, and then the visitors departed; not, however, until Lady Hampton had accepted from Sir Oswald an invitation to spend a week at Darrell Court. Sir Francis and Lady Allroy were coming—the party would be a very pleasant one; and Sir Oswald said he would give a grand ball in the course of the week—a piece of intelligence which delighted the captain and Miss Rocheford greatly.

Then Lady Hampton and her niece set out. Sir Oswald held Elinor's hand rather longer than strict etiquette required.

"How like she is to my dead love!" he thought, and his adieu was more than cordial.

As they drove home, Lady Hampton gazed at her niece with a look of triumph.

"You have a splendid chance, Elinor," she said; "no girl ever had a better. What do you think of Darrell Court?"

"It is a palace, aunt—a magnificent, stately palace. I have never seen anything like it before."

"It may be yours if you play your cards well, my dear."

"How?" cried the girl. "I thought it was to be Miss Darrell's. Every one says she is her uncle's heiress."

"People need not make too sure of it. I do not think so. With a little management, Sir Oswald will propose to you, I am convinced."

The girl's face fell.

"But, aunt, he is so old."

"He is only just fifty, Elinor. No girl in her senses would ever call that old. It is just the prime of life."

"I like Captain Langton so much the better," she murmured.

"I have no doubt that you do, my dear; but there must be no nonsense about liking or disliking. Sir Oswald's income must be quite twenty thousand per annum, and if you manage well, all that may be yours. But you must place yourself under my directions, and do implicitly what I tell you, if so desirable a result is to be achieved."

CHAPTER XIV
PAULINE'S LOVE FOR DARRELL COURT

Miss Darrell preserved a dignified silence during dinner; but when the servants had withdrawn, Sir Oswald, who had been charmed with his visitors, said:

"I am delighted, Pauline, that you have secured a young lady friend. You will be pleased with Miss Rocheford."

Pauline made no reply; and Sir Oswald, never thinking that it was possible for one so gentle and lovely as Miss Rocheford to meet with anything but the warmest praise, continued:

"I consider that Lady Hampton has done us all a great favor in bringing her charming niece with her. Were you not delighted with her, Pauline?"

Miss Darrell made no haste to reply; but Sir Oswald evidently awaited an answer.

"I do not like Miss Rocheford," she said at length; "it would be quite useless to pretend that I do."

Miss Hastings looked up in alarm. Captain Langton leaned back in his chair, with a smile on his lips—he always enjoyed Pauline's "scenes" when her anger was directed against any one but himself; Sir Oswald's brow darkened.

"Pray, Miss Darrell, may I ask why you do not like her?"

"Certainly. I do not like her for the same reason that I should not like a diet of sugar. Miss Rocheford is very elegant and gentle, but she has no opinions of her own; every wind sways her; she has no ideas, no force of character. It is not possible for me to really like such a person."

"But, my dear Pauline," interposed Miss Hastings, "you should not express such very decided opinions; you should be more reticent, more tolerant."

"If I am not to give my opinion," said Pauline, serenely, "I should not be asked for it."

"Pray, Miss Hastings, do not check such delightful frankness," cried Sir Oswald, angrily, his hands trembling, his face darkening with an angry frown.

He said no more; but the captain, who thought he saw a chance of recommending himself to Miss Darrell's favor, observed, later on in the evening:

"I knew you would not like our visitor, Miss Darrell. She was not of the kind to attract you."

"Sir Oswald forced my opinion from me," she said; "but I shall not listen to one word of disparagement of Miss Rocheford from you, Captain Langton. You gave her great attention, you flattered her, you paid her many compliments; and now, if you say that you dislike her, it will simply be deceitful, and I abominate deceit."

It was plain that Pauline had greatly annoyed Sir Oswald. He liked Miss Rocheford very much; the sweet, yielding, gentle disposition, which Pauline had thought so monotonous, delighted him. Miss Rocheford was so like that lost, dead love of his—so like! And for this girl, who tried his patience every hour of the day, to find fault with her! It was too irritating; he could not endure it. He was very cold and distant to Pauline for some time, but the young girl was serenely unconscious of it.

In one respect she was changing rapidly. The time had been when she had been indifferent to Darrell Court, when she had thought with regret of the free, happy life in the Rue d'Orme, where she could speak lightly of the antiquity and grandeurs of the race from which she had sprung; but all that was altered now. It could not be otherwise, considering how romantic, how poetical, how impressionable she was, how keenly alive to everything beautiful and noble. She was living here in the very cradle of the race, where every tree had its legend, every stone its story; how could she be indifferent while the annals of her house were filled with noble retrospects? The Darrells had numbered great warriors and statesmen among their number. Some of the noblest women in England had been Darrells; and Pauline had learned to glory in the old stories, and to feel her heart beat with pride as she remembered that she, too, was a Darrell.

So, likewise, she had grown to love the Court for its picturesque beauty, its stately magnificence, and the time came soon when almost every tree and shrub was dear to her.

It was Pauline's nature to love deeply and passionately if she loved at all; there was no lukewarmness about her. She was incapable of those gentle, womanly likings that save all wear and tear of passion. She could not love in moderation; and very soon the love of Darrell Court became a passion with her. She sketched the mansion from twenty different points of view, she wrote verses about it; she lavished upon it the love which some girls lavish upon parents, brothers, sisters, and friends.

She stood one day looking at it as the western sunbeams lighted it up until it looked as though it were bathed in gold. The stately towers and turrets, the flower-wreathed balconies, the grand arched windows, the Gothic porch, all made up a magnificent picture; the fountains were playing in the sunlit air, the birds singing in the stately trees. She turned to Miss Hastings, and the governess saw tears standing warm and bright in the girl's eyes.

"How beautiful it is!" she said. "I cannot tell you—I have no words to tell you—how I love my home."

The heart of the gentle lady contracted with sudden fear.

"It is very beautiful," she said; "but, Pauline, do not love it too much; remember how very uncertain everything is."

"There can be nothing uncertain about my inheritance," returned the girl. "I am a Darrell—the only Darrell left to inherit it. And, oh! Miss Hastings, how I love it! But it is not for its wealth that I love it; it is my heart that is bound to it. I love it as I can fancy a husband loves his wife, a mother her child. It is everything to me."

"Still," said Miss Hastings, "I would not love it too well; everything is so uncertain."

"But not that," replied Pauline, quickly. "My uncle would never dare to be so unjust as to leave Darrell Court to any one but a Darrell. I am not in the least afraid—not in the least."

CHAPTER XV
BREACH BETWEEN UNCLE AND NIECE

A few days later the tranquillity of Darrell Court was at an end. The invited guests were expected, and Sir Oswald had determined to do them all honor. The state-apartments, which had not been used during his tenure, were all thrown open; the superb ball-room, once the pride of the county, was redecorated; the long, empty corridors and suites of apartments reserved for visitors, were once more full of life. Miss Hastings was the presiding genius; Pauline Darrell took far less interest in the preparations.

"I am glad," she said, one morning, "that I am to see your 'world,' Sir Oswald. You despise mine; I shall be anxious to see what yours is like."

The baronet answered her testily:

"I do not quite understand your remarks about 'worlds.' Surely we live under the same conditions."

"Not in the same world of people," she opposed; "and I am anxious to see what yours is like."

"What do you expect to find in what you are pleased to call my world, Pauline?" he asked, angrily.

"Little truth, and plenty of affectation; little honor, and plenty of polish; little honesty, and very high-sounding words; little sincerity, and plenty of deceit."

"By what right do you sit in judgment?" he demanded.

"None at all," replied Pauline; "but as people are always speaking ill of the dear, honest world in which I have lived, I may surely be permitted to criticise the world that is outside it."

Sir Oswald turned away angrily; and Miss Hastings sighed over the girl's willfulness.

"Why do you talk to Sir Oswald in a fashion that always irritates him?" she remonstrated.

"We live in a free country, and have each of us freedom of speech."

"I am afraid the day will come when you will pay a sad price for yours."

But Pauline Darrell only laughed. Such fears never affected her; she would sooner have expected to see the heavens fall at her feet than that Sir Oswald should not leave Darrell Court to her—his niece, a Darrell, with the Darrell face and the Darrell figure, the true, proud features of the race. He would never dare to do otherwise, she thought, and she would not condescend to change either her thought or speech to please him.

"The Darrells do not know fear," she would say; "there never yet was an example of a Darrell being frightened into anything."

So the breach between the uncle and the niece grew wider every day. He could not understand her; the grand, untrained, undisciplined, poetical nature was beyond him—he could neither reach its heights nor fathom its depths. There were times when he thought that, despite her outward coldness and pride, there was within a soul of fire, when he dimly understood the magnificence of the character he could not read, when he suspected there might be some souls that could not be narrowed or forced into a common groove. Nevertheless he feared her; he was afraid to trust, not the honor, but the fame of his race to her.

"She is capable of anything," he would repeat to himself again and again. "She would fling the Darrell revenues to the wind; she would transform Darrell Court into one huge observatory, if astronomy pleased her—into one huge laboratory, if she gave herself to chemistry. One thing is perfectly clear to me—she can never be my heiress until she is safely married."

And, after great deliberation—after listening to all his heart's pleading in favor of her grace, her beauty, her royal generosity of character, the claim of her name and her truth—he came to the decision that if she would marry Captain Langton, whom he loved perhaps better than any one else in the world, he would at once make his will, adopt her, and leave her heiress of all that he had in the world.

One morning the captain confided in him, telling him how dearly he loved his beautiful niece, and then Sir Oswald revealed his intentions.

"You understand, Aubrey," he said—"the girl is magnificently beautiful—she is a true Darrell; but I am frightened about her. She is not like other girls; she is wanting in tact, in knowledge of the world, and both are essential. I hope you will win her. I shall die content if I leave Darrell Court in your hands, and if you are her husband. I could not pass her over to make you my heir; but if you can persuade her to marry you, you can take the name of Darrell, and you can guide and direct her. What do you say, Aubrey?"

"What do I say?" stammered the captain. "I say this—that I love her so dearly that I would marry her if she had not a farthing. I love her so that language cannot express the depth of my affection for her."

The captain was for a few minutes quite overcome—he had been so long dunned for money, so hardly pressed, so desperate, that the chance of twenty thousand a year and Darrell Court was almost too much for him. His brow grew damp, and his lips pale. All this might be his own if he could but win the consent of this girl. Yet he feared her; the proud, noble face, the grand, dark eyes rose before him, and seemed to rebuke him for his presumptuous hope. How was he to win her? Flattery, sweet, soft words would never do it. One scornful look from her sent his ideas "flying right and left."

"If she were only like other girls," he thought, "I could make her my wife in a few weeks."

Then he took heart of grace. Had he not been celebrated for his good fortune among the fair sex? Had he not always found his handsome person, his low, tender voice, his pleasing manner irresistible? Who was this proud, dark-eyed girl that she should measure the depths of his heart and soul, and find them wanting? Surely he must be superior to the artists in shabby coats by whom she had been surrounded. And yet he feared as much as he hoped.

"She has such a way of making me feel small," he said to himself; "and if that kind of feeling comes over me when I am making her an offer, it will be of no use to plead my suit."

But what a prospect—master of Darrell Court and twenty thousand per annum! He would endure almost any humiliation to obtain that position.

"She must have me," he said to himself—"she shall have me! I will force her to be my wife!"

Why, if he could but announce his engagement to Miss Darrell, he could borrow as much money as would clear off all his liabilities! And how much he needed money no one knew better than himself. He had paid this visit to the Court because there were two writs out against him in London, and, unless he could come to some settlement of them, he knew what awaited him.

And all—fortune, happiness, wealth, freedom, prosperity—depended on one word from the proud lips that had hardly ever spoken kindly to him. He loved her, too—loved her with a fierce, desperate love that at times frightened himself.

"I should like you," said Sir Oswald, at the conclusion of their interview, "to have the matter settled as soon as you can; because, I tell you, frankly, if my niece does not consent to marry you, I shall marry myself. All my friends are eagerly solicitous for me to do so; they do not like the prospect of seeing a grand old inheritance like this fall into the hands of a willful, capricious girl. But I tell you in confidence, Aubrey, I do not wish to marry. I am a confirmed old bachelor now, and it would be a sad trouble to me to have my life changed by marriage. Still I would rather marry than that harm should come to Darrell Court."

"Certainly," agreed the captain.

"I do not mind telling you still further that I have seen a lady whom, if I marry at all, I should like to make my wife—in fact, she resembles some one I used to know long years ago. I have every reason to believe she is much admired and sought after; so that I want you to settle your affairs as speedily as possible. Mind, Aubrey, they must be settled—there must be no deferring, no putting off; you must have an answer—yes or no—very shortly; and you must not lose an hour in communicating that answer to me."

"I hope it will be a favorable one," said Aubrey Langton; but his mind misgave him. He had an idea that the girl had found him wanting; he could not forget her first frank declaration that she did not like him.

"If she refuses me, have I your permission to tell Miss Darrell the alternative?" he asked of Sir Oswald.

The baronet thought deeply for some minutes, and then said:

"Yes; it is only fair and just that she should know it—that she should learn that if she refuses you she loses all chance of being my heiress. But do not say anything of the lady I have mentioned."

The visitors were coming on Tuesday, and Thursday was the day settled for the ball.

"All girls like balls," thought Captain Langton. "Pauline is sure to be in a good temper then, and I will ask her on Thursday night."

But he owned to himself that he would rather a thousand times have faced a whole battalion of enemies than ask Pauline Darrell to be his wife.

CHAPTER XVI
THE QUEEN OF THE BALL

It was many years since Darrell Court had been so gay. Sir Oswald had resolved that the ball should be one that should reflect credit on the giver and the guests. He had ordered a fine band of music and a magnificent banquet. The grounds were to be illuminated, colored lamps being placed among the trees; the ball-room was a gorgeous mass of brilliant bloom—tier after tier of magnificent flowers was ranged along the walls, white statues gleaming from the bright foliage, and little fountains here and there sending up their fragrant spray.

Sir Oswald had sent to London for some one to superintend the decorations; but they were not perfected until Miss Darrell, passing through, suggested first one alteration, and then another, until the originators, recognizing her superior artistic judgment and picturesque taste, deferred to her, and then the decorations became a magnificent work of art.

Sir Oswald declared himself delighted, and the captain's praises were unmeasured. Then, and then only, Miss Darrell began to feel some interest in the ball; her love of beauty was awakened and pleased—there was something more in the event than the mere gratification of seeing people dance.

The expected visitors had arrived on the Tuesday—Lady Hampton, radiant with expected victory; Elinor, silent, thoughtful, and more gentle than ever, and consequently more pleasing.

Lady Hampton was delighted with the idea of the ball.

"You must make a bold stroke for a husband on that evening, Elinor," she said. "You shall have a superb dress, and I shall quite expect you to receive and accept an offer from Sir Oswald."

Elinor Rocheford raised her eyes. There was something wistful in their expression.

"Oh, aunt," she said, "I like the captain so much better!"

Lady Hampton did not lose her good humor—Elinor was not the first refractory girl she had brought to her senses.

"Never mind about liking the captain, my dear; that is only natural. He is not in love with you. I can see through the whole business. If Darrell Court goes to Miss Darrell, he will marry her. He can marry no girl without money, because he is, I know, over head and ears in debt. Major Penryn was speaking of him to-day. The only way to prevent his marriage with Miss Darrell is for you to take Sir Oswald yourself."

Elinor's face flushed.

Lady Hampton certainly understood the art of evoking the worst feelings. Jealousy, envy, and dislike stirred faintly in the gentle heart of her niece.

"I hope you will do your very best to win Sir Oswald's affections," continued Lady Hampton, "for I should not like to see Darrell Court fall into the hands of that proud girl."

"Nor should I," assented Miss Rocheford.

The evening of the ball arrived at last, and Lady Hampton stood like a fairy godmother in Elinor's dressing-room, superintending the toilet that was to work such wonders. Lady Hampton herself looked very imposing in her handsome dress of black velvet and point lace, with diamond ornaments. Elinor's dress was a triumph of art. Her fresh, fair, gentle loveliness shone to perfection, aided by her elaborate costume of white silk and white lace, trimmed with green and silver leaves. The ornaments were all of silver—both fringe and leaves; the headdress was a green wreath with silver flowers. Nothing could have been more elegant and effective. There was a gentle flush on the fair face and a light in the blue eyes.

"That will do, Elinor," said Lady Hampton, complacently. "Your dress is perfection. I have no fear now—you will have no rival."

Perhaps Lady Hampton had never disliked Pauline Darrell more than on that night, for the magnificent beauty of the girl had never been so apparent. Sir Oswald had given his niece *carte blanche* in respect to preparation for the ball, but she had not at first taken sufficient interest in the matter to send to London, as he wished, for a dress. Later on she had gone to the large wardrobe, where the treasures accumulated by the Ladies Darrell lay. Such shining treasures of satin, velvet, silk, cashmere, and such profusion of laces and ornaments were there! She selected a superb costume—a magnificent amber brocade, embroidered with white flowers, gorgeous, beautiful, artistic. It was a dress that had been made for some former Lady Darrell.

How well it became her! The amber set off her dark beauty as a golden frame does a rich picture. The dress required but little alteration; it was cut square, showing the white, stately, graceful neck, and the sleeves hung after the Grecian fashion, leaving the round, white arms bare. The light shining upon the dress changed with every movement; it was as though the girl was enveloped in sunbeams. Every lady present envied that dress, and pronounced it to be gorgeous beyond comparison.

Pauline's rich curls of dark hair were studded with diamond stars, and a diamond necklace clasped her white throat—this was Sir Oswald's present. Her artistic taste had found yet further scope; for she had enhanced the beauty of her dress by the addition of white daphnes shrouded in green leaves.

Sir Oswald looked at her in admiration—her magnificent beauty, her queenly figure, her royal grace and ease of movement, her splendid costume, all impressed him. From every fold of her shining dress came a rich, sweet, subtle perfume; her usually pale face had on it an unwonted flush of delicate rose-leaf color.

"If she would but be like that sweet Elinor!" thought Sir Oswald. "I could not wish for a more beautiful mistress for Darrell Court."

She stood by his side while he received his guests, and her dignified ease delighted him.

"Had she been some Eastern queen," he thought, "her eccentricities would have hurt no one. As it is——" and Sir Oswald concluded his sentence by a grave shake of the head.

The captain, pleased with Miss Rocheford's graceful loveliness, had been amusing himself by paying her some very choice compliments, and she was delighted with them.

"If Sir Oswald were only like him!" she thought; and Aubrey Langton, meeting the timid, gentle glance, said to himself that he must be careful—he had no wish to win the girl's heart—he should be quite at a loss to know what to do with it.

When he saw Pauline his courage almost failed him.

"How am I to ask that magnificent girl to marry me?" he said.

Sir Oswald had expressed a wish that Aubrey and Pauline would open the ball; it would give people an idea of what he wished, he thought, and prevent other gentlemen from "turning her head" by paying her any marked attention. Yet he knew how difficult it would be for any one to win Pauline's regard. She made no objection when he expressed his wish to her, but she did not look particularly pleased.

Captain Langton understood the art of dancing better perhaps than the art of war; he was perfect in it—even Pauline avowed it. With him dancing was the very poetry of motion. The flowers, the lights, the sweet, soft music, the fragrance, the silvery sound of laughter, the fair faces and shining jewels of the ladies, all stirred and warmed Pauline's imagination; they brought bright and vivid fancies to her, and touched the poetical beauty-loving soul. A glow came over her face, a light into her proud, dark eyes, her lips were wreathed in smiles—no one had ever seen Pauline so beautiful before.

"You enjoy this, do you not?" said Aubrey Langton, as he watched her beautiful face.

"I shall do so," she replied, "very much indeed;" and at what those words implied the captain's courage fell to zero.

He saw how many admiring eyes followed her; he knew that all the gentlemen in the room were envying him his position with Miss Darrell. He knew that, pretty as some of the girls were, Pauline outshone them as the sun outshines the stars; and he knew that she was queen of the *fete*—queen of the ball.

"This is the first time you have met many of the county people, is it not?" he asked.

She looked round indifferently.

"Yes, it is the first time," she replied.

"Do you admire any of the men? I know how different your taste is from that of most girls. Is there any one here who has pleased you?"

She laughed.

"I cannot tell," she answered; "you forget this is the first dance. I have had no opportunity of judging."

"I believe that I am jealous already," he observed.

She looked at him; her dark eyes made his heart beat, they seemed to look through him.

"You are what?" she asked. "Captain Langton, I do not understand."

He dared not repeat the words.

"I wish," he said, with a deep sigh, "that I had all the talent and all the wealth in the world."

"For what reason?" she inquired.

"Because you would care for me then."

"Because of your talent and wealth!" she exclaimed. "No, that I should not."

"But I thought you admired talent so much," he said, in surprise.

"So I do; but mere talent would never command my respect, nor mere wealth."

"The two together might," he suggested.

"No. You would not understand me, Captain Langton, were I to explain. Now this dance is over, and I heard you engage Miss Rocheford for the next."

"And you," he said, gloomily—"what are you going to do?"

"To enjoy myself," she replied; and, from the manner in which her face brightened when he left her, the captain feared she was pleased to be quit of him.

CHAPTER XVII
PAULINE'S BRIGHT FANCIES

The ball at Darrell Court was a brilliant success. Sir Oswald was delighted, Lady Hampton complimented him so highly.

"This is just as it ought to be, Sir Oswald," she said. "One who can give such entertainments as this should not think of retiring from a world he is so well qualified to adorn. Confess, now, that under the influence of that music you could dance yourself."

Sir Oswald laughed.

"I must plead guilty," he said. "How beautiful Miss Rocheford looks to-night!"

"It is well for you, Sir Oswald, that you have not heard all the compliments that the dear child has lavished on you; they would have made you vain."

Sir Oswald's face brightened with pleasure.

"Is your niece pleased? I am very glad indeed. It was more to give her pleasure than from any other motive that I gave the ball."

"Then you have succeeded perfectly. Now, Sir Oswald, do you not see that what I said was true—that an establishment like this requires a mistress? Darrell Court always led the hospitalities of the county. It is only since no lady has lived here that it has fallen into the background."

"It shall be in the background no longer," said Sir Oswald. "I think my first ball is a very successful one. How happy everybody looks!"

But of all that brilliant company, Pauline Darrell was queen. There were men present who would have given anything for one smile from her lips. They admired her, they thought her beautiful beyond comparison, but they did not feel quite at ease with her. She was somewhat beyond them; they did not understand her. She did not blush, and glow, and smile when they said pretty things to her. When they gave her their most brilliant small-talk, she had nothing to give them in return. A soul quite different from theirs looked at them out of her dark, proud eyes. They said to themselves that she was very beautiful, but that she required softening, and that something lovable and tender was wanting in her. She was a queen to be worshiped, an empress to receive all homage, but not a woman to be loved. So they thought who were not even capable of judging such capacity for love as hers.

She was also not popular with the ladies. They thought her very superb; they admired her magnificent dress; but they pronounced her proud and reserved. They said she gave herself airs, that she took no pains to make friends; and they did not anticipate any very great rejoicings when Darrell Court should belong to her. The elder ladies pronounced that judgment on her; the younger ones shrank abashed, and were slightly timid in her presence.

Sir Oswald, it was noticed, led Miss Rocheford in to supper, and seemed to pay her very great attention. Some of the ladies made observations, but others said it was all nonsense; if Sir Oswald had ever intended to marry, he would have married years ago, and his choice would have fallen on a lady of mature age, not on a slight, slender girl. Besides—and who could find an answer to such an argument?—was it not settled that Miss Darrell was to be his heiress? There was no doubt about that.

The baronet's great affection for Aubrey Langton was also known. More than one of the guests present guessed at the arrangement made, and said that in all probability Miss Darrell would marry the captain, and that they would have the Court after Sir Oswald's death.

The banquet was certainly a magnificent one. The guests did full justice to the costly wines, the rare and beautiful fruits, the *recherche* dishes prepared with so much skill and labor. When supper was ended, the dancers returned to the ball-room, but Miss Darrell was already rather weary of it all.

She stole away during the first dance after supper. The lamps were lighted in the conservatory, and shed a soft, pearly light over the fragrant flowers; the great glass doors at the end were open, and beyond lay the moonlight, soft, sweet, and silvery, steeping the flowers, the trees, and the long grass in its mild light. Without, all was so calm, so still; there was the evening sky with its myriad stars, so calm and so serene; close to the doors stood great sheaves of white lilies, and just inside was a nest of fragrant daphnes and jessamines.

Pauline stood lost in delight; the perfume seemed to float in from the moonlight and infold her. This quiet, holy, tranquil beauty touched her heart as the splendor of the ball-room could not; her soul grew calm and still; she seemed nearer happiness than she had ever been before.

"How beautiful the world is!" she thought. She raised her face, so serenely placid and fair in the moonlight; the silver radiance fell upon it, adding all that was needed to make it perfect, a blended softness and tenderness. The gorgeous, golden-hued dress falling around her, glistened, gleamed, and glowed; her diamonds shone like flames. No artist ever dreamed of a fairer picture than this girl in the midst of the moonlight and the flowers.

Bright fancies thronged her mind. She thought of the time when she should be mistress of that rich domain. No mercenary delight made her heart thrill; it was not the prospect of being rich that delighted her; it was a nobler pride—delight in the grand old home where heroes had lived and died, earnest thoughts of how she would care for it, how she would love it as some living thing when it should be her own.

Her own! Verily her lines were cast in pleasant places! She dreamed great things—of the worthy deeds she would do, of the noble charities she would carry out, the magnificent designs she would bring to maturity when Darrell Court should be hers.

It was not that she wished for it at once. She did not love Sir Oswald—their natures were too antagonistic for that; but she did not wish—indeed, she was incapable of wishing—that his life should be shortened even for one hour. She only remembered that in the course of time this grand inheritance must be hers. How she would help those artist-friends of her father's! What orders she would give them, what pictures she would buy, what encouragement she would give to art and literature! How she would foster genius! How she would befriend the clever and gifted poor ones of the earth!

The beautiful moonlight seemed to grow fairer, the blue, starry heavens nearer, as the grand and gracious possibilities of her life revealed themselves to her. Her heart grew warm, her soul trembled with delight.

And then—then there would be something dearer and fairer than all this—something that comes to every woman—her birthright—something that would complete her life, that would change it, that would make music of every word, and harmony of every action. The time would come when love would find her out, when the fairy prince would wake her from her magic sleep. She was pure and spotless as the white lilies standing near her; the breath of love had never passed over her. There had been no long, idle conversations with young girls on the subject of love and lovers; her heart was a blank page. But there came to her that night, as she stood dreaming her maiden dreams among the flowers, an idea of how she could love, and of what manner of man he would be who should win her love.

Was she like Undine? Were there depths in her heart and soul which could not be reached until love had brought them to light? She felt in herself great capabilities that had never yet been exercised or called into action. Love would complete her life; it would be the sun endowing the flowers with life, warmth, and fragrance.

What manner of man must he be who would wake this soul of hers to perfect life? She had seen no one yet capable of doing so. The mind that mastered hers must be a master-mind; the soul that could bring her soul into subjection must be a grand soul, a just soul, noble and generous.

Ah, well, the moonlight was fair, and the flowers were fair. Soon, perhaps, this fair dream of hers might be realized, and then— —

CHAPTER XVIII
REJECTED

A shadow came between Pauline and the moonlight, and a quiet voice said:

"Miss Darrell, I am so glad to find you here, and alone!"

Looking up, she saw Aubrey Langton standing by her side. Aubrey's fair, handsome face was flushed, and there was the fragrance of the wine-cup about him, for the gallant captain's courage had failed him, and he had to fortify himself.

He had seen Miss Darrell go into the conservatory, and he understood her well enough to be sure that she had gone thither in search of quiet. Here was his opportunity. He had been saying to himself all day that he must watch for his opportunity. Here it was; yet his courage failed him, and his heart sank; he would have given anything to any one who would have undertaken the task that lay before him. There was so much at stake—not only love, but wealth, fortune, even freedom—there was so much to be won or lost, that he was frightened.

However, as he said to himself, it had to be done. He went back to the dining-room and poured out for himself a tumbler of the baronet's generous old wine, which made his heart glow, and diffused warmth through his whole frame, and then he went on his difficult errand. He walked quietly through the conservatory, and saw Pauline standing at the doors.

He was not an artist, he had nothing of the poet about him, but the solemn beauty of that picture did touch him—the soft, sweet moonlight, the sheaves of white lilies, the nest of daphnes, and that most beautiful face raised to the starry sky.

He stood for some minutes in silence; a dim perception of his own unworthiness came over him. Pauline looked as though she stood in a charmed circle, which he almost feared to enter.

Then he went up to her and spoke. She was startled; she had been so completely absorbed in her dreams, and he was the last person on earth with whom she could identify them.

"I hope I have not startled you," he said. "I am so glad to find you here, Miss Darrell. There is something I wish to say to you."

Perhaps that beautiful, calm night-scene had softened her; she turned to him with a smile more gentle than he had ever seen on her face before.

"You want to tell me something—I am ready to listen, Captain Langton. What is it?"

He came nearer to her. The sweet, subtle perfume from the flowers at her breast reached him, the proud face that had always looked proudly on him, was near his own.

He came one step nearer still, and then Pauline drew back with a haughty gesture that seemed to scatter the light in her jewels.

"I can hear perfectly well," she said, coldly. "What is it you have to tell me?"

"Pauline, do not be unkind to me. Let me come nearer, where I may kneel at your feet and pray my prayer."

His face flushed, his heart warmed with his words; all the passionate love that he really felt for her woke within him. There was no feigning, no pretense—it was all reality. It was not Darrell Court he was thinking of, but Pauline, peerless, queenly Pauline; and in that moment he felt that he could give his whole life to win her.

"Let me pray my prayer," he repeated; "let me tell you how dearly I love you, Pauline—so dearly and so well that if you send me from you my life will be a burden to me, and I shall be the most wretched of men."

She did not look proud of angry, but merely sorry. Her dark eyes drooped, her lips even quivered.

"You love me," she rejoined—"really love me, Captain Langton?"

He interrupted her.

"I loved you the first moment that I saw you. I have admired others, but I have seen none like you. All the deep, passionate love of my heart has gone out to you; and, if you throw it from you, Pauline, I shall die."

"I am very sorry," she murmured, gently.

"Nay, not sorry. Why should you be sorry? You would not take a man's life, and hold it in the hollow of your hand, only to fling it away. You may have richer lovers, you may have titles and wealth offered to you, but you will never have a love truer or deeper than mine."

There was a ring of truth about his words, and they haunted her.

"I know I am unworthy of you. If I were a crowned king, and you, my peerless Pauline, the humblest peasant, I should choose you from the whole world to be my wife. But I am only a soldier—a poor soldier. I have but one treasure, and that I offer to you—the deepest, truest love of my heart. I would that I were a king, and could woo you more worthily."

She looked up quickly—his eyes were drinking in the beauty of her face; but there was something in them from which she shrank without knowing why. She would have spoken, but he went on, quickly:

"Only grant my prayer, Pauline—promise to be my wife—promise to love me—and I will live only for you. I will give you my heart, my thoughts, my life. I will take you to bright sunny lands, and will show you all that the earth holds beautiful and fair. You shall be my queen, and I will be your humblest slave."

His voice died away in a great tearless sob—he loved her so dearly, and there was so much at stake. She looked at him with infinite pity in her dark eyes. He had said all that he could think of; he had wooed her as eloquently as he was able; he had done his best, and now he waited for some word from her.

There were tenderness, pity, and surprise in her musical voice as she spoke to him.

"I am so sorry, Captain Langton. I never thought you loved me so well. I never dreamed that you had placed all your heart in your love."

"I have," he affirmed. "I have been reckless; I have thrown heart, love, manhood, life, all at your feet together. If you trample ruthlessly on them, Pauline, you will drive me to desperation and despair."

"I do not trample on them," she said, gently; "I would not wrong you so. I take them up in my hands and restore them to you, thanking you for the gift."

"What do you mean, Pauline?" he asked, while the flush died from his face.

"I mean," she replied, softly, "that I thank you for the gift you have offered me, but that I cannot accept it. I cannot be your wife, for I do not love you."

He stood for some minutes dazed by the heavy blow; he had taken hope from her gentle manner, and the disappointment was almost greater than he could bear.

"It gives me as much pain to say this," she continued, "as it gives you to hear it; pray believe that."

"I cannot bear it!" he cried. "I will not bear it! I will not believe it! It is my life I ask from you, Pauline—my life! You cannot send me from you to die in despair!"

His anguish was real, not feigned. Love, life, liberty, all were at stake. He knelt at her feet; he covered her white, jeweled hands with kisses and with hot, passionate tears. Her keen womanly instinct told her there was no feigning in the deep, broken sob that rose to his lips.

"It is my life!" he repeated. "If you send me from you, Pauline, I shall be a desperate, wicked man."

"You should not be so," she remarked, gently; "a great love, even if it be unfortunate, should ennoble a man, not make him wicked."

"Pauline," he entreated, "you must unsay those words. Think that you might learn to love me in time. I will be patient—I will wait long years for you—I will do anything to win you; only give me some hope that in time to come you will be mine."

"I cannot," she said; "it would be so false. I could never love you, Captain Langton."

He raised his face to hers.

"Will you tell me why? You do not reject me because I am poor—you are too noble to care for wealth. It is not because I am a soldier, with nothing to offer you but a loving heart. It is not for these things. Why do you reject me, Pauline?"

"No, you are right; it is not for any of those reasons; they would never prevent my being your wife if I loved you."

"Then why can you not love me?" he persisted.

"For many reasons. You are not at all the style of man I could love. How can you doubt me? Here you are wooing me, asking me to be your wife, offering me your love, and my hand does not tremble, my heart does not beat; your words give me no pleasure, only pain; I am conscious of nothing but a wish to end the interview. This is not love, is it, Captain Langton?"

"But in time," he pleaded—"could you not learn to care for me in time?"

"No, I am quite sure. You must not think I speak to pain you, but indeed you are the last man living with whom I could fall in love, or whom I could marry. If you were, as you say, a king, and came to me with a crown to offer, it would make no difference. It is better, as I am sure you will agree, to speak plainly."

Even in the moonlight she saw how white his face had grown, and what a sudden shadow of despair had come into his eyes. He stood silent for some minutes.

"You have unmanned me," he said, slowly, "but, Pauline, there is something else for you to hear. You must listen to me for your own sake," he added; and then Aubrey Langton's face flushed, his lips grew dry and hot, his breath came in short quick gasps—he had played a manly part, but now he felt that what he had to say would sound like a threat.

He did not know how to begin, and she was looking at him with those dark, calm eyes of hers, with that new light of pity on her face.

"Pauline," he said, hoarsely, "Sir Oswald wishes for this marriage. Oh, spare me—love me—be mine, because of the great love I bear you!"

"I cannot," she returned; "in my eyes it is a crime to marry without love. What you have to say of Sir Oswald say quickly."

"But you will hate me for it," he said.

"No, I will not be so unjust as to blame you for Sir Oswald's fault."

"He wishes us to marry; he is not only willing, but it would give him more pleasure than anything else on earth; and he says—do not blame me, Pauline—that if you consent he will make you mistress of Darrell Court and all his rich revenues."

She laughed—the pity died from her face, the proud, hard expression came back.

"He must do that in any case," she said, haughtily. "I am a Darrell; he would not dare to pass me by."

"Let me speak frankly to you, Pauline, for your own sake—your own sake, dear, as well as mine. You err—he is not so bound. Although the Darrell property has always descended from father to son, the entail was destroyed fifty years ago, and Sir Oswald is free to leave his property to whom he likes. There is only one imperative condition—whoever takes it must take with it the name of Darrell. Sir Oswald told me that much himself."

"But he would not dare to pass me—a Darrell—by, and leave it to a stranger."

"Perhaps not; but, honestly, Pauline, he told me that you were eccentric—I know that you are adorable—and that he would not dare to leave Darrell Court to you unless you were married to some one in whom he felt confidence—and that some one, Pauline, is your humble slave here, who adores you. Listen, dear—I have not finished. He said nothing about leaving the Court to a stranger; but he did say that unless we were married he himself should marry."

She laughed mockingly.

"I do not believe it," she said. "If he had intended to marry, he would have done so years ago. That is merely a threat to frighten me; but I am not to be frightened. No Darrell was ever a coward—I will not be coerced. Even if I liked you, Captain Langton, I would not marry you after that threat."

He was growing desperate now. Great drops stood on his brow—his lips were so hot and tremulous that he could hardly move them.

"Be reasonable, Pauline. Sir Oswald meant what he said. He will most certainly marry, and, when you see yourself deprived of this rich inheritance, you will hate your folly—hate and detest it."

"I would not purchase twenty Darrell Courts at the price of marrying a man I do not like," she said, proudly.

"You think it an idle threat—it is not so. Sir Oswald meant it in all truth. Oh, Pauline, love, riches, position, wealth, honor—all lie before you; will you willfully reject them?"

"I should consider it dishonor to marry you for the sake of winning Darrell Court, and I will not do it. It will be mine without that; and, if not, I would rather a thousand times go without it than pay the price named, and you may tell Sir Oswald so."

There was no more pity—no more tenderness in the beautiful face. It was all aglow with scorn, lighted with pride, flushed with contempt. The spell of the sweet moonlight was broken—the Darrell spirit was aroused— the fiery Darrell pride was all ablaze.

He felt angry enough to leave her at that moment and never look upon her again; but his position was so terrible, and he had so much at stake. He humbled himself again and again—he entreated her in such wild, passionate tones as must have touched one less proud.

"I am a desperate man, Pauline," he cried, at last; "and I pray you, for Heaven's sake, do not drive me to despair."

But no words of his had power to move her; there was nothing but scorn in the beautiful face, nothing but scorn in the willful, passionate heart.

"Sir Oswald should have known better than to use threats to a Darrell!" she said, with a flash of her dark eyes; and not the least impression could Aubrey Langton make upon her.

He was silent at last in sheer despair. It was all over; he had no more hope. Life had never held such a brilliant chance for any man, and now it was utterly lost. Instead of wealth, luxury, happiness, there was nothing before him but disgrace. He could almost have cursed her as she stood there in the moonlight before him. A deep groan, one of utter, uncontrollable anguish escaped his lips. She went nearer to him and started back in wonder at the white, settled despair on his face.

"Captain Langton," she said, quietly, "I am sorry—I am sorry—I am indeed sorry—that you feel this so keenly. Let me comfort you."

He appealed to her again more passionately than ever, but she interrupted him.

"You mistake me," she said; "I am grieved to see you suffer, but I have no thought of altering my mind. Let me tell you, once and for all, I would rather die than marry you, because I have neither liking nor respect for you; but your sorrow I cannot but feel for."

"You have ruined me," he said, bitterly, "and the curse of a broken-hearted man will rest upon you!"

"I do not think the Darrells are much frightened at curses," she retorted; and then, in all the magnificence of her shining gems and golden-hued dress, she swept from the spot.

Yes, he was ruined, desperate. Half an hour since, entering that conservatory, he had wondered whether he should leave it a happy, prosperous man. He knew now that there was nothing but blank, awful despair, ruin and shame, before him. He had lost her, too, and love and hate fought fiercely in his heart. He buried his face in his hands and sobbed aloud.

A ruined man! Was ever so splendid a chance lost? It drove him mad to think of it! All was due to the willful caprice of a willful girl.

Then he remembered that time was passing, and that he must tell Sir Oswald that he had failed—utterly, ignominiously failed. He went back to the ball-room and saw the baronet standing in the center of a group of gentlemen. He looked anxiously at the captain, and at his approach the little group fell back, leaving them alone.

"What news, Aubrey?" asked Sir Oswald.

"The worst that I can possibly bring. She would not even hear of it."

"And you think there is no hope either now or at any future time?"

"I am, unfortunately, sure of it. She told me in plain words that she would rather die than marry me, and she laughed at your threats."

Sir Oswald's face flushed; he turned away haughtily.

"The consequence be on her own head!" he said, as he moved away. "I shall make Elinor Rocheford an offer to-night," he added to himself.

The captain was in no mood for dancing; the music and light had lost all their charms. The strains of a beautiful German waltz filled the ball-room. Looking round, he saw Pauline Darrell, in all the sheen of her jewels and the splendor of her golden-hued dress, waltzing with Lord Lorrimer. Her beautiful face was radiant; she had evidently forgotten all about him and the threat that was to disinherit her.

Sir Oswald saw her too as he was searching for Elinor—saw her radiant, triumphant, and queenly—and almost hated her for the grand dower of loveliness that would never now enhance the grandeur of the Darrells. He found Elinor Rocheford with Lady Hampton. She had been hoping that the captain would ask her to dance again. She looked toward him with a feint smile, but was recalled to order by a gesture from Lady Hampton.

Sir Oswald, with a low bow, asked if Miss Rocheford would like a promenade through the rooms. She would fain have said "No," but one look from her aunt was sufficient. She rose in her quiet, graceful way, and accompanied him.

They walked to what was called the white drawing-room, and there, standing before a magnificent Murillo, the gem of the Darrell collection, Sir Oswald Darrell made Elinor Rocheford a quiet offer of his hand and fortune.

Just as quietly she accepted it; there was no blushing, no trembling, no shrinking. He asked her to be Lady Darrell, and she consented. There was very little said of love, although his wooing was chivalrous and deferential. He had secured his object—won a fair young wife for himself, and punished the proud, defiant, willful girl who had laughed at his threats. After some little time he led his fair companion back to Lady Hampton.

"Miss Rocheford has done me very great honor," he said; "she has consented to be my wife. I will give myself the pleasure of waiting upon you to-morrow, Lady Hampton, when I shall venture to ask for a happy and speedy conclusion to my suit."

Lady Hampton, with a gentle movement of her fan, intended to express emotion, murmured a few words, and the interview was ended.

"I congratulate you, Elinor," she said. "You have secured a splendid position; no girl in England could have done better."

"Yes," returned Elinor Rocheford, "I ought to be ticketed, 'Sold to advantage;'" and that was the only bitter thing the young girl ever said of her brilliant marriage.

Of course Lady Hampton told the delightful news to a few of her dearest friends; and these, watching Pauline Darrell that night in the splendor of her grand young beauty, the sheen of her jewels, and the glitter of her rich amber dress, knew that her reign was ended, her chance of the inheritance gone.

CHAPTER XIX
PAULINE THREATENS VENGEANCE

"Pray do not leave us, Miss Hastings; I wish you to hear what I have to say my niece, if you will consent to remain;" and Sir Oswald placed a chair for the gentle, amiable lady, who was so fearful of coming harm to her willful pupil.

Miss Hastings took it, and looked apprehensively at the baronet. It was the morning after the ball, and Sir Oswald had sent to request the presence of both ladies in the library.

Pauline looked fresh and brilliant; fatigue had not affected her. She had taken more pains than usual with her toilet; her dress was a plain yet handsome morning costume. There was no trace of fear on her countenance; the threats of the previous night had made no impression upon her. She looked calmly at Sir Oswald's flushed, agitated face.

"Pray be seated, Miss Darrell," he said; "it is you especially whom I wish to see."

Pauline took a chair and looked at him with an air of great attention. Sir Oswald turned the diamond ring on his finger.

"Am I to understand, Miss Darrell," he asked, "that you refused Captain Langton last evening?"

"Yes," she replied, distinctly.

"Will you permit me to ask why?" he continued.

"Because I do not love him, Sir Oswald. I may even go further, and say I do not respect him."

"Yet he is a gentleman by birth and education, handsome, most agreeable in manner, devoted to you, and my friend."

"I do not love him," she said again; "and the Darrells are too true a race to marry without love."

The allusion to his race pleased the baronet, in spite of his anger.

"Did Captain Langton give you to understand the alternative?" asked Sir Oswald. "Did he tell you my resolve in case you should refuse him?"

She laughed a clear, ringing laugh, in which there was a slight tinge of mockery. Slight though it was, Sir Oswald's face flushed hotly as he heard it.

"He told me that you would disinherit me if I did not marry him; but I told him you would never ignore the claim of the last living Darrell—you would not pass me over and make a stranger your heir."

"But did he tell you my intentions if you refused him?"

Again came the musical laugh that seemed to irritate Sir Oswald so greatly.

"He talked some nonsense about your marrying," said Pauline: "but that of course I did not believe."

"And why did you not believe it, Miss Darrell?"

"Because I thought if you had wished to marry you would have married before this," she replied.

"And you think," he said, his face pale with passion, "that you may do as you like—that your contempt for all proper laws, your willful caprice, your unendurable pride, are to rule every one? You are mistaken, Miss Darrell. If you had consented to marry Aubrey Langton, I would have made you my heiress, because I should have known that you were in safe hands, under proper guidance; as it is—as you have refused in every instance to obey me, as you have persisted in ignoring every wish of mine—it is time we came to a proper understanding. I beg to announce to you the fact that I am engaged to be married—that I have offered my hand and heart to a lady who is as gentle as you are the reverse."

A dread silence followed the words; Pauline bore the blow like a true Darrell, never flinching, never showing the least dismay. After a time she raised her dark, proud eyes to his face.

"If your marriage is for your happiness, I wish you joy," she said, simply.

"There is no doubt but that it will add greatly to my happiness," he put in, shortly.

"At the same time," resumed Pauline, "I must tell you frankly that I do not think you have used me well. You told me when I came here that I was to be heiress of Darrell Court. I have grown to love it, I have shaped my life in accordance with what you said to me, and I do not think it fair that you should change your intentions."

"You have persistently defied me," returned the baronet; "you have preferred your least caprice to my wish; and now you must reap your reward. Had you been dutiful, obedient, submissive, you might have made yourself very dear to me. Pray, listen." He raised his fine white hand with a gesture that demanded silence. "My marriage need not make any difference as regards your residence here. As you say, you are a Darrell, and my niece, so your home is here; and, unless you make yourself intolerable, you shall always have a home suitable to your position. But, as I can never hope that you will prove an agreeable companion to the lady who honors me by becoming my wife, I should be grateful to Miss Hastings if she would remain with you."

Miss Hastings bowed her head; she was too deeply grieved for words.

"It is my wish that you retain your present suite of rooms," continued Sir Oswald; "and Lady Darrell, when she comes, will, I am sure, try to make everything pleasant for you. I have no more to say. As for expressing any regret for the part you have acted toward my young friend, Aubrey Langton, it is useless—we will let the matter drop."

All the Darrell pride and passion had been slowly gathering in Pauline's heart; a torrent of burning words rose to her lips.

"If you wish to marry, Sir Oswald," she said, "you have a perfect right to do so—no one can gainsay that; but I say you have acted neither justly nor fairly to me. As for the stranger you would bring to rule over me, I shall hate her, and I will be revenged on her. I shall tell her that she is taking my place; I shall speak my mind openly to her; and, if she chooses to marry you, to help you to punish me, she shall take the consequences."

Sir Oswald laughed.

"I might be alarmed by such a melodramatic outburst," he said, "but that I know you are quite powerless;" and with a profound bow to Miss Hastings, Sir Oswald quitted the library.

Then Pauline's anger burst forth; she grew white with rage.

"I have not been fairly used," she cried. "He told me Darrell Court was to be mine. My heart has grown to love it; I love it better than I love anything living."

Miss Hastings, like a sensible woman, refrained from saying anything on the subject—from reminding her that she had been warned time after time, and had only laughed at the warning. She tried to offer some soothing words, but the girl would not listen to them. Her heart and soul were in angry revolt.

"I might have been a useful woman," she said, suddenly, "if I had had this chance in life; I might have been happy myself, and have made others happy. As it is, I swear that I will live only for vengeance."

She raised her beautiful white arm and jeweled hand.

"Listen to me," she said; "I will live for vengeance—not on Sir Oswald— if he chooses to marry, let him—but I will first warn the woman he marries, and then, if she likes to come here as Lady Darrell, despite my warning, let her. I will take such vengeance on her as suits a Darrell—nothing commonplace—nothing in the way of poisoning—but such revenge as shall satisfy even me."

In vain Miss Hastings tried to soothe her, to calm her, the torrent of angry words had their way.

Then she came over to Miss Hastings, and, placing her hand on her shoulder, asked:

"Tell me, whom do you think Sir Oswald is going to marry?"

"I cannot imagine—unless it is Miss Rocheford."

"Elinor Rocheford—that mere child! Let her beware!"

CHAPTER XX
CAPTAIN LANGTON DESPERATE

A short period of calm fell upon Darrell Court. Miss Darrell's passion seemed to have exhausted itself.

"I will never believe," she said one day to Miss Hastings, "that Sir Oswald meant what he said. I am beginning to think it was merely a threat— the Darrells are all hot-tempered."

But Miss Hastings had heard more than she liked to tell her pupil, and she knew that what the baronet had said was not only quite true, but that preparations for the marriage had actually commenced.

"I am afraid it was no threat, Pauline," she said, sadly.

"Then let the new-comer beware," said the girl, her face darkening. "Whoever she may be, let her beware. I might have been a good woman, but this will make me a wicked one. I shall live only for revenge."

A change came over her. The improvement that Miss Hastings had so fondly noticed, and of which she had been so proud, died away. Pauline seemed no longer to take any interest in reading or study. She would sit for hours in gloomy, sullen silence, with an abstracted look on her face. What was passing in her mind no one knew. Miss Hastings would go to her, and try to rouse her; but Pauline grew impatient.

"Do leave me in peace," she would say. "Leave me to my own thoughts. I am framing my plans."

And the smile that came with the words filled poor Miss Hastings with terrible apprehensions as to the future of her strange, willful pupil.

The captain was still at the Court. He had had some vague idea of rushing off to London; but a letter from one of his most intimate friends warned him to keep out of the way until some arrangement could be made about his affairs. More than one angry creditor was waiting for him; indeed, the gallant captain had brought his affairs to such a pass that his appearance in London without either money or the hope of it would have been highly dangerous.

He was desperate. Sir Oswald had hinted to him, since the failure of their plan, that he should not be forgotten in his will. He would have borrowed money from him but for that hint; but he did not care to risk the loss of many thousand pounds for the sake of fifteen hundred.

Fifteen hundred—that was all he wanted. If he could have gone back to London the betrothed husband of Pauline Darrell, he could have borrowed as many thousands; but that chance was gone; and he could have cursed the girlish caprice that deprived him of so splendid a fortune. In his heart fierce love and fierce hate warred together; there were times when he felt that he loved Pauline with a passion words could not describe; and at other times he hated her with something passing common hate. They spoke but little; Miss Darrell spent as much time as possible in her own rooms. Altogether the domestic atmosphere at Darrell Court had in it no sunshine; it was rather the brooding, sullen calm that comes before a storm.

The day came when the Court was invaded by an army of workmen, when a suit of rooms was fitted up in the most superb style, and people began to talk of the coming change. Pauline Darrell kept so entirely aloof from all gossip, from all friends and visitors, that she was the last to hear on whom Sir Oswald's choice had fallen. But one day the baronet gave a dinner-party at which the ladies of the house were present, and there was no mistaking the allusions made.

Pauline Darrell's face grew dark as she listened. So, then, the threat was to be carried out, and the grand old place that she had learned to love with the deepest love of her heart was never to be hers! She gave no sign; the proud face was very pale, and the dark eyes had in them a scornful gleam, but no word passed her lips.

Sir Oswald was radiant, he had never been seen in such high spirits; his friends had congratulated him, every one seemed to approve so highly of his resolution; a fair and gentle wife was ready for him—one so fair and gentle that it seemed to the old man as though the lost love of his youth had returned to him. Who remembered the bitter, gnawing disappointment of the girl who had cared so little about making herself friends?

The baronet was so delighted, and everything seemed so bright and smiling, that he resolved upon an act of unusual generosity. His guests went away early, and he retired to the library for a few minutes. The captain followed the ladies to the drawing-room, and, while pretending to read, sat watching Pauline's face, and wondering how he was to pay his debts.

To ask for the loan of fifteen hundred pounds would be to expose his affairs to Sir Oswald. He must confess then that he had gambled on the turf and at play. If once the stately old baronet even suspected such a thing, there was no further hope of a legacy—the captain was quite sure of that. His anxiety was terrible, and it was all occasioned by that proud, willful girl whose beautiful face was turned resolutely from him.

Sir Oswald entered the room with a smile on his face, and, going up to Aubrey Langton, slipped a folded paper into his hands.

"Not a word of thanks," he said; "if you thank me, I shall be offended."

And Aubrey, opening the paper, found that it was a check for five hundred pounds.

"I know what life in London costs," said Sir Oswald; "and you are my old friend's son."

Five hundred pounds! He was compelled to look exceedingly grateful, but it was difficult. The gift was very welcome, but there was this great drawback attending it—it was not half sufficient to relieve him from his embarrassments, and it would quite prevent his asking Sir Oswald for a loan. He sighed deeply in his dire perplexity.

Still smiling, the baronet went to the table where Pauline and Miss Hastings sat. He stood for some minutes looking at them.

"I must not let you hear the news of my good fortune from strangers," he said; "it is only due to you that I should inform you that in one month from to-day I hope to have the honor and happiness of making Miss Elinor Rocheford my wife."

Miss Hastings in a few cautious words wished him joy; Pauline's white lips opened, but no sound escaped them. Sir Oswald remained for some minutes talking to Miss Hastings, and then he crossed the room and rang the bell.

"Pauline, my dearest child!" whispered the anxious governess.

Miss Darrell looked at her with a terrible smile.

"It would have been better for her," she said, slowly, "that she had never been born."

"Pauline!" cried the governess. But she said no more.

A footman entered the room, to whom Sir Oswald spoke.

"Go to my study," he said, "and bring me a black ebony box that you will find locked in my writing-table. Here are the keys."

The man returned in a few minutes, bearing the box in his hands. Sir Oswald took it to the table where the lamps shone brightly.

"Aubrey," he said, "will you come here? I have a commission for you."

Captain Langton followed him to the table, and some remark about the fashion of the box drew the attention of all present to it. Sir Oswald raised the lid, and produced a diamond ring.

"You are going over to Audleigh Royal to-morrow, Aubrey," he said; "will you leave this with Stamford, the jeweler? I have chosen a new setting for the stone. I wish to present it to Miss Hastings as a mark of my deep gratitude to her."

Miss Hastings looked up in grateful wonder. Sir Oswald went on talking about the contents of the ebony box. He showed them many quaint treasures that it contained; among other things he took out a roll of bank-notes.

"That is not a very safe method of keeping money, Sir Oswald," said Miss Hastings.

"No, you are right," he agreed. "Simpson's clerk paid it to me the other day; I was busy, and I put it there until I had time to take the numbers of the notes."

"Do you keep notes without preserving a memorandum of their numbers, Sir Oswald?" inquired Aubrey Langton. "That seems to me a great risk."

"I know it is not prudent; but there is no fear. I have none but honest and faithful servants about me. I will take the numbers and send the notes to the bank to-morrow."

"Yes," said Miss Hastings, quietly, "it is better to keep temptation from servants."

"There is no fear," he returned. "I always put the box away, and I sleep with my keys under my pillow."

Sir Oswald gave Captain Langton a few directions about the diamond, and then the ladies withdrew.

"Sir Oswald," said Captain Langton, "let me have a cigar with you to-night. I must not thank you, but if you knew how grateful I feel— —"

"I will put away the box first, and then we will have a glass of wine, Aubrey."

The baronet went to his study, and the captain to his room; but in a few minutes they met again, and Sir Oswald ordered a bottle of his choicest Madeira. They sat talking for some time, and Sir Oswald told Aubrey all his plans—all that he intended to do. The young man listened, with envy and dissatisfaction burning in his heart. All these plans, these hopes, these prospects, might have been his but for that girl's cruel caprice.

They talked for more than an hour; and then Sir Oswald complained of feeling sleepy.

"The wine does not seem to have its usual flavor to-night," he said; "there is *something wrong* with this bottle."

"I thought the same thing," observed Aubrey Langton; "but I did not like to say so. I will bid you good-night, as you are tired. I shall ride over to Audleigh Royal early in the morning, so I may not be here for breakfast."

They shook hands and parted, Sir Oswald murmuring something about his Madeira, and the captain feeling more desperate than ever.

CHAPTER XXI
MYSTERIOUS ROBBERY

The sun shone on Darrell Court; the warmth and brightness of the day were more than pleasant. The sunbeams fell on the stately trees, the brilliant flowers. There was deep silence in the mansion. Captain Langton had been gone some hours. Sir Oswald was in his study. Pauline sat with Miss Hastings under the shade of the cedar on the lawn. She had a book in her hands, but she had not turned a page. Miss Hastings would fain have said something to her about inattention, but there was a look in the girl's face that frightened her—a proud, hard, cold look that she had never seen there before.

Pauline Darrell was not herself that morning. Miss Hastings had told her so several times. She had asked her again and again if she was ill—if she was tired—and she had answered drearily, "No." Partly to cheer her, the governess had suggested that they should take their books under the shade of the cedar tree. She had assented wearily, without one gleam of animation.

Out there in the sunlight Miss Hastings noticed how cold and white Pauline's face was, with its hard, set look—there was a shadow in the dark eyes, and, unlike herself, she started at every sound. Miss Hastings watched her keenly. She evinced no displeasure at being so watched; but when the elder lady went up to her and said, gently:

"Pauline, you are surely either ill or unhappy?"

"I am neither—I am only thinking," she returned, impatiently.

"Then your thoughts must be very unpleasant ones—tell them to me. Nothing sends away unpleasant ideas so soon as communicating them to others."

But Miss Darrell had evidently not heard the words; she had relapsed into deep meditation, and Miss Hastings thought it better to leave her alone. Suddenly Pauline looked up.

"Miss Hastings," she said, "I suppose a solemn promise, solemnly given, can never be broken?"

"It never should be broken," replied the governess. "Instances have been known where people have preferred death to breaking such a promise."

"Yes, such deaths have been known. I should imagine," commented Pauline, with a gleam of light on her face, "that no Darrell ever broke his or her word when it had been solemnly given."

"I should imagine not," said Miss Hastings.

But she had no clew to her pupil's musings or to the reason of her question.

So the noon-day shadows crept on. Purple-winged butterflies coquetted with the flowers, resting on the golden breasts of the white lilies, and on the crimson leaves of the rose; busy bees murmured over the rich clove carnations; the birds sang sweet, jubilant songs, and a gentle breeze stirred faintly the leaves on the trees. For once Pauline Darrell seemed blind to the warm, sweet summer beauty; it lay unheeded before her.

Miss Hastings saw Sir Oswald coming toward them; a murmur of surprise came from her lips.

"Pauline," she said, "look at Sir Oswald—how ill he seems. I am afraid something is wrong."

He drew near to them, evidently deeply agitated.

"I am glad to find you here, Miss Hastings," he said; "I am in trouble. Nay, Pauline, do not go; my troubles should be yours."

For the girl had risen with an air of proud weariness, intending to leave them together. At his words—the kindest he had spoken to her for some time—she took her seat again; but the haughty, listless manner did not change.

"I am nearly sixty years of age," said Sir Oswald, "and this is the first time such a trouble has come to me. Miss Hastings, do you remember that conversation of ours last night, over that roll of notes in the ebony box?"

"I remember it perfectly, Sir Oswald."

"I went this morning to take them from the box, to take their numbers and send them to the bank, and I could not find them—they were gone."

"Gone!" repeated Miss Hastings. "It is impossible! You must be mistaken; you must have overlooked them. What did they amount to?"

"Exactly one thousand pounds," he replied. "I cannot understand it. You saw me replace the notes in the box?"

"I did; I watched you. You placed them in one corner. I could put my finger on the place," said Miss Hastings.

"I locked the box and carried it with my own hands to my study. I placed it in the drawer of my writing-table, and locked that. I never parted with my keys to any one; as is my invariable rule, I placed them under my pillow. I slept soundly all night, and when I woke I found them there. As I tell you I have been to the box, and the notes are gone. I cannot understand it, for I do not see any indication of a theft, and yet I have been robbed."

Miss Hastings looked very thoughtful.

"You have certainly been robbed," she said. "Are you sure the keys have never left your possession?"

"Never for one single moment," he replied.

"Has any one in the house duplicate keys?" she asked.

"No. I bought the box years ago in Venice; it has a peculiar lock—there is not one in England like it."

"It is very strange," said Miss Hastings. "A thousand pounds is no trifle to lose."

Pauline Darrell, her face turned to the flowers, uttered no word.

"You might show some little interest, Pauline," said her uncle, sharply; "you might have the grace to affect it, even if you do not feel it."

"I am very sorry indeed," she returned, coldly. "I am grieved that you have had such a loss."

Sir Oswald looked pacified.

"It is not so much the actual loss of the money that has grieved me," he said; "I shall not feel it. But I am distressed to think that there should be a thief among the people I have loved and trusted."

"What a solemn council!" interrupted the cheery voice of Aubrey Langton. "What gloomy conspirators!"

Sir Oswald looked up with an air of great relief.

"I am so glad you are come, Aubrey; you can advise me what to do."

And the baronet told the story of his loss.

Captain Langton was shocked, amazed; he asked a hundred questions, and then suggested that they should drive over to Audleigh Royal and place the affair in the hands of the chief inspector of police.

"You said you had not taken the numbers of the notes; I fear it will be difficult to trace them," he said, regretfully. "What a strange, mysterious robbery. Is there any one you suspect, Sir Oswald?"

No; in all the wide world there was not one that the loyal old man suspected of robbing him.

"My servants have always been to me like faithful old friends," he said, sadly; "there is not one among them who would hold out his hand to steal from me."

Captain Langton suggested that, before going to Audleigh Royal, they should search the library.

"You may have made some mistake, sir," he said. "You were tired last night, and it is just possible that you may have put the money somewhere else, and do not remember it."

"We will go at once," decided Sir Oswald.

Miss Hastings wished them success; but the proud face directed toward the flowers was never turned to them. The pale lips were never unclosed to utter one word.

After the gentlemen had left them, when Miss Hastings began to speak eagerly of the loss, Pauline raised her hand with a proud gesture.

"I have heard enough," she said. "I do not wish to hear one word more."

The robbery created a great sensation; inspectors came from Audleigh Royal, and a detective from Scotland Yard, but no one could throw the least light upon the subject. The notes could not be traced; they had been paid in from different sources, and no one had kept a list of the numbers.

Even the detective seemed puzzled. Sir Oswald had locked up the notes in the box at night, he had kept the keys in his own possession, and he had found in the morning that the box was still locked and the notes were gone. It was a nine days' wonder. Captain Langton gave all the help he could, but as all search seemed useless and hopeless, it was abandoned after a time, and at the end of the week Captain Langton was summoned to London, and all hope of solving the mystery was relinquished.

CHAPTER XXII
FULFILLING THE CONTRACT

The preparations for the wedding went on with great activity; the rooms prepared for the bride were a marvel of luxury and beauty. There was a boudoir with rose-silk and white-lace hangings, adorned with most exquisite pictures and statues, with rarest flowers and most beautiful ornaments—a little fairy nook, over which every one went into raptures except Pauline; she never even looked at the alterations, she never mentioned them nor showed the least interest in them. She went on in her cold, proud, self-contained manner, hiding many thoughts in her heart.

"Miss Hastings," she said, one morning, "you can do me a favor. Sir Oswald has been saying that we must call at the Elms to see Lady Hampton and Miss Rocheford. I should refuse, but that the request exactly suits my plans. I wish to see Miss Rocheford; we will drive over this afternoon. Will you engage Lady Hampton in conversation while I talk to her niece?"

"I will do anything you wish, Pauline," returned Miss Hastings; "but, my dear child, be prudent. I am frightened for you—be prudent. It will be worse than useless for you to make an enemy of the future Lady Darrell. I would do anything to help you, anything to shield you from sorrow or harm, but I am frightened on your account."

Caresses and demonstrations of affection were very rare with Pauline; but now she bent down with a softened face and kissed the anxious brow.

"You are very good to me," she said. "You are the only one in the wide world who cares for me."

And with the words there came to her such a sense of loneliness and desolation as no language could describe. Of what use had been her beauty, of which her poor father had been so proud—of what avail the genius with which she was so richly dowered?

No one loved her. The only creature living who seemed to enter into either her joys or her sorrows was the kind-hearted, gentle governess.

"You must let me have my own way this time, Miss Hastings. One peculiarity of the Darrells is that they must say what is on their minds. I intend to do so now; it rests with you whether I do it in peace or not."

After that Miss Hastings knew all further remonstrance was useless. She made such arrangements as Pauline wished, and that afternoon they drove over to the Elms. Lady Hampton received them very kindly; the great end and aim of her life was accomplished—her niece was to be Lady Darrell, of Darrell Court. There was no need for any more envy or jealousy of Pauline. The girl who had so lately been a dangerous rival and an enemy to be dreaded had suddenly sunk into complete insignificance. Lady Hampton even thought it better to be gracious, conciliatory, and kind; as Elinor had to live with Miss Darrell, it was useless to make things disagreeable.

So Lady Hampton received them kindly. Fruit from the Court hothouses and flowers from the Court conservatories were on the table. Lady Hampton insisted that Miss Hastings should join her in her afternoon tea, while Pauline, speaking with haughty grace, expressed a desire to see the Elms garden.

Lady Hampton was not sorry to have an hour's gossip with Miss Hastings, and she desired Elinor to show Miss Darrell all their choicest flowers.

Elinor looked half-frightened at the task. It was wonderful to see the contrast that the two girls presented—Pauline tall, slender, queenly, in her sweeping black dress, all passion and magnificence; Miss Rocheford, fair, dainty, golden-haired, and gentle.

They walked in silence down one of the garden-paths, and then Miss Rocheford said, in her low, sweet voice:

"If you like roses, Miss Darrell, I can show you a beautiful collection."

Then for the first time Pauline's dark eyes were directed toward her companion's face.

"I am a bad dissembler, Miss Rocheford," she said, proudly. "I have no wish to see your flowers. I came here to see you. There is a seat under yonder tree. Come with me, and hear what I have to say."

Elinor followed, looking and feeling terribly frightened. What had this grand, imperious Miss Darrell to say to her? They sat down side by side under the shade of a large magnolia tree, the white blossoms of which filled the air with sweetest perfume; the smiling summer beauty rested on the landscape. They sat in silence for some minutes, and then Pauline turned to Elinor.

"Miss Rocheford," she said, "I am come to give you a warning—the most solemn warning you have ever received—one that if you have any common sense you will not refuse to heed. I hear that you are going to marry my uncle, Sir Oswald. Is it true?"

"Sir Oswald has asked me to be his wife," Elinor replied, with downcast eyes and a faint blush.

Pauline's face gleamed with scorn.

"There is no need for any of those pretty airs and graces with me," she said. "I am going to speak stern truths to you. You, a young girl, barely twenty, with all your life before you—surely you cannot be so shamelessly untrue as even to pretend that you are marrying an old man like my uncle for love? You know it is not so—you dare not even pretend it."

Elinor's face flushed crimson.

"Why do you speak so to me, Miss Darrell?" she gasped.

"Because I want to warn you. Are you not ashamed—yes, I repeat the word, ashamed—to sell your youth, your hope of love, your life itself, for money and title? That is what you are doing. You do not love Sir Oswald. How should you? He is more than old enough to be your father. If he were a poor man, you would laugh his offer to scorn; but he is old and rich, and you are willing to marry him to become Lady Darrell, of Darrell Court. Can you, Elinor Rocheford, look me frankly in the face, and say it is not so?"

No, she could not. Every word fell like a sledge-hammer on her heart, and she knew it was all true. She bent her crimson face, and hid it from Pauline's clear gaze.

"Are you not ashamed to sell yourself? If no truth, no honor, no loyalty impels you to end this barter, let fear step in. You do not love my uncle. It can give you no pain to give him up. Pursue your present course, and I warn you. Darrell Court ought to be mine. I am a Darrell, and when my uncle took me home it was as his heiress. For a long period I have learned to consider Darrell Court as mine. It is mine," she continued—"mine by right, for I am a Darrell—mine by right of the great love I bear it—mine by every law that is just and right! Elinor Rocheford, I warn you, beware how you step in between me and my birthright—beware! My uncle is only marrying you to punish me; he has no other motive. Beware how you lend yourself to such punishment! I am not asking you to give up any love. If you loved him, I would not say one word; but it is not a matter of love—only of sale and barter. Give it up!"

"How can you talk so strangely to me, Miss Darrell? I cannot give it up; everything is arranged."

"You can if you will. Tell my uncle you repent of the unnatural compact you have made. Be a true woman—true to the instinct Heaven has placed in your heart. Marry for love, nothing else—pure, honest love—and then you will live and die happy. Answer me—will you give it up?"

"I cannot," murmured the girl.

"You will not, rather. Listen to me. I am a true Darrell, and a Darrell never breaks a word once pledged. If you marry my uncle, I pledge my word that I will take a terrible vengeance on you—not a commonplace one, but one that shall be terrible. I will be revenged upon you if you dare to step in between me and my just inheritance! Do you hear me?"

"I hear. You are very cruel, Miss Darrell. You know that I cannot help myself. I must fulfill my contract."

"Very well," said Pauline, rising; "then I have no more to say. But remember, I have given you full, fair, honest warning. I will be revenged upon you."

And Miss Darrell returned to the house, with haughty head proudly raised, while Elinor remained in the garden, bewildered and aghast.

Two things happened. Elinor never revealed a word of what had transpired, and three weeks from that day Sir Oswald Darrell married her in the old parish church of Audleigh Royal.

CHAPTER XXIII
NO COMPROMISE WITH PAULINE

It was evident to Miss Hastings that Sir Oswald felt some little trepidation in bringing his bride home. He had, in spite of himself, been somewhat impressed by his niece's behavior. She gave no sign of disappointed greed or ambition, but she bore herself like one who has been unjustly deprived of her rights.

On the night of the arrival every possible preparation had been made for receiving the baronet and his wife. The servants, under the direction of Mr. Frampton, the butler, were drawn up in stately array. The bells from the old Norman church of Audleigh Royal pealed out a triumphant welcome; flags and triumphal arches adorned the roadway. The Court was looking its brightest and best; the grand old service of golden plate, from which in olden times, kings and queens had dined, was displayed. The rooms were made bright with flowers and warm with fires. It was a proud coming home for Lady Darrell, who had never known what a home was before. Her delicate face flushed as her eyes lingered on the splendor around her. She could not repress the slight feeling of triumph which made her heart beat and her pulse thrill as she remembered that this was all her own.

She bowed right and left, with the calm, suave smile that never deserted her. As she passed through the long file of servants she tried her best to be most gracious and winning; but, despite her delicate, grave, and youthful loveliness, they looked from her to the tall, queenly girl whose proud head was never bent, and whose dark eyes had in them no light of welcome. It might be better to bow to the rising sun, but many of them preferred the sun that was setting.

Sir Oswald led his young wife proudly through the outer rooms into the drawing-room.

"Welcome home, my dear Elinor!" he said. "May every moment you spend in Darrell Court be full of happiness!"

She thanked him. Pauline stood by, not looking at them. After the first careless glance at Lady Darrell, which seemed to take in every detail of her costume, and to read every thought of her mind, she turned carelessly away.

Lady Darrell sat down near the fire, while Sir Oswald, with tender solicitude, took off her traveling-cloak, his hands trembling with eagerness.

"You will like to rest for a few minutes before you go to your rooms, Elinor," he said.

Then Miss Hastings went up to them, and some general conversation about traveling ensued. That seemed to break the ice. Lady Darrell related one or two little incidents of their journey, and then Sir Oswald suggested that she should go to her apartments, as the dinner-bell would ring in half an hour. Lady Darrell went away, and Sir Oswald soon afterward followed.

Pauline had turned to one of the large stands of flowers, and was busily engaged in taking the dying leaves from a beautiful plant bearing gorgeous crimson flowers.

"Pauline," said the governess, "my dear child!"

She was startled. She expected to find the girl looking sullen, angry, passionate; but the splendid face was only lighted by a gleam of intense scorn, the dark eyes flashing fire, the ruby lips curling and quivering with disdain. Pauline threw back her head with the old significant movement.

"Miss Hastings," she said, "I would not have sold myself as that girl has done for all the money and the highest rank in England."

"My dear Pauline, you must not, really, speak in that fashion. Lady Darrell undoubtedly loves her husband."

The look of scorn deepened.

"You know she does not. She is just twenty, and he is nearly sixty. What love—what sympathy can there be between them?"

"It is not really our business, my dear; we will not discuss it."

"Certainly not; but as you are always so hard upon what you call my world—the Bohemian world, where men and women speak the truth—it amuses me to find flaws in yours."

Miss Hastings looked troubled; but she knew it was better for the passionate torrent of words to be poured out to her. Pauline looked at her with that straight, clear, open, honest look before which all affectation fell.

"You tell me, Miss Hastings, that I am deficient in good-breeding—that I cannot take my proper place in your world because I do not conform to its ways and its maxims. You have proposed this lady to me as a model, and you would fain see me regulate all my thoughts and words by her. I would rather die than be like her! She may be thoroughly lady-like—I grant that she is so—but she has sold her youth, her beauty, her love, her life, for an old man's money and title. I, with all my *brusquerie*, as you call it, would have scorned such sale and barter."

"But, Pauline— —" remonstrated Miss Hastings.

"It is an unpleasant truth," interrupted Pauline, "and you do not like to hear it. Sir Oswald is Baron of Audleigh Royal and master of Darrell Court; but if a duke, thirty years older, had made this girl an offer, she would have accepted him, and have given up Sir Oswald. What a world, where woman's truth is so bidden for?"

"My dear Pauline, you must not, indeed, say these things; they are most unlady-like."

"I begin to think that all truth is unlady-like," returned the girl, with a laugh. "My favorite virtue does not wear court dress very becomingly."

"I have never heard that it affects russet gowns either," said Miss Hastings. "Oh, Pauline, if you would but understand social politeness, social duties! If you would but keep your terrible ideas to yourself! If you would but remember that the outward bearing of life must be as a bright, shining, undisturbed surface! Do try to be more amiable to Lady Darrell!"

"No!" exclaimed the girl, proudly. "I have warned her, and she has chosen to disregard my warning. I shall never assume any false appearance of amiability or friendship for her; it will be war to the knife! I told her so, and she chose to disbelieve me. I am a Darrell, and the Darrells never break their word."

Looking at her, the unstudied grace of her attitude, the perfect pose, the grand face with its royal look of scorn, Miss Hastings felt that she would rather have the girl for a friend than an enemy.

"I do hope, for your own sake, Pauline," she said, "that you will show every respect to Lady Darrell. All your comfort will depend upon it. You must really compromise matters."

"Compromise matters!" cried Pauline. "You had better tell the sea to compromise with the winds which have lashed it into fury. There can be no compromise with me."

The words had scarcely issued from her lips when the dinner-bell sounded, and Lady Darrell entered in a beautiful evening dress of white and silver. Certainly Sir Oswald's choice did him great credit. She was one of the most delicate, the most graceful of women, fair, caressing, insinuating—one of those women who would never dream of uttering barbarous truth when elegant fiction so much better served their purpose—who loved fine clothes, sweet perfumes, costly jewels—who preferred their own comfort in a graceful, languid way to anything else on earth—who expected to be waited upon and to receive all homage—who deferred to men with a graceful, sweet submission that made them feel the deference a compliment—who placed entire reliance upon others—whom men felt a secret delight in ministering to, because they appeared so weak—one of those who moved cautiously and graciously with subtle harmonious action, whose hands were always soft and jeweled, whose touch was light and gentle—a woman born to find her place in the lap of luxury, who shuddered at poverty or care.

Such was Elinor Darrell; and she entered the drawing-room now with that soft, gliding movement that seemed always to irritate Pauline. She drew a costly white lace shawl over her fair shoulders—the rich dress of silver and white was studded with pearls. She looked like a fairy vision.

"I think," she said to Miss Hastings, in her quiet, calm way, "that the evening is cold."

"You have just left a warm country, Lady Darrell," was the gentle reply. "The South of France is blessed with one of the most beautiful climates in the world."

"It was very pleasant," said Lady Darrell, with a dreamy little sigh. "You have been very quiet, I suppose? We must try to create a little more gayety for you."

She looked anxiously across the room at Pauline; but that young lady's attention was entirely engrossed by the crimson flowers of the beautiful plant. Not one line of the superb figure, not one expression of the proud face, was lost upon Lady Darrell.

"I have been saying to Sir Oswald," she continued, looking intently at the costly rings shining on her fingers, "that youth likes gayety—we must have a series of parties and balls."

"Is she beginning to patronize me?" thought Pauline.

She smiled to herself—a peculiar smile which Lady Darrell happened to catch, and which made her feel very uncomfortable; and then an awkward silence fell over them, only broken by the entrance of Sir Oswald, and the announcement that dinner was served.

CHAPTER XXIV
A RICH GIFT DECLINED

The bride's first dinner at home was over, and had been a great success. Lady Darrell had not evinced the least emotion; she had married for her present social position—for a fine house, troops of servants, beautiful, warm, fragrant rooms, choice wines, and luxurious living; it was only part and parcel of what she expected, and intended to have. She took the chair of state provided for her, and by the perfect ease and grace of her manner proved that she was well fitted for it.

Sir Oswald watched her with keen delight, only regretting that years ago he had not taken unto himself a wife. He was most courtly, most deferential, most attractive. If Lady Darrell did occasionally feel weary, and the memory of Aubrey Langton's face rose between her and her husband, she made no sign.

When the three ladies withdrew, she made no further efforts to conciliate Pauline. She looked at her, but seemed almost afraid to speak. Then she opened a conversation with Miss Hastings, and the two persevered in their amiable small talk until Pauline rose and went to the piano, the scornful glance on her face deepening.

"This is making one's self amiable!" she thought. "What a blessing it would be if people would speak only when they had something sensible to say!"—

She sat down before the piano, but suddenly remembered that she had not been asked to do so, and that she was no longer mistress of the house—a reflection sufficiently galling to make her rise quickly, and go to the other end of the room.

"Pauline," said Lady Darrell, "pray sing for us. Miss Hastings tells me you have a magnificent voice."

"Have I? Miss Hastings is not so complimentary when she speaks to me alone."

Then a sudden resolution came to Lady Darrell. She rose from her seat, and, with the rich robe of silver and white sweeping around her, she went to the end of the room where Pauline was standing, tall, stately, and statuesque, turning over the leaves of a book. The contrast between the two girls—the delicate beauty of the one, and the grand loveliness of the other— was never more strongly marked.

Lady Darrell laid her white hand, shining with jewels, on Pauline's arm. She looked up into her proud face.

"Pauline," she said, gently, "will you not be friends? We have to live together—will you be friends?"

"No!" replied Miss Darrell, in her clear, frank voice. "I gave you warning. You paid no heed to it. We shall never be friends."

A faint smile played round Lady Darrell's lips.

"But, Pauline, do you not see how useless all your resentment against me is now? My marriage with Sir Oswald has taken place, and you and I shall have to live together perhaps for many years—it would be so much better for us to live in peace."

The proud face wore its haughtiest look.

"It would be better for you, perhaps, Lady Darrell, but it can make no difference to me."

"It can, indeed. Now listen to reason—listen to me!" and in her eagerness Lady Darrell once more laid her hand on the girl's arm. Her face flushed as Pauline drew back, with a look of aversion, letting the jeweled hand fall. "Listen, Pauline!" persevered Lady Darrell. "You know all this is nonsense—sheer nonsense. My position now is established. You can do nothing to hurt me—Sir Oswald will take good care of that. Any attempt that you may make to injure me will fall upon yourself; besides, you know you can do nothing." In spite of her words, Lady Darrell looked half-fearfully at the girl's proud, defiant face. "You may have all kinds of tragic plans for vengeance in your mind, but there are no secrets in my life that you can find out to my discredit—indeed, you cannot injure me in any possible way." She seemed so sure of it, yet her eyes sought Pauline's with an anxious, questioning fear. "Now, I, on the contrary," she went on, "can do much for you—and I will. You are young, and naturally wish to enjoy your life. You shall. You shall have balls and parties, dresses—everything that you can wish for, if you will only be friends with me."

She might as well have thrown drops of oil on an angry ocean to moderate its wrath.

"Lady Darrell," was the sole reply, "you are only wasting your time and mine. I warned you. Twenty years may elapse before my vengeance arrives, but it will come at last."

She walked away, leaving the brilliant figure of the young bride alone in the bright lamp-light. She did not leave the room, for Sir Oswald entered at the moment, carrying a small, square parcel in his hand. He smiled as he came in.

"How pleasant it is to see so many fair faces!" he said. "Why, my home has indeed been dark until now."

He went up to Lady Darrell, as she stood alone. All the light in the room seemed to be centered on her golden hair and shining dress. He said:

"I have brought the little parcel, Elinor, thinking that you would prefer to give your beautiful present to Pauline herself. But," he continued, "why are you standing, my love? You will be tired."

She raised her fair, troubled face to his, with a smile.

"Moreover, it seems to me that you are looking anxious," he resumed. "Miss Hastings, will you come here, please? Is this an anxious look on Lady Darrell's face?"

"I hope not," said the governess, with a gentle smile.

Then Sir Oswald brought a chair, and placed his wife in it; he next obtained a footstool and a small table. Lady Darrell, though half-ashamed of the feeling, could not help being thankful that Pauline did not notice these lover-like attentions.

"Now, Miss Hastings," spoke Sir Oswald, "I want you to admire Lady Darrell's taste."

He opened the parcel. It contained a morocco case, the lid of which, upon a spring being touched, flew back, exposing a beautiful suite of rubies set in pale gold.

Miss Hastings uttered a little cry of delight.

"How very beautiful!" she said.

"Yes," responded Sir Oswald, holding them up to the light, "they are, indeed. I am sure we must congratulate Lady Darrell upon her good taste. I suggested diamonds or pearls, but she thought rubies so much better suited to Pauline's dark beauty; and she is quite right."

Lady Darrell held up the shining rubies with her white fingers, but she did not smile; a look of something like apprehension came over the fair face.

"I hope Pauline will like them," she said, gently.

"She cannot fail to do so," remarked Sir Oswald, with some little *hauteur.* "I will tell her that you want to speak to her."

He went over to the deep recess of the large window, where Pauline sat reading. He had felt very sure that she would be flattered by the rich and splendid gift. There had been some little pride, and some little pomp in his manner as he went in search of her, but it seemed to die away as he looked at her face. That was not the face of a girl who could be tempted, pleased, or coaxed with jewels. Insensibly his manner changed.

"Pauline," he said, gently, "Lady Darrell wishes to speak to you."

There was evidently a struggle in her mind as to whether she should comply or not, and then she rose, and without a word walked up to the little group.

"What do you require, Lady Darrell?" she asked; and Miss Hastings looked up at her with quick apprehension.

The fair face of Lady Darrell looked more troubled than pleased. Sir Oswald stood by, a little more stately and proud than usual—proud of his niece, proud of his wife, and pleased with himself.

"I have brought you a little present, Pauline, from Paris," said Lady Darrell. "I hope it will give you pleasure."

"You were kind to remember me," observed Pauline.

Sir Oswald thought the acknowledgment far too cool and calm.

"They are the finest rubies I have seen, Pauline; they are superb stones."

He held them so that the light gleamed in them until they shone like fire. The proud, dark eyes glanced indifferently at them.

"What have you to say to Lady Darrell, Pauline?" asked Sir Oswald, growing angry at her silence.

The girl's beautiful lip curled.

"Lady Darrell was good to think of me," she said, coldly; "and the jewels are very fine; but they are not suitable for me."

Her words, simple as they were, fell like a thunder-cloud upon the little group.

"And pray why not?" asked Sir Oswald, angrily.

"Your knowledge of the world is greater than mine, and will tell you better than I can," she replied, calmly. "Three months since they would have been a suitable present to one in the position I held then; now they are quite out of place, and I decline them."

"You decline them!" exclaimed Lady Darrell, hardly believing that it was in human nature to refuse such jewels.

Pauline smiled calmly, repeated the words, and walked away.

Sir Oswald, with an angry murmur, replaced the jewels in the case and set it aside.

"She has the Darrell spirit," he said to his wife, with an awkward smile; and she devoutly hoped that her husband would not often exhibit the same.

CHAPTER XXV
A TRUE DARRELL

The way in which the girl supported her disappointment was lofty in the extreme. She bore her defeat as proudly as some would have borne a victory. No one could have told from her face or her manner that she had suffered a grievous defeat. When she alluded to the change in her position, it was with a certain proud humility that had in it nothing approaching meanness or envy.

It did not seem that she felt the money-loss; it was not the disappointment about mere wealth and luxury. It was rather an unbounded distress that she had been set aside as unworthy to represent the race of the Darrells—that she, a "real" Darrell, had been forced to make way for what, in her own mind, she called a "baby-faced stranger"—that her training and education, on which her dear father had prided himself, should be cast in her face as unworthy and deserving of reproach. He and his artist-friends had thought her perfection; that very "perfection" on which they had prided themselves, and for which they had so praised and flattered her, was the barrier that had stood between her and her inheritance.

It was a painful position, but her manner of bearing it was exalted. She had not been a favorite—the pride, the truth, the independence of her nature had forbidden that. She had not sought the liking of strangers, nor courted their esteem; she had not been sweet and womanly, weeping with those who wept, and rejoicing with those who rejoiced; she had looked around her with a scorn for conventionalities that had not sat well upon one so young—and now she was to pay the penalties for all this. She knew that people talked about her—that they said she was rightly punished, justly treated—that it was a blessing for the whole county to have a proper Lady Darrell at Darrell Court She knew that among all the crowds who came to the Court there was not one who sympathized with her, or who cared in the least for her disappointment. No Darrell ever showed greater bravery than she did in her manner of bearing up under disappointment. Whatever she felt or thought was most adroitly concealed. The Spartan boy was not braver; she gave no sign. No humiliation seemed to touch her, she carried herself loftily; nor could any one humiliate her when she did not humiliate herself. Even Sir Oswald admired her.

"She is a true Darrell," he said to Miss Hastings; "what a grand spirit the girl has, to be sure!"

The Court was soon one scene of gayety. Lady Darrell seemed determined to enjoy her position. There were garden-parties at which she appeared radiant in the most charming costumes, balls where her elegance and delicate beauty, her thoroughbred grace, made her the queen; and of all this gayety she took the lead. Sir Oswald lavished every luxury upon her— her wishes were gratified almost before they were expressed.

Lady Hampton, calling rather earlier than usual one day, found her in her luxurious dressing-room, surrounded by such treasures of silk, velvet, lace, jewels, ornaments of every description of the most costly and valuable kind, that her ladyship looked round in astonishment.

"My dearest Elinor," she said, "what are you doing? What beautiful confusion!"

Lady Darrell raised her fair face, with a delicate flush and a half-shy glance.

"Look, aunt," she said, "I am really overwhelmed."

"What does it mean?" asked Lady Hampton.

"It means that Sir Oswald is too generous. These large boxes have just arrived from Paris; he told me they were a surprise for me—a present from him. Look at the contents—dresses of all kinds, lace, ornaments, fans, slippers, gloves, and such *articles of luxury* as can be bought only in Paris. I am really ashamed."

"Sir Oswald is indeed generous," said Lady Hampton; then she looked round the room to see if they were quite alone.

The maid had disappeared.

"Ah, Elinor," remarked Lady Hampton, "you are indeed a fortunate woman; your lines have fallen in pleasant places. You might have looked all England over and not have found such a husband. I am quite sure of one thing—you have everything a woman's heart can desire."

"I make no complaint," said Lady Darrell.

"My dear child, I should imagine not; there are few women in England whose position equals yours."

"I know it," was the calm reply.

"And you may really thank me for it; I certainly worked hard for you, Elinor. I believe that if I had not interfered you would have thrown yourself away on that Captain Langton."

"Captain Langton never gave me the chance, aunt; so we will not discuss the question."

"It was a very good thing for you that he never did," remarked her ladyship. "Mrs. Bretherton was saying to me the other day what a very fortunate girl you were—how few of us have our heart's desire."

"You forget one thing, aunt. Even if I have everything I want, still my heart is empty," said the girl, wearily.

Lady Hampton smiled.

"You must have your little bit of sentiment, Elinor, but you are too sensible to let it interfere with your happiness. How are you getting on with that terrible Pauline? I do dislike that girl from the very depths of my heart."

Lady Darrell shrugged her delicate shoulders.

"There is a kind of armed neutrality between us at present," she said. "Of course, I have nothing to fear from her, but I cannot help feeling a little in dread of her, aunt."

"How is that?" asked Lady Hampton, contemptuously. "She is a girl I should really delight to thwart and contradict; but, as for being afraid of her, I consider Frampton, the butler, a far more formidable person. Why do you say that, Elinor?"

"She has a way with her—I cannot describe it—of making every one else feel small. I cannot tell how she does it, but she makes me very uncomfortable."

"You have more influence over Sir Oswald than any one else in the world; if she troubles you, why not persuade him to send her away?"

"I dare not," said Lady Darrell; "besides, I do not think he would ever care to do that."

"Then you should be mistress of her, Elinor—keep her in her place."

Lady Darrell laughed aloud.

"I do not think even your skill could avail here, aunt. She is not one of those girls you can extinguish with a frown."

"How does she treat you, Elinor? Tell me honestly," said Lady Hampton.

"I can hardly describe it. She is never rude or insolent; if she were, appeal to Sir Oswald would be very easy. She has a grand, lofty way with her—an imperious carriage and bearing that I really think he admires. She ignores me, overlooks me, and there is a scornful gleam in her eyes at times, when she does look at me, which says more plainly than words, 'You married for money.'"

"And you did a very sensible thing, too, my dear. I wish, I only wish I had the management of Miss Darrell; I would break her spirit, if it is to be broken."

"I do not think it is," said Lady Darrell, rising as though she were weary of the discussion. "There is nothing in her conduct that any one could find fault with, yet I feel she is my enemy."

"Wait a while," returned Lady Hampton; "her turn will come."

And from that day the worthy lady tried her best to prejudice Sir Oswald against his proud, beautiful, wayward niece.

CHAPTER XXVI
A PUZZLING QUESTION

"Does Miss Darrell show any signs of disappointment?" inquired Lady Hampton one day of Miss Hastings.

Miss Hastings, although she noticed a hundred faults in the girl which she would fain have corrected, had nevertheless a true, strong, and warm affection for her pupil; she was not one therefore to play into the enemy's hand; and, when Lady Darrell fixed her eyes upon her, full of eagerness and brightened by curiosity, Miss Hastings quietly resolved not to gratify her.

"Disappointment about what?" she asked. "I do not understand you, Lady Hampton."

"About the property," explained Lady Hampton, impatiently. "She made so very sure of it. I shall never forget her insolent confidence. Do tell me, is she not greatly annoyed and disappointed?"

"Not in the way you mean, Lady Hampton. She has never spoken of such a thing."

Her ladyship felt piqued; she would have preferred to hear that Pauline did feel her loss, and was grieving over it. In that case she would have been kind to her, would have relented; but the reflection that her pride was still unbending annoyed her, and she mentally resolved to try if she could not force the girl into some expression of her feelings. It was not an amiable resolve, but Lady Hampton was not naturally an amiable woman.

Fortune favored her. That very day, as she was leaving the Court, she saw Pauline standing listlessly by the lake side feeding the graceful white swans. She went up to her with a malicious smile, only half-vailed by her pretended friendly greeting.

"How do you do, Miss Darrell? You are looking very melancholy. There is nothing the matter, I hope?"

For any one to attempt to humiliate Pauline was simply a waste of time; the girl's natural character was so dignified that all attempts of the kind fell through or told most upon her assailants. She answered Lady Hampton with quiet politeness, her dark eyes hardly resting for a moment upon her.

"You do not seem to find much occupation for your leisure hours," continued Lady Hampton. "You are making the round of the grounds, I suppose? They are very beautiful. I am afraid that you must feel keenly how much my niece has deprived you of."

It was not a lady-like speech; but Lady Hampton felt irresistibly impelled to make it—the proud, defiant, beautiful face provoked her. Pauline merely smiled; she had self-control that would have done honor to one much older and more experienced.

"Your niece has deprived me of nothing, Lady Hampton," she returned, with a curl of the lip, for which the elder lady could have shaken her. "I possess one great advantage of which no one living can deprive me—that is, the Darrell blood runs in my veins."

And, with a bow, she walked away, leaving her ladyship more angry than she would have cared to own. So Pauline met all her enemies. Whatever she might suffer, they should not triumph over her. Even Sir Oswald felt himself compelled to yield to her an admiration that he had never given before.

He was walking one evening on the terrace. The western sunbeams, lingering on the grand old building, brightened it into beauty. Flowers, trees, and shrubs were all in their fullest loveliness. Presently Sir Oswald, leaning over the balustrade of the terrace, saw Pauline sketching in the grounds below. He went to her, and looked over her shoulder. She was just completing a sketch of the great western tower of the Court; and he was struck with the vivid beauty of the drawing.

"You love Darrell Court, Pauline?" he said, gently.

She raised her face to his for a minute; the feud between them was forgotten. She only remembered that he was a Darrell, and she his nearest of kin.

"I do love it, uncle," she said, "as pilgrims love their favorite shrine. It is the home of beauty, of romance, the cradle of heroes; every stone is consecrated by a legend. Love is a weak word for what I feel."

He looked at the glowing face, and for a few moments a doubt assailed him as to whether he had done right in depriving this true Darrell of her inheritance.

"But, Pauline," he said, slowly, "you would never have——"

She sprang from her seat with a quickness that almost startled him. She had forgotten all that had happened; but now it all returned to her with a bitter pang that could not be controlled.

"Hush, Sir Oswald!" she cried, interrupting him; "it is too late for us to talk about Darrell Court now. Pray do not misunderstand me; I was only expressing my belief."

She bent down to take up her drawing materials.

"I do not misunderstand you, child," he said, sadly. "You love it because it is the home of a race you love, and not for its mere worth in money."

Her dark eyes seemed to flash with fire; the glorious face had never softened so before.

"You speak truly," she said; "that is exactly what I mean."

Then she went away, liking Sir Oswald better than she had ever liked him in her life before. He looked after her half-sadly.

"A glorious girl!" he said to himself; "a true Darrell! I hope I have not made a mistake."

Lady Darrell made no complaint to her husband of Pauline; the girl gave her no tangible cause of complaint. She could not complain to Sir Oswald that Pauline's eyes always rested on her with a scornful glance, half-humorous, half-mocking. She could not complain of that strange power Miss Darrell exercised of making her always "feel so small." She would gladly have made friends with Miss Darrell; she had no idea of keeping up any species of warfare; but Pauline resisted all her advances. Lady Darrell had a strange kind of half-fear, which made her ever anxious to conciliate.

She remarked to herself how firm and steadfast Pauline was; there was no weakness, no cowardice in her character; she was strong, self-reliant; and, discerning that, Lady Darrell asked herself often, "What will Pauline's vengeance be?"

The question puzzled her far more than she would have cared to own. What shape would her vengeance assume? What could she do to avoid it? When would it overtake her?

Then she would laugh at herself. What was there to fear in the wildly-uttered, dramatic threats of a helpless girl? Could she take her husband from her? No; it was not in any human power to do that. Could she take her wealth, title, position, from her? No; that was impossible. Could she make her unhappy? No, again; that did not seem to be in her power. Lady Darrell would try to laugh, but one look at the beautiful, proud face, with its dark, proud eyes and firm lips, would bring the coward fear back again.

She tried her best to conciliate her. She was always putting little pleasures, little amusements, in her way, of which Pauline never availed herself. She was always urging Sir Oswald to make her some present or to grant her some indulgence. She never interfered with her; even when suggestions from her would have been useful, she never made them. She was mistress of the house, but she allowed the utmost freedom and liberty to this girl, who never thanked her, and who never asked her for a single favor.

Sir Oswald admired this grace and sweetness in his wife more than he had ever admired anything else. Certainly, contrasted with Pauline's blunt, abrupt frankness, these pretty, bland, suave ways shone to advantage. He saw that his wife did her best to conciliate the girl, that she was always kind and gracious to her. He saw, also, that Pauline never responded; that nothing ever moved her from the proud, defiant attitude she had from the first assumed.

He said to himself that he could only hope; in time things must alter; his wife's caressing ways must win Pauline over, and then they would be good friends.

So he comforted himself, and the edge of a dark precipice was for a time covered with flowers.

The autumn and winter passed away, spring-tide opened fair and beautiful, and Miss Hastings watched her pupil with daily increasing anxiety. Pauline never spoke of her disappointment; she bore herself as though it had never happened, her pride never once giving way; but, for all that, the governess saw that her whole character and disposition was becoming warped. She watched Pauline in fear. If circumstances had been propitious to her, if Sir Oswald would but have trusted her, would but have had more patience with her, would but have awaited the sure result of a little more knowledge and experience, she would have developed into a noble and magnificent woman, she would have been one of the grandest Darrells that ever reigned at the old Court. But Sir Oswald had not trusted her; he had not been willing to await the result of patient training; he had been impetuous and hasty, and, though Pauline was too proud to own it, the disappointment preyed upon her until it completely changed her. It was all the deeper and more concentrated because she made no sign.

This girl, noble of soul, grand of nature, sensitive, proud, and impulsive, gave her whole life to one idea—her disappointment and the vengeance due to it; the very grandeur of her virtues helped to intensify her faults; the very strength of her character seemed to deepen and darken the idea over which she brooded incessantly by night and by day. She was bent on vengeance.

CHAPTER XXVII
SIR OSWALD'S DOUBTS

It was the close of a spring day. Lady Hampton had been spending it at Darrell Court, and General Deering, an old friend of Sir Oswald's, who was visiting in the neighborhood, had joined the party at dinner. When dinner was over, and the golden sunbeams were still brightening the beautiful rooms, he asked Sir Oswald to show him the picture-gallery.

"You have a fine collection," he said—"every one tells me that; but it is not only the pictures I want to see, but the Darrell faces. I heard the other day that the Darrells were generally acknowledged to be the handsomest race in England."

The baronet's clear-cut, stately face flushed a little.

"I hope England values us for something more useful than merely handsome faces," he rejoined, with a touch of *hauteur* that made the general smile.

"Certainly," he hastened to say; "but in this age, when personal beauty is said to be on the decrease, it is something to own a handsome face."

The picture-gallery was a very extensive one; it was wide and well lighted, the floor was covered with rich crimson cloth, white statues gleamed from amid crimson velvet hangings, the walls were covered with rare and valuable pictures. But General Deering saw a picture that day in the gallery which he was never to forget.

Lady Hampton was not enthusiastic about art unless there was something to be gained by it. There was nothing to excite her cupidity now, her last niece being married, so her ladyship could afford to take matters calmly; she reclined at her ease on one of the crimson lounges, and enjoyed the luxury of a quiet nap.

The general paused for a while before some of Horace Vernet's battle-pieces; they delighted him. Pauline had walked on to the end of the gallery, and Lady Darrell, always anxious to conciliate her, had followed. The picture that struck the general most were the two ladies as they stood side by side—Lady Darrell with the sheen of gold in her hair, the soft luster of gleaming pearls on her white neck, the fairness of her face heightened by its dainty rose-leaf bloom, her evening dress of sweeping white silk setting off the graceful, supple lines of her figure, all thrown into such vivid light by the crimson carpet on which she stood and the background of crimson velvet; Pauline like some royal lady in her trailing black robes, with the massive coils of her dark hair wound round the graceful, haughty head, and her grand face with its dark, glorious eyes and rich ruby lips. The one looked fair, radiant, and charming as a Parisian coquette; the other like a Grecian goddess, superb, magnificent, queenly, simple in her exquisite beauty—art or ornaments could do nothing for her.

"Look," said the general to Sir Oswald, "that picture surpasses anything you have on your walls."

Sir Oswald bowed.

"What a beautiful girl your niece is!" the old soldier continued. "See how her face resembles this of Lady Edelgitha Darrell. Pray do not think me impertinent, but I cannot imagine, old friend, why you married, so devoted to bachelor life as you were, when you had a niece so beautiful, so true a Darrell, for your heiress. I am puzzled now that I see her."

"She lacked training," said Sir Oswald.

"Training?" repeated the general, contemptuously. "What do you call training? Do you mean that she was not experienced in all the little trifling details of a dinner-table—that she could not smile as she told graceful little untruths? Training! Why, that girl is a queen among women; a noble soul shines in her grand face, there is a royal grandeur of nature about her that training could never give. I have lived long, but I have never seen such a woman."

"She had such strange, out-of-the-way, unreal notions, I dared not—that is the truth—I dared not leave Darrell Court to her."

"I hope you have acted wisely," said the general; "but, as an old friend and a true one, I must say that I doubt it."

"My wife, I am happy to say, has plenty of common sense," observed Sir Oswald.

"Your wife," returned the general, looking at the sheen of the golden hair and the shining dress, "is pretty, graceful, and amiable, but that girl has all the soul; there is as much difference between them as between a golden buttercup and a dark, stately, queenly rose. The rose should have been ruler at Darrell Court, old friend."

Then he asked, abruptly:

"What are you going to do for her, Sir Oswald?"

"I have provided for her," he replied.

"Darrell Court, then, and all its rich revenues go to your wife, I presume?"

"Yes, to my wife," said Sir Oswald.

"Unconditionally?" asked the general.

"Most certainly," was the impatient reply.

"Well, my friend," said the general, "in this world every one does as he or she likes; but to disinherit that girl, with the face and spirit of a true Darrell, and to put a fair, amiable blonde stranger in her place, was, to say the least, eccentric—the world will deem it so, at any rate. If I were forty years younger I would win Pauline Darrell, and make her love me. But we must join the ladies—they will think us very remiss."

"Sweet smiles, no mind, an amiable manner, no intellect, prettiness after the fashion of a Parisian doll, to be preferred to that noble, truthful, queenly girl! Verily tastes differ," thought the general, as he watched the two, contrasted them, and lost himself in wonder over his friend's folly.

He took his leave soon afterward, gravely musing on what he could not understand—why his old friend had done what seemed to him a rash, ill-judged deed.

He left Sir Oswald in a state of great discomfort. Of course he loved his wife—loved her with a blind infatuation that did more honor to his heart than his head—but he had always relied so implicitly on the general's judgment. He found himself half wishing that in this, the crowning action of his life, he had consulted his old friend.

He never knew how that clever woman of the world, Lady Hampton, had secretly influenced him. He believed that he had acted entirely on his own clear judgment; and now, for the first time, he doubted that.

"You look anxious, Oswald," said Lady Darrell, as she bent down and with her fresh, sweet young lips touched his brow. "Has anything troubled you?"

"No, my darling," he replied; "I do not feel quite well, though. I have had a dull, nervous heaviness about me all day—a strange sensation of pain too. I shall be better to-morrow."

"If not," she said, sweetly, "I shall insist on your seeing Doctor Helmstone. I am quite uneasy about you."

"You are very kind to me," he responded, gratefully.

But all her uneasiness did not prevent her drawing the white lace round her graceful shoulders and taking up the third volume of a novel in which she was deeply interested, while Sir Oswald, looking older and grayer than he had looked before, went into the garden for a stroll.

The sunbeams were so loth to go; they lingered even now on the tips of the trees and the flowers; they lingered on the lake and in the rippling spray of the fountains. Sir Oswald sat down by the lake-side.

Had he done wrong? Was it a foolish mistake—one that he could not undo? Was Pauline indeed the grand, noble, queenly girl his friend thought her? Would she have made a mistress suitable for Darrell Court, or had he done right to bring this fair, blonde stranger into his home—this dearly-loved young wife? What would she do with Darrell Court if he left it to her? The great wish of his heart for a son to succeed him had not been granted to him; but he had made his will, and in it he had left Darrell Court to his wife.

He looked at the home he had loved so well. Ah, cruel death! If he could but have taken it with him, or have watched over it from another world! But when death came he must leave it, and a dull, uneasy foreboding came over him as to what he should do in favor of this idolized home.

As he looked at it, tears rose to his eyes; and then he saw Pauline standing a little way from him, the proud, beautiful face softened into tenderness, the dark eyes full of kindness. She went up to him more affectionately than she had ever done in her life; she knelt on the grass by his side.

"Uncle," she said, quietly, "you look very ill; are you in trouble?"

He held out his hands to her; at the sound of her voice all his heart seemed to go out to this glorious daughter of his race.

"Pauline," he said, in a low, broken voice, "I am thinking about you—I am wondering about you. Have I done—I wonder, have I done wrong?"

A clear light flashed into her noble face.

"Do you refer to Darrell Court?" she asked. "If you do, you have done wrong. I think you might have trusted me. I have many faults, but I am a true Darrell. I would have done full justice to the trust."

"I never thought so," he returned, feebly; "and I did it all for the best, as I imagined, Pauline."

"I know you did—I am sure you did," she agreed, eagerly; "I never thought otherwise. It was not you, uncle. I understand all that was brought to bear upon you. You are a Darrell, honorable, loyal, true; you do not understand anything that is not straightforward. I do, because my life has been so different from yours."

He was looking at her with a strange, wavering expression in his face; the girl's eyes, full of sympathy, were turned on him.

"Pauline," he said, feebly, "if I have done wrong—and, oh, I am so loth to believe it—you will forgive me, my dear, will you not?"

For the first time he held out his arms to her; for the first time she went close to him and kissed his face. It was well that Lady Hampton was not there to see. Pauline heard him murmur something about "a true Darrell—the last of the Darrells," and when she raised her head she found that Sir Oswald had fallen into a deep, deadly swoon.

CHAPTER XXVIII
READING OF THE WILL

Assistance was soon procured, and Sir Oswald was carried to his room; Doctor Helmstone was sent for, and when he arrived the whole house was in confusion. Lady Darrell wrung her hands in the most graceful distress.

"Now, Elinor," said Lady Hampton, "pray do not give way to anything of that kind. It is a fortunate thing for you that I am here. Let me beg of you to remember that, whatever happens, you are magnificently provided for, Sir Oswald told me as much. There is really no need to excite yourself in that fashion."

While Lady Darrell, with a few graceful exclamations and a very pretty show of sorrow, managed to attract all possible sympathy, Pauline moved about with a still, cold face, which those best understood who knew her nature. It seemed incredible to the girl that anything unexpected should happen to her uncle. She had only just begun to love him; that evening had brought those two proud hearts closer together than they had ever been; the ice was broken; each had a glimmering perception of the real character of the other—a perception that in time would have developed into perfect love. It seemed too hard that after he had just begun to like her—that as soon as a fresh and genuine sentiment was springing up between them—he must die.

For it had come to that. Care, skill, talent, watching, were all in vain; he must die. Grave-faced doctors had consulted about him, and with professional keenness had seen at once that his case was hopeless. The ailment was a sudden and dangerous one—violent inflammation of the lungs. No one could account for the sudden seizure. Sir Oswald had complained of pain during the day, but no one thought that it was anything of a serious nature. His manner, certainly, had been strange, with a sad pathos quite unlike himself; but no one saw in that the commencement of a mortal illness.

Lady Hampton frequently observed how fortunate it was that she was there. To all inquiries as to the health of her niece, she replied, "Poor, dear Lady Darrell is bearing up wonderfully;" and with the help of pathetic little speeches, the frequent use of a vinaigrette, a few tears, and some amiable self-condolence, that lady did bear up.

Strange to say, the one who felt the keenest sorrow, the deepest regret, the truest pain, was the niece with whom Sir Oswald had continually found fault, and whom he had disinherited. She went about with a sorrow on her face more eloquent than words. Lady Hampton said it was all assumed; but Lady Darrell said, more gently, that Pauline was not a girl to assume a grief which she did not feel.

So the baronet died after a week of severe illness, during which he never regained the power of speech, nor could make himself intelligible. The most distressing thing was that there was evidently something which he wished to say—something which he desired to make them understand. When Pauline was in the room his eyes followed her with a wistful glance, pitiful, sad, distressing; he evidently wished to say something, but had not the power.

With that wish unexpressed he died, and they never knew what it was. Only Pauline thought that he meant, even at the last, to ask her forgiveness and to do her justice.

Darrell Court was thrown into deepest mourning; the servants went about with hushed footsteps and sorrowful faces. He had been kind to them, this stately old master; and who knew what might happen under the new *regime?* Lady Hampton was, she assured every one, quite overwhelmed with business. She had to make all arrangements for the funeral, to order all the mourning, while Lady Darrell was supposed to be overwhelmed with sorrow in the retirement of her own room.

One fine spring morning, while the pretty bluebells were swaying in the wind, and the hawthorn was shining pink and white on the hedges, while the birds sang and the sun shone, Sir Oswald Darrell was buried, and the secret of what he had wished to say or have done was buried with him.

At Lady Darrell's suggestion, Captain Langton was sent for to attend the funeral. It was a grand and stately procession. All the *elite* of the county were there, all the tenantry from Audleigh Royal, all the friends who had known Sir Oswald and respected him.

"Was he the last of the Darrells?" one asked of another; and many looked at the stately, dark-eyed girl who bore the name, wondering how he had left his property, whether his niece would succeed him, or his wife take all. They talked of this in subdued whispers as the funeral *cortege* wound its way to the church, they talked of it after the coffin had been lowered into the vault, and they talked of it as the procession made its way back to Darrell Court.

As Lady Hampton said, it was a positive relief to open the windows and let the blessed sunshine in, to draw up the heavy blinds, to do away with the dark, mourning aspect of the place.

Everything had been done according to rule—no peer of the realm could have had a more magnificent funeral. Lady Hampton felt that in every respect full honor had been done both to the living and the dead.

"Now," she wisely remarked, "there is nothing to be done, save to bear up as well as it is possible."

Then, after a solemn and dreary dinner, the friends and invited guests went away, and the most embarrassing ceremony of all had to be gone through—the reading of the will.

Mr. Ramsden, the family solicitor, was in attendance. Captain Langton, Lady Darrell, Lady Hampton, and Miss Darrell took their seats. Once or twice Lady Hampton looked with a smile of malicious satisfaction at the proud, calm face of Pauline. There was nothing there to gratify her—no queen could have assisted at her own dethronement with prouder majesty or prouder grace. Some of the old retainers, servants who had been in the family from their earliest youth, said there was not one who did not wish in his heart that Pauline might have Darrell Court.

Lady Darrell, clad in deepest mourning, was placed in a large easy-chair in the center of the group, her aunt by her side. She looked extremely delicate and lovely in her black sweeping robes.

Pauline, who evidently thought the ceremony an empty one, as far as she was concerned, stood near the table. She declined the chair that Captain Langton placed for her. Her uncle was dead; she regretted him with true, unfeigned, sincere sorrow; but the reading of his will had certainly nothing to do with her. There was not the least shadow on her face, not the least discomposure in her manner. To look at her one would never have thought she was there to hear the sentence of disinheritance.

Lady Darrell did not look quite so tranquil; everything was at stake for her. She held her dainty handkerchief to her face lest the trembling of her lips should be seen.

Mr. Ramsden read the will, and its contents did not take any one much by surprise. The most important item was a legacy of ten thousand pounds to Captain Aubrey Langton. To Pauline Darrell was left an annuity of five hundred pounds per annum, with the strict injunction that she should live at Darrell Court until her marriage; if she never married, she was to reside there until her death. To all his faithful servants Sir Oswald left legacies and annuities. To his well-beloved wife, Elinor, he bequeathed all else—Darrell Court, with its rich dependencies and royal revenues, his estate in Scotland, his house in town, together with all the valuable furniture, plate, jewelry, pictures, all the moneys that had accumulated during his life-time—all to her, to hold at her will and pleasure; there was no restriction, no condition to mar the legacy.

To the foregoing Sir Oswald had added a codicil; he left Miss Hastings one hundred pounds per annum, and begged of her to remain at Darrell Court as companion to Lady Darrell and his niece.

Then the lawyer folded up the parchment, and the ceremony was ended.

"A very proper will," said Lady Hampton; "it really does poor dear Sir Oswald credit."

They hastened to congratulate Lady Darrell; but Captain Langton, it was noticed, forgot to do so—he was watching Pauline's calm, unconcerned departure from the room.

CHAPTER XXIX
WAITING FOR REVENGE

There was a slight, only a very slight difference of opinion between Lady Darrell and her aunt after the reading of the will. Lady Hampton would fain have given up the Elms, and have gone to live at Darrell Court.

"Sir Oswald's will is a very just one," she said, "admirable in every respect; but I should never dream, were I in your place, Elinor, of keeping that proud girl here. Let her go. I will come and live with you. I shall make a better chaperon than that poor, faded Miss Hastings."

But Lady Darrell was eager to taste the sweets of power, and she knew how completely her aunt would take every vestige of it from her.

She declared her intention to adhere most strictly to the terms of the will.

"And, aunt," she continued, with firmness quite new to her, "it would be so much better, I think, for you to keep at the Elms. People might make strange remarks if you came here to live with me."

Lady Hampton was shrewd enough to see that she must abide by her niece's decision.

The captain was to remain only two days at Darrell Court, and Lady Darrell was anxious to spend some little time with him.

"I like the captain, aunt," she said; "he amuses me."

Lady Hampton remembered how she had spoken of him before, and it was not her intention that her beautiful niece should fling away herself and her magnificent fortune on Aubrey Langton.

"She is sure to marry again," thought the lady; "and, dowered as she is, she ought to marry a duke, at least."

She represented to her that it was hardly etiquette for her, a widow so young, and her loss being so recent, to entertain a handsome young officer.

"I do not see that the fact of his being handsome makes any difference, aunt," said Lady Darrell; "still, if you think I must remain shut up in my room while the captain is here, of course, I will remain so, though it seems very hard."

"Appearances are everything," observed Lady Hampton, sagely; "and you cannot be too careful at first."

"Does he seem to pay Pauline any attention?" asked the young widow, eagerly.

"I have never heard them exchange more than a few words—indeed the circumstance has puzzled me, Elinor. I have seen him look at her as though he worshiped her and as though he hated her. As for Miss Darrell, she seems to treat him with contemptuous indifference."

"I used to think he liked her," said Lady Darrell, musingly.

"He liked the future heiress of Darrell Court," rejoined Lady Hampton. "All his love has gone with her prospects, you may rely upon it."

Lady Darrell, brought up in a school that would sacrifice even life itself for the sake of appearances, knew there was no help for her enforced retirement. She remained in her rooms until the young officer had left the Court.

Lady Hampton was not the only one who felt puzzled at Pauline's behavior to the captain. Miss Hastings, who understood her pupil perhaps better than any one, was puzzled. There was somewhat of a calm, unutterable contempt in her manner of treating him. He could not provoke her; no matter what he said, she would not be provoked into retort. She never appeared to remember his existence; no one could have been more completely ignored; and Captain Langton himself was but too cognizant of the fact. If he could have but piqued or aroused her, have stung her into some exhibition of feeling, he would have been content; but no statue could have been colder, no queen prouder. If any little attention was required at her hands she paid it, but there was no denying the fact that it was rendered in such a manner that the omission would have been preferable.

On the evening of his departure Lady Hampton went down to wish him farewell; she conveyed to him Lady Darrell's regret at not being able to do the same.

"I am very sorry," said the captain; "though, of course, under the circumstances, I could hardly hope for the pleasure of seeing Lady Darrell. Perhaps you will tell her that in the autumn, with her permission, I shall hope to revisit the Court."

Lady Hampton said to herself that she should take no such message. The dearest wish of her heart was that the gallant captain should never be seen there again. But she made some gracious reply, and then asked, suddenly:

"Have you seen Miss Darrell? Have you said good-by to her?"

Aubrey Langton looked slightly confused.

"I have not seen her to-day," he replied.

Lady Hampton smiled very graciously.

"I will send for her," she said; and when, in answer to her summons, a servant entered, she asked that Miss Darrell might be requested to favor her with her presence in the library. It did not escape her keen observation that Captain Langton would rather have avoided the interview.

Pauline entered with the haughty grace so natural to her; her proud eyes never once glanced at the captain; he was no more to her than the very furniture in the room.

"You wished to see me, Lady Hampton," she said, curtly.

"Yes—that is, Captain Langton wishes to say good-by to you; he is leaving Darrell Court this morning."

There was the least possible curl of the short upper lip. Lady Hampton happened to catch the glance bestowed upon Pauline by their visitor. For a moment it startled her—it revealed at once such hopeless passionate love and such strong passionate hate. Pauline made no reply; the queenly young figure was drawn up to its full height, the thoughtful face was full of scorn. The captain concealed his embarrassment as he best could, and went up to her with outstretched hands.

"Good-by, Miss Darrell," he said; "this has been a very sad time for you, and I deeply sympathize with you. I hope to see you again in the autumn, looking better—more like yourself."

Lady Hampton was wont to declare that the scene was one of the finest she had ever witnessed. Pauline looked at him with that straight, clear, calm gaze of hers, so terribly searching and direct.

"Good-by," she said, gravely, and then, utterly ignoring the outstretched hands, she swept haughtily from the room.

Lady Hampton did not attempt to conceal her delight at the captain's discomfiture.

"Miss Darrell is very proud," he said, laughing to hide his confusion. "I must have been unfortunate enough to displease her."

But Lady Hampton saw his confusion, and in her own mind she wondered what there was between these two—why he should appear at the same time to love and to hate her—above all, why she should treat him with such sovereign indifference and contempt.

"It is not natural," she argued to herself; "young girls, as a rule, admire—nay, take an uncommon interest in soldiers. What reason can she have for such contemptuous indifference?"

How little she dreamed of the storm of rage—of passion—of anger—of love—of fury, that warred in the captain's soul!

He was ten thousand pounds richer, but it was as a drop in the ocean to him. If it had been ten thousand per annum he might have been grateful. Ten thousand pounds would discharge every debt he had in the world, and set him straight once more; he might even lead the life he had always meant to lead for two or three years, but then the money would be gone. On the other hand, if that girl—that proud, willful, defiant girl—would but have married him, Darrell Court, with all its rich dependencies, would have been his. The thought almost maddened him.

How he loathed her as he rode away! But for her, all this grand inheritance would have been his. Instead of riding away, he would now be taking possession and be lord and master of all. These stables with the splendid stud of horses would be his—his the magnificent grounds and gardens—the thousand luxuries that made Darrell Court an earthly paradise. All these would have been his but for the obstinacy of one girl. Curses deep and burning rose to his lips; yet, for his punishment, he loved her with a love that mastered him in spite of his hate—that made him long to throw himself at her feet, while he could have slain her for the wrong he considered that she had done him.

Lady Hampton could not refrain from a few remarks on what she had witnessed.

"Has Captain Langton been so unfortunate as to offend you, Miss Darrell?" she asked of Pauline. "I thought your adieus were of the coldest."

"Did you? I never could see the use of expressing regret that is not really felt."

"Perhaps not; but it is strange that you should not feel some little regret at losing such a visitor."

To this remark Pauline deigned nothing save an extra look of weariness, which was not lost upon Lady Hampton.

"Pauline," said Miss Hastings, one morning, "I do not think you are compelled by the terms of Sir Oswald's will to reside at Darrell Court whether you like it or not. There could be no possible objection to your going away for a change."

The beautiful, restless face was turned to her.

"I could not leave Darrell Court even if I would," she returned.

"Why not? There is really nothing to detain you here."

"I am waiting," said the girl, her dark eyes lit by a fire that was not pleasant to see—"I am waiting here for my revenge."

"Oh, Pauline!" cried Miss Hastings, in real distress. "My dear child, you must forget such things. I do not like to hear such a word from your lips."

Pauline smiled as she looked at her governess, but there was something almost terrible in the calm smile.

"What do you think I am living here for—waiting here in patience for? I tell you, nothing but the vengeance I have promised myself—and it shall be mine!"

CHAPTER XXX
WILL FATE AID PAULINE?

Six months had passed since Sir Oswald's death, and his widow had already put away her cap and heavy weeds. Six months of retirement, she considered, were a very handsome acknowledgment of all her husband's love and kindness. She was in a state of serene and perfect self-content—everything had gone well with her. People had expressed their admiration of her devotion to his memory. She knew that in the eyes of the world she was esteemed faultless. And now it seemed to Lady Darrell that the time was come in which she might really enjoy herself, and reap the reward of her sacrifice.

The "armed neutrality" between Pauline and herself still continued. Each went her own way—their interests never clashed. Lady Darrell rather preferred that Pauline should remain at the Court. She had a vague kind of fear of her, a vague dread that made her feel safer where Pauline was, and where she could know something of her. Whole days would pass without their meeting; but, now that there was to be a little more gayety at Darrell Court, the two must expect to be brought into daily communication.

Lady Darrell was an amiable woman. It was true she had a small soul, capable of maintaining small ideas only. She would have liked to be what she called "comfortable" with Pauline—to live on sisterly terms with her—to spend long hours in discussing dress, ornaments, fashionable gossip—to feel that there was always some one at hand to listen to her and to amuse her. She, in her turn, would have been most generous. She would have made ample presents of dresses and jewels to such a friend; she would have studied her comfort and interests. But to expect or to hope for a companion of that kind in Pauline was as though some humble little wood-blossom could hope to train itself round a grand, stately, sad passion-flower.

Lady Darrell's worldly knowledge and tact were almost perfect; yet they could never reveal to her the depths of a noble nature like Pauline's. She could sooner have sounded the depths of the Atlantic than the grand deep of that young girl's heart and soul; they would always be dead letters to her—mysteries she could not solve. One morning the impulse was strong upon her to seek Pauline, to hold a friendly conversation with her as to half-mourning; but when she reached the door of the study her courage gave way, and she turned abruptly, feeling rather than knowing why the discussion of dress and mere personal appearance must prove distasteful to Miss Darrell.

Little by little Lady Darrell began to take her place in the grand world; she was too wise and wary to do it all at once. The degrees were almost imperceptible; even Lady Hampton, one of the most fastidious of critics, was obliged to own to herself that her niece's conduct was highly creditable. The gradations in Lady Darrell's spirits were as carefully regulated as the gradations of color in her dress; with deep lavender and black ribbons she was mildly sorrowful, the lighter grew the lavender the lighter grew her heart. On the first day she wore a silver gray brocade she laughed outright, and the sound of that laugh was the knell of all mourning.

Visitors began to arrive once more at Darrell Court, but Lady Darrell still exercised great restraint over herself. Her invitations were at first confined to matrons of mature age. "She did not feel equal to the society of gentlemen yet."

There was a grand chorus of admiration for the nice feeling Lady Darrell displayed. Then elderly gentlemen—husbands of the matrons—were admitted; and, after a time, "braw wooers began to appear at the hall," and then Lady Darrell's reign began in real earnest.

From these admiring matrons, enthusiastic gentlemen, ardent lovers, and flattering friends Pauline stood aloof. How she despised the whole of them was to be gathered only from her face; she never expressed it in words. She did not associate with them, and they repaid her behavior by the most hearty dislike.

It was another proof of "dear Lady Darrell's sweet temper" that she could live in peace with this haughty, abrupt, willful girl. No one guessed that the bland, amiable, suave, graceful mistress of Darrell Court stood in awe of the girl who had been disinherited to make way for her.

"Pauline," said Miss Hastings, one day, "I want you to accustom yourself to the idea of leaving Darrell Court; for I do not think there is any doubt but that sooner or later Lady Darrell will marry again."

"I expect it," she returned. "Poor Sir Oswald! His home will go to strangers, his name be extinct. How little he foresaw this when he married!"

"Let it take place when it may, the Court can be no home for you then," continued Miss Hastings.

Pauline raised her hand with a warning gesture.

"Do not say another word, Miss Hastings; I cannot listen. Just as criminals were fastened to the rack, bound to the wheel, tied to the stake, I am bound here—awaiting my revenge!"

"Oh, Pauline, if you would but forego such strange speech! This longing for vengeance is in your heart like a deadly canker in a fair flower. It will end badly."

The beautiful face with its defiant light was turned toward her.

"Do not attempt to dissuade me," she said. "Your warning is useless, and I do not like to grieve you. I acquainted Lady Darrell with my determination before she married my uncle for his money. She persisted in doing it. Let her take the consequences—bear the penalty. If she had acted a true womanly part—if she had refused him, as she ought to have done—he would have had time for reflection, he would not have disinherited me in his anger, and Darrell Court would have descended to a Darrell, as it ought to have done."

"If you could but forget the past, Pauline!"

"I cannot—it is part of my life now. I saw two lives before me once—the one made noble, grand, and gracious by this inheritance, which I should have known so well how to hold; the other darkened by disappointment and shadowed by revenge. You know how some men wait for the fair fruition of a fair hope—for the dawn of success—for the sunshine of perfect prosperity; so do I wait for my revenge. We Darrells never do things by halves; we are not even moderate. My heart, my soul, my life—which might have been, I grant, filled with high impulses—are concentrated on revenge."

Though the words she spoke were so terrible, so bitter, there was no mean, vindictive, or malign expression on that beautiful face; rather was it bright with a strange light. Mistaken though the idea might be, Pauline evidently deemed herself one chosen to administer justice.

Miss Hastings looked at her.

"But, Pauline," she said, gravely, "who made you Lady Darrell's judge?"

"Myself," she replied. "Miss Hastings, you often speak of justice; let me ask, was this matter fair? My uncle was irritated against me because I would not marry a man I detested and loathed; in his anger he formed the project of marriage to punish me. He proposed to Elinor Rocheford, and, without any love for him, she agreed to marry him. I went to her, and warned her not to come between me and my rightful inheritance. I told her that if she did I would be revenged. She laughed at my threat, married my uncle, and so disinherited me. Now, was it fair that I should have nothing, she all—that

I, a Darrell, should see the home of my race go to strangers? It is not just, and I mean to take justice into my hands."

"But, Pauline," opposed Miss Hastings, "if Lady Darrell had not accepted Sir Oswald, some one else would."

"Are such women common, then?" she demanded, passionately. "I knew evil enough of your world, but I did not know this. This woman is sweet-voiced, her face is fair, her hair is golden, her hands are white and soft, her manners caressing and gentle; but you see her soul is sordid — it was not large enough to prevent her marrying an old man for his money. Something tells me that the vengeance I have promised myself is not far off."

Miss Hastings wrung her hands in silent dismay.

"Oh, for something to redeem you, Pauline — something to soften your heart, which is hardening into sin!"

"I do not know of any earthly influence that could, as you say, redeem me. I know that I am doing wrong. Do not think that I have transformed vice into virtue and have blinded myself. I know that some people can rise to a far grander height; they would, instead of seeking vengeance, pardon injuries. I cannot — I never will. There is no earthly influence that can redeem me, because there is none stronger than my own will."

The elder lady looked almost hopelessly at the younger one. How was she to cope with this strong nature — a nature that could own a fault, yet by strength of will persevere in it? She felt that she might as well try to check the angry waves of the rising tide as try to control this willful, undisciplined disposition.

How often in after years these words returned to her mind: "I know of no earthly influence stronger than my own will."

Miss Hastings sat in silence for some minutes, and then she looked at the young girl.

"What shape will your vengeance take, Pauline?" she asked, calmly.

"I do not know. Fate will shape it for me; my opportunity will come in time."

"Vengeance is a very high-sounding word," observed Miss Hastings, "but the thing itself generally assumes very prosaic forms. You would not descend to such a vulgar deed as murder, for instance; nor would you avail yourself of anything so commonplace as poison."

"No," replied Pauline, with contempt; "those are mean revenges. I will hurt her where she has hurt me—where all the love of her heart is garnered; there will I wound her as she has wounded me. Where she can feel most there I mean to strike, and strike home."

"Then you have no definite plan arranged?" questioned Miss Hastings.

"Fate will play into my hands when the time comes," replied Pauline. Nor could the governess extract aught further from her.

CHAPTER XXXI
FATE FAVORS PAULINE

Autumn, with its golden grain, its rich fruits, and its luxuriant foliage, had come and gone; then Christmas snow lay soft and white on the ground; and still Captain Langton had not paid his promised visit to Darrell Court. He sent numerous cards, letters, books, and music, but he did not appear himself. Once more the spring flowers bloomed; Sir Oswald had been lying for twelve months in the cold, silent family vault. With the year of mourning the last of Lady Darrell's gracefully expressed sorrow vanished—the last vestige of gray and lavender, of jet beads and black trimmings, disappeared from her dresses; and then she shone forth upon the world in all the grace and delicate loveliness of her fair young beauty.

Who could number her lovers or count her admirers? Old and young, peer and commoner, there was not one who would not have given anything he had on earth to win the hand of the beautiful and wealthy young widow.

Lady Hampton favored the suit of Lord Aynsley, one of the wealthiest peers in England. He had met Lady Darrell while on a visit at the Elms, and was charmed with her. So young, fair, gifted, accomplished, so perfect a mistress of every art and grace, yet so good and amiable—Lord Aynsley thought that he had never met with so perfect a woman before.

Lady Hampton was delighted.

"I think, Elinor," she said, "that you are one of the most fortunate of women. You have a chance now of making a second and most brilliant marriage. I think you must have been born under a lucky star."

Lady Darrell laughed her soft, graceful little laugh.

"I think, auntie," she returned, "that, as I married the first time to please you, I may marry now to please myself and my own heart."

"Certainly," said her ladyship, dubiously; "but remember what I have always told you—sentiment is the ruin of everything."

And, as Lady Hampton spoke, there came before her the handsome face of Aubrey Langton. She prayed mentally that he might not appear again at Darrell Court until Lord Aynsley had proposed and had been accepted.

But Fate was not kind to her.

The next morning Lady Darrell received a letter from the captain, saying that, as the summer was drawing near, he should be very glad to pay his long-promised visit to Darrell Court. He hoped to be with them on Thursday evening.

Lady Darrell's fair face flushed as she read. He was coming, then, this man who above all others had taken her fancy captive—this man whom, with all her worldly scheming, she would have married without money if he had but asked her. He was coming, and he would see her in all the glory of her prosperity. He would be almost sure to fall in love with her; and she—well, it was not the first time that she whispered to her own heart how gladly she would love him. She was too excited by her pleasant news to be quite prudent. She must have a confidante—she must tell some one that he was coming.

She went to the study, where Miss Hastings and Pauline were busily engaged with some water-colors. She held the open letter in her hand.

"Miss Hastings, I have news for you," she said. "I know that all that interested Sir Oswald is full of interest for you. Pauline, you too will be pleased to hear that Captain Langton is coming. Sir Oswald loved him very much."

Pauline knew that, and had cause to regret it.

"I should be much pleased," continued Lady Darrell, "if, without interfering with your arrangements, you could help me to entertain him."

Miss Hastings looked up with a smile of assent.

"Anything that lies in my power," she said, "I shall be only too happy to do; but I fear I shall be rather at a loss how to amuse a handsome young officer like Captain Langton."

Lady Darrell laughed, but looked much pleased.

"You are right," she said—"he is handsome. I do not know that I have ever seen one more handsome."

Then she stopped abruptly, for she caught the gleam of Pauline's scornful smile—the dark eyes were looking straight at her. Lady Darrell blushed crimson, and the smile on Pauline's lips deepened.

"I see my way now," she said to herself. "Time, fate, and opportunity will combine at last."

"And you, Pauline," inquired Lady Darrell, in her most caressing manner—"you will help me with my visitor—will you not?"

"Pardon me, I must decline," answered Miss Darrell.

"Why, I thought Captain Langton and yourself were great friends!" cried Lady Darrell.

"I am not answerable for your thoughts, Lady Darrell," said Pauline.

"But you—you sing so beautifully! Oh, Pauline, you must help me!" persisted Lady Darrell.

She drew nearer to the girl, and was about to lay one white jeweled hand on her arm, but Pauline drew back with a haughty gesture there was no mistaking.

"Pray understand me, Lady Darrell," she said—"all arts and persuasions are, as you know, lost on me. I decline to do anything toward entertaining your visitor, and shall avoid him as much as possible."

Lady Darrell looked up, her face pale, and with a frightened look upon it.

"Why do you speak so, Pauline? You must have some reason for it. Tell me what it is."

No one had ever heard Lady Darrell speak so earnestly before.

"Tell me!" she repeated, and her very heart was in the words.

"Pardon me if I keep my counsel," said Pauline. "There is wisdom in few words."

Then Miss Hastings, always anxious to make peace, said:

"Do not be anxious, Lady Darrell; Pauline knows that some of the unpleasantness she had with Sir Oswald was owing to Captain Langton. Perhaps that fact may affect her view of his character."

Lady Darrell discreetly retired from the contest.

"I am sure you will both do all you can," she said, in her most lively manner. "We must have some charades, and a ball; we shall have plenty of time to talk this over when our guests arrive." And, anxious to go before Pauline said anything more, Lady Darrell quitted the room.

"My dear Pauline," said Miss Hastings, "if you would——"

But she paused suddenly, for Pauline was sitting with a rapt expression on her face, deaf to every word.

Such a light was in those dark eyes, proud, triumphant, and clear—such a smile on those curved lips; Pauline looked as though she could see into futurity, and as though, while the view half frightened, it pleased her.

Suddenly she rose from her seat, with her hands clasped, evidently forgetting that she was not alone.

"Nothing could be better," she said. "I could not have asked of fate or fortune anything better than this."

When Miss Hastings, wondering at her strange, excited manner, asked her a question, she looked up with the vague manner of one just aroused from deep sleep.

"What are you thing of, Pauline?" asked Miss Hastings.

"I am thinking," she replied, with a dreamy smile, "what good fortune always attends those who know how to wait. I have waited, and what I desired is come."

Thursday came at last. Certainly Lady Darrell had spared neither time nor expense in preparing for her visitor; it was something like a warrior's home-coming—the rarest of wines, the fairest of flowers, the sweetest of smiles awaiting him. Lady Darrell's dress was the perfection of good taste—plain white silk trimmed with black lace, with a few flowers in her golden hair. She knew that she was looking her best; it was the first time that the captain had seen her in her present position, so she was anxious to make the most favorable impression on him.

"Welcome once more to Darrell Court!" she said, holding out one white hand in greeting.

"It seems like a welcome to Paradise," said the captain, profanely; and then he bowed with the grace of a Chesterfield over the little hand that he still held clasped in his own.

CHAPTER XXXII
CAPTAIN LANGTON ACCEPTED

Lady Darrell was obliged to own herself completely puzzled. All the girls she had ever known had not only liked admiration, but had even sought it; she could not understand why Pauline showed such decided aversion to Captain Langton. He was undeniably handsome, graceful, and polished in manner; Lady Darrell could imagine no one more pleasant or entertaining. Why should Pauline show such great distaste for his society, and such avoidance of him?

There were times, too, when she could not quite understand Aubrey Langton. She had seen him look at Pauline with an expression not merely of love, but with something of adoration in his eyes; and then again she would be startled by a look of something more fierce and more violent even than hate. She herself was in love with him; nor was she ashamed to own the fact even to herself. She could let her heart speak now—its voice had been stifled long enough; still she would have liked to know the cause of Pauline's avoidance of him.

On the second day of his visit Lady Darrell gave a grand dinner-party. Lady Hampton, who viewed the captain's arrival with great disfavor, was, as a matter of course, to be present. All the neighbors near were invited, and Pauline, despite her dislike, saw that she must be present.

Lady Darrell took this opportunity of appearing, for the first time since Sir Oswald's death, *en grande toilette*. She wore a dress of blue brocade, a marvel of color and weaving, embroidered with flowers, the very delicacy of which seemed to attract notice. She wore the Darrell diamonds, her golden head being wreathed with a tiara of precious stones. She looked marvelously bright and radiant; her face was flushed with the most delicate bloom, her eyes were bright with happiness. The guests remarked to each other how lovely their young hostess was.

But when Pauline entered the room, Lady Darrell was eclipsed, even as the light of the stars is eclipsed by that of the sun. Pauline wore no jewels; the grand beauty of her face and figure required none. The exquisite head and graceful, arched neck rose from the clouds of gray tulle like some superb flower from the shade of its leaves; her dress was low, showing the white neck and statuesque shoulders; the dark, clustering hair was drawn back from the noble brow, a pomegranate blossom glowing in the thick coils. Graceful and dignified she looked, without glitter of jewels or dress—simple, perfect in the grandeur of her own loveliness.

She was greatly admired; young men gazed at her from a distance with an expression almost of infatuation, while the ladies whispered about her; yet no one had the courage to pay her any great attention, from the simple fact that Lady Hampton had insinuated that the young widow did not care much about Miss Darrell. Some felt ill at ease in her presence; her proud, dark eyes seemed to detect every little false grace and affectation, all paltry little insincerities seemed to be revealed to her.

Yet Pauline on this occasion did her best. Despite Sir Oswald's false judgment of her, there was an innate refinement about her, and it showed itself to-night. She talked principally to old Lady Percival, who had known her mother, and who professed and really felt the most profound liking and affection for Pauline; they talked during dinner and after dinner, and then, seeing that every one was engaged, and that no one was likely to miss her, Pauline slipped from the room and went out.

She gave a long sigh of relief as she stood under the broad, free sky; flowers and birds, sunshine and shade, the cool, fragrant gloaming, were all so much more beautiful, so much more to her taste, than the warm, glittering rooms. In the woods a nightingale was singing. What music could be compared to this? The white almond blossoms were falling as she went down to the lakeside, where her dreams were always fairest.

"I wonder," mused the girl, "why the world of nature is so fair, and the world of men and women so stupid and so inane."

"Pauline," said a voice near her, "I have followed you; I could not help doing so."

She turned hastily, and saw Captain Langton, his face flushed, his eyes flaming with a light that was not pleasant to see.

"How have you dared to do so?" she demanded.

"I dare do anything," he replied, "for you madden me. Do you hear? You madden me!"

She paid no more heed to his words than she did to the humming of the insects in the grass.

"You shall hear me!" he cried. "You shall not turn away your haughty head! Look at me—listen to me, or I will——"

"Or you will murder me," she interrupted. "It will not be the first time you have used that threat. I shall neither look at you nor listen to you."

"Pauline, I swear that you are driving me mad. I love you so dearly that my life is a torment, a torture to me; yet I hate you so that I could almost trample your life out under my feet. Be merciful to me. I know that I may woo and win this glittering widow. I know that I may be master of Darrell Court—she has let me guess that much—but, Pauline, I would rather marry you and starve than have all the world for my own."

She turned to him, erect and haughty, her proud face flushing, her eyes so full of scorn that their light seemed to blind him.

"I did not think," she said, "that you would dare to address such words to me. If I had to choose this instant between death and marrying you, I would choose death. I know no words in which I can express my scorn, my contempt, my loathing for you. If you repeat this insult, it will be at your peril. Be warned."

"You are a beautiful fiend!" he hissed. "You shall suffer for your pride!"

"Yes," she said, calmly; "go and marry Lady Darrell. I have vowed to be revenged upon her; sweeter vengeance I could not have than to stand by quietly while she marries you."

"You are a beautiful fiend!" he hissed again, his face white with rage, his lips dry and hot.

Pauline turned away, and he stood with deeply muttered imprecations on his lips.

"I love her and I hate her," he said; "I would take her in my arms and carry her away where no one in the world could see her beautiful face but myself. I could spend my whole life in worshiping her—yet I hate her. She has ruined me—I could trample her life out. 'Go and marry Lady Darrell,' she said; I will obey her."

He returned to the house. No one noticed that his face was paler than usual, that his eyes were shadowed and strange; no one knew that his breath came in hot gasps, and that his heart beat with great irregular throbs.

"I will woo Lady Darrell and win her," he said, "and then Pauline shall suffer."

What a contrast that graceful woman, with her fair face and caressing manner, presented to the girl he had just left, with her passionate beauty and passionate scorn! Lady Darrell looked up at him with eyes of sweetest welcome.

"You have been out in the grounds," she said, gently; "the evening is very pleasant."

"Did you miss me, Lady Darrell—Elinor?" he asked, bending over her chair.

He saw a warm blush rising in her cheeks, and in his heart he felt some little contempt for the conquest so easily made.

"Did you miss me, Elinor?" he repeated. "You must let me call you Elinor—I think it is the sweetest name in all the world."

It was almost cruel to trifle with her, for, although she was conventional to the last degree, and had but little heart, still what heart she had was all his. It was so easy to deceive her, too; she was so ready to believe in him and love him that her misplaced affection was almost pitiable. She raised her blue eyes to his; there was no secret in them for him.

"I am very glad my name pleases you," she said; "I never cared much for it before."

"But you will like it now?" he asked; and then bending over her chair, he whispered something that sent a warm, rosy flush over her face and neck.

Every one noticed the attention he paid her; Lady Hampton saw it, and disliked him more than ever. Lord Aynsley saw it, and knew that all hope of winning the beautiful widow was over for him. People made their comments upon it, some saying it would be an excellent match, for Sir Oswald had been much attached to Captain Langton, others thinking that Lady Darrell, with her fair face and her large fortune, might have done better. There was something, too, in the captain's manner which puzzled simple-hearted people—something of fierce energy, which all the softness of word and look could not hide.

"There is not much doubt of what will be the next news from Darrell Court," said one to another.

No one blamed the young widow for marrying again, but there was a general expression of disappointment that she had not done better.

Those dwelling in the house foresaw what was about to take place. Aubrey Langton became the widow's shadow. Wherever she went he followed her; he made love to her with the most persevering assiduity, and it seemed to be with the energy of a man who had set himself a task and meant to go through with it.

He also assumed certain airs of mastership. He knew that he had but to speak one word, and Darrell Court would be his. He spoke in a tone of authority, and the servants had already begun to look upon him as their master.

Silent, haughty, and reserved, Pauline Darrell stood aside and watched—watched with a kind of silent triumph which filled Miss Hastings with wonder—watched and spoke no word—allowed her contempt and dislike to be seen in every action, yet never uttered one word—watched like a beautiful, relentless spirit of fate.

Throughout the bright, long summer months Aubrey Langton staid on at Darrell Court, and at last did what he intended to do—proposed to Lady Darrell. He was accepted. It was the end of July then, but, yielding to her regard for appearances, it was agreed that no further word should be said of marriage until the spring of the following year.

CHAPTER XXXIII
"I HAVE HAD MY REVENGE!"

It was a warm, beautiful morning, with a dull haze lying over the fair summer earth; and Pauline Darrell, finding even the large, airy rooms too warm, went out to seek her favorite shade—the shelter of the great cedar tree. As she sat with her book in her hand—of which she never turned a page—Miss Hastings watched her, wondering at the dark shadow that had fallen over her beauty, wondering at the concentration of thought in her face, wondering whether this shadow of disappointment would darken all her life or if it would pass away, wondering if the vengeance to which she had vowed herself was planned yet; and to them, so silent and absorbed, came the pretty, bright vision of Lady Darrell, wearing a white morning dress with blue ribbons in her golden hair. The brightness and freshness of the morning seemed to linger on her fair face, as she drew near them with a smile on her lips, and a look of half-proud shyness in her eyes.

"I am glad you are both here," she said; "I have something to tell you." The blush and the smile deepened. "Perhaps you can guess what it is. Miss Hastings, you are smiling—Pauline, you do not look at me. Captain Langton has asked me to be his wife, and I have consented."

Then she paused. Miss Hastings congratulated her, and wished her much happiness. Pauline started at first, clasping her hands while her face grew white, and then she recovered herself and kept perfect silence.

"Pauline," said Lady Darrell, "I am very happy; do not shadow my happiness. Will you not wish me joy?"

"I cannot," replied the girl, in a trembling voice; "you will have no joy."

Then, seeing Lady Darrell's wondering face, she seemed to recover herself more completely.

"I will wish you," she said, bitterly, "as much happiness as you deserve."

"That would be but little," returned Lady Darrell, with a faint laugh; "I do not hold myself a particularly deserving person."

Then Miss Hastings, thinking they might come to a better understanding alone, went away, leaving them together.

Lady Darrell went up to the girl. She laid her hands on her arm appealingly, and raised her face with a pleading expression.

"Pauline," she said, her lips trembling with emotion, "after all, I was your uncle's wife; for his sake you might show me a little kindness. Marriage is a tie for life, not a bond for one day. Oh, Pauline, Pauline, if there is any reason why I should not marry Aubrey Langton, tell it—for Heaven's sake, tell it! Your manner is always so strange to him; if you know anything against him, tell me now before it is too late—tell me!"

There fell over them a profound silence, broken only by the sweet, cheery music of a bird singing in the cedar tree, and the faint sighing of the wind among the leaves.

"Tell me, for Heaven's sake!" repeated Lady Darrell, her grasp tightening on Pauline's arm.

"I have nothing to tell," was the curt reply. "Pray do not hold my arm so tightly, Lady Darrell; I have nothing to tell."

"Do not deceive me—there must be some reason for your strange manner. Tell it to me now, before it is too late."

There was almost an agony of pleading in her face and voice, but Pauline turned resolutely away, leaving her beneath the cedar alone.

"I must be mistaken," Lady Darrell thought. "What can she know of him? I must be wrong to doubt him; surely if I doubt him I shall doubt Heaven itself. It is her manner—her awkward manner—nothing more."

And she tried her best to dismiss all thoughts of Pauline from her mind, and give herself to her newly-found happiness.

"Pauline," said Miss Hastings, sorrowfully, when she rejoined the girl, "I cannot understand you."

"I do not quite understand myself," returned Miss Darrell. "I did not think I had any weakness or pity in my heart, but I find it is there."

"You frighten me," said Miss Hastings. "What makes you so strange? O, Pauline, throw it off, this black shadow that envelopes you, and forget this idea of vengeance which has so completely changed you!"

She looked up with a smile—a hard, bitter smile.

"I shall have had my revenge," she said, gloomily, "when she has married him."

Nor could any entreaties, any prayers of the kind-hearted woman move her to say more.

Whether the mysterious and uncertain aspect of things preyed upon Miss Hastings' mind, whether she grieved over her pupil and allowed that grief to disturb her, was never revealed, but in the month of August she became seriously ill—not ill enough to be obliged to keep her room, but her health and her strength failed her, and day by day she became weaker and less able to make any exertion.

Lady Darrell sent for Doctor Helmstone, and he advised Miss Hastings to go to the sea-side at once, and to remain there during the autumn. At her earnest request Pauline consented to accompany her.

"The change will do you good as well as myself," said the anxious lady; and Miss Darrell saw that she was thinking how much better it would be that she should leave Darrell Court.

"I will go," she said. "I know what you are thinking of. My vengeance is nearly accomplished. There is no reason now why I should remain here."

After many consultations it was agreed that they should go to the pretty little watering-place called Omberleigh. Many things recommended it; the coast was sheltered, the scenery beautiful, the little town itself very quiet, the visitors were few and of the higher class. It was not possible to find a prettier spot than Omberleigh.

Lady Darrell was generosity itself! In her quiet, amiable way she liked Miss Hastings as well as she was capable of liking any one. She insisted upon making all kinds of arrangements for the governess—she was to have every comfort, every luxury.

"And you must do nothing," she said, in her most caressing manner, "but try to get well. I shall expect to see you looking quite young and blooming when you return."

Lady Darrell had already written to Omberleigh, and, through an agent there, had secured beautiful apartments. When Miss Hastings half remonstrated with her, she laughed.

"I have nothing to do," she said, "but make every one happy; and it is my duty to find you always a comfortable home."

Lady Darrell looked, as she was in those days, a most happy woman. She seemed to have grown younger and fairer. The height of her ambition, the height of her happiness, was reached at last. She was rich in the world's goods, and it was in her power to make the man she loved rich and powerful too. She was, for the first time in her life, pleasing her own heart; and happiness made her more tender, more amiable, more considerate and thoughtful for others.

Lady Hampton mourned over the great mistake her niece was making. She had whispered in confidence to all her dear friends that Elinor was really going to throw herself away on the captain after all. It was such a pity, she said, when Lord Aynsley was so deeply in love with her.

"But then," she concluded, with a sigh, "it is a matter in which I cannot interfere."

Yet, looking at Lady Darrell's bright, happy face, she could not quite regret the captain's existence.

"You will not be lonely, Lady Darrell," said Miss Hastings, the evening before her journey.

She never forgot the light that spread over the fair young face—the intense happiness that shone in the blue eyes.

"No," she returned, with a sigh of unutterable content, "I shall never be lonely again. I have thoughts and memories that keep my heart warm—all loneliness or sorrow is over for me."

On the morrow Miss Darrell and the governess were to go to Omberleigh, but the same night Lady Darrell went to Pauline's room.

"I hope you will excuse me," she said, when the girl looked up in haughty surprise. "I want to say a few words to you before you go."

The cool, formal terms on which they lived were set aside, and for the first time Lady Darrell visited Pauline in her room.

"I want to ask you one great favor," continued Lady Darrell. "Will you promise me that Miss Hastings shall not want for anything? She is far from strong."

"I shall consider Miss Hastings my own especial charge," said Pauline.

"But you must allow me to help you. I have a very great affection for her, and desire nothing better than to prove it by kind actions."

"Miss Hastings would be very grateful to you if she knew it," said Pauline.

"But I do not want her to be grateful. I do not want her to know anything about it. With all her gentleness, Miss Hastings has an independence quite her own—an independence that I respect greatly; but it is quite possible, you know, Pauline, to manage an invalid—to provide good wine and little delicacies."

"I will do all that myself," observed the young girl.

Lady Darrell went nearer to her.

"Pauline," she said, gently, "you have always repelled every effort of mine; you would not be friends with me. But now, dear—now that I am so much happier, that I have no cloud in my sky save the shadow of your averted face—be a little kinder to me. Say that you forgive me, if I have wronged you."

"You have wronged me, Lady Darrell, and you know it. For me to talk of forgiveness is only a farce; it is too late for that. I have had my revenge!"

Lady Darrell looked up at her with a startled face.

"What is that you say, Pauline?"

"I repeat it," said the girl, huskily—"I have had my revenge!"

"What can you mean? Nothing of moment has happened to me. You are jesting, Pauline."

"It would be well for you if I were," said the girl; "but I tell you in all truth I have had my revenge!"

And those words sounded in Lady Darrell's ears long after Pauline had left Darrell Court.

CHAPTER XXXIV
THE STRANGER ON THE SANDS

The tide was coming in, the sun setting over the sea; the crimson and golden light seemed to be reflected in each drop of water until the waves were one mass of heaving roseate gold; a sweet western wind laden with rich, aromatic odors from the pine woods seemed to kiss the waves as they touched the shore and broke into sheets of beautiful white foam. It was such a sunset and such a sea—such a calm and holy stillness. The golden waters stretched out as far and wide as the eye could reach. The yellow sands were clear and smooth; the cliffs that bounded the coast were steep and covered with luxuriant green foliage. Pauline Darrell had gone to the beach, leaving Miss Hastings, who already felt much better, to the enjoyment of an hour's solitude.

There was a small niche in one of the rocks, and the young girl sat down in it, with the broad, beautiful expanse of water spread out before her, and the shining waves breaking at her feet. She had brought a book with her, but she read little; the story did not please her. The hero of it was too perfect. With her eyes fixed on the golden, heaving expanse of water, she was thinking of the difference between men in books and men in real life. In books they were all either brave or vicious—either very noble or very base.

She passed in review all the men she had ever known, beginning with her kind-hearted, genial father, the clever humorist artist, who could define a man's character in an epigram so skillfully. He was no hero of romance; he liked his cigar, his "glass," and his jest. She thought of all his rugged, picturesque artist-comrades, blunt of speech, honest of heart, open-handed, generous, self-sacrificing men, who never envied a comrade's prosperity, nor did even their greatest enemy an evil turn; yet they were not heroes of romance. She thought of Sir Oswald—the stately gentleman of the old school, who had held his name and race so dear, yet had made so fatal an error in his marriage and will. She thought of the captain, handsome and polished in manner, and her face grew pale as she remembered him. She thought of Lord Aynsley, for whom she had a friendly liking, not unmixed with wonder that he could so deeply love the fair, soft-voiced, inane Lady Darrell.

Then she began to reflect how strange it was that she had lived until now, yet had never seen a man whom she could love. Her beautiful lips curled in scorn as she thought of it.

"If ever I love any one at all," she said to herself, "it must be some one whom I feel to be my master. I could not love a man who was weak in body, soul, heart, or mind. I must feel that he is my master; that my soul yields to his; that I can look up to him as the real guiding star of my life, as the guide of my actions. If ever I meet such a man, and vow to love him, what will my love do for me? I do not think I could fall in love with a book-hero either; they are too coldly perfect. I should like a hero with some human faults, with a touch of pride capable of being roused into passion."

Suddenly, as the thought shaped itself in her mind, she saw a tall figure crossing the sands—the figure of a man, walking quickly.

He stopped at some little distance from the cliff, and then threw himself on the sand. His eyes were fixed on the restless, beautiful sea; and she, attracted by his striking masculine beauty, the statuesque attitude, the grand, free grace of the strong limbs, the royal carriage of the kingly head, watched him. In the Louvre she had seen some marvelous statues, and he reminded her of them. There was one of Antinous, with a grand, noble face, a royal head covered with clusters of hair, and the stranger reminded her of it.

She looked at him in wonder. She had seen picturesque-looking men—dandies, fops—but this was the first time she had ever seen a noble and magnificent-looking man.

"If his soul is like his face," she thought to herself, "he is a hero."

She watched him quite unconsciously, admiration gradually entering her heart.

"I should like to hear him speak," she thought. "I know just what kind of voice ought to go with that face."

It was a dreamy spot, a dreamy hour, and he was all unconscious of her presence. The face she was watching was like some grand, harmonious poem to her; and as she so watched there came to her the memory of the story of Lancelot and Elaine. The restless golden waters, the yellow sands, the cliffs, all faded from her view, and she, with her vivid imagination, saw before her the castle court where Elaine first saw him, lifted her eyes and read his lineaments, and then loved him with a love that was her doom. The face on which she gazed was marked by no great and guilty love—it was the face of Lancelot before his fall, when he shone noblest, purest, and grandest of all King Arthur's knights.

"It was for his face Elaine loved him," thought the girl—"grand and noble as is the face on which the sun shines now."

Then she went through the whole of that marvelous story; she thought of the purity, the delicate grace, the fair loveliness of Elaine, as contrasted with the passionate love which, flung back upon itself, led her to prefer death to life—of that strange, keen, passionate love that so suddenly changed the whole world for the maid of Astolat.

"And I would rather be like her," said the girl to herself; "I would rather die loving the highest and the best than live loving one less worthy."

It had seized her imagination, this beautiful story of a deathless love.

"I too could have done as Elaine did," she thought; "for love cannot come to me wearing the guise it wears to others. I could read the true nobility of a man's soul in his face; I could love him, asking no love in return. I could die so loving him, and believing him greatest and best."

Then, as she mused, the sunlight deepened on the sea, the rose became purple, the waters one beaming mass of bright color, and he who had so unconsciously aroused her sleeping soul to life rose and walked away over the sands. She watched him as he passed out of sight.

"I may never see him again," she thought; "but I shall remember his face until I die."

A great calm seemed to fall over her; the very depths of her heart had been stirred. She had been wondering so short a time before if she should ever meet any one at all approaching the ideal standard of excellence she had set up in her mind. It seemed like an answer to her thoughts when he crossed the sands.

"I may never see him again," she said; "but I shall always remember that I have met one whom I could have loved."

She sat there until the sun had set over the waters and the moon had risen; and all the time she saw before her but one image—the face that had charmed her as nothing in life had ever done before. Then, startled to find that it had grown so late, she rose and crossed the sands. Once she turned to look at the sea, and a curious thought came to her that there, by the side of the restless, shining waters, she had met her fate. Then she tried to laugh at the notion.

"To waste one's whole heart in loving a face," she thought, "would be absurd. Yet the sweetest of all heroines—Elaine—did so."

A great calm, one that lulled her brooding discontent, that stilled her angry despair, that seemed to raise her above the earth, that refined and beautified every thought, was upon her. She reached home, and Miss Hastings, looking at the beautiful face on which she had never seen so sweet an expression, so tender a light before, wondered what had come over her. So, too, like Elaine—

All night his face before her lived,

and the face was

Dark, splendid, sparkling in the silence, full
Of noble things.

All unconsciously, all unknowingly, the love had come to her that was to work wonders—the love that was to be her redemption.

CHAPTER XXXV
THE STORY OF ELAINE

Miss Hastings laid down the newspaper, with a quick glance of pleased surprise.

"I am glad that I came to Omberleigh," she said. "Imagine, Pauline, who is here. You have heard me speak of the St. Lawrences. I educated Laura St. Lawrence, and she married well and went to India. Her husband holds a very high appointment there. Lady St. Lawrence is here with her son, Sir Vane. I am so pleased."

"And I am pleased for you," responded Pauline, with the new gentleness that sat so well upon her.

"I must go and see them," continued Miss Hastings. "They are staying at Sea View. We can soon find out where Sea View is."

"St. Lawrence!" said Pauline, musingly; "I like the name; it has a pleasant sound."

"They are noble people who bear it," observed Miss Hastings. "Lady St. Lawrence was always my ideal of a thoroughbred English gentlewoman. I never heard how it was, but the greater part of their fortune was lost when Sir Arthur died. He left but this one son, Vane; and, although he has the title, he has but little to support it with. I know their family estates were all sold. Lady St. Lawrence has a small fortune of her own; but it is not much."

Again Pauline repeated the name to herself—"Vane St. Lawrence!"—thinking there was a sound as of half-forgotten music in it. That was a name that would have suited the face she had watched on the sands.

"Vane St. Lawrence!"

Unconsciously to herself she had said the words aloud. Miss Hastings looked up quickly.

"Did you speak, my dear?" she asked; and Pauline wondered to find her face suddenly grow warm with a burning blush.

"I think," said Miss Hastings, presently, "that I should like to visit them at once. Lady St. Lawrence may not be staying long, and I should never forgive myself if I were to miss her. Will you come with me, Pauline?"

"Yes, willingly."

She was ready to go anywhere, to do anything, with that great, wonderful love, that great, grand calm, filling her heart and soul.

For the first time the sight of her own magnificent loveliness pleased her.

"I may see him again," she thought to herself with almost child-like simplicity, "and I should like him to think of me."

She took more pains than she had ever taken before; and the picturesque taste that was part of her character greatly assisted her. Her dress was of purple silk, plain, rich, and graceful; her hat, with its drooping purple plume, looked like a crown on the beautiful head. She could no more help looking royal and queenly than she could help the color of her eyes and hair. Miss Hastings looked up with a smile of surprise, the proud face was so wonderfully beautiful—the light that never yet shone on land or sea was shining on it.

"Why, Pauline," she said, laughing, "Lady St. Lawrence will think I am taking the Queen of Sheba in disguise! What strange change is coming over you, child?"

What indeed? Was it the shadow of the love that was to redeem her—to work wonders in her character? Was it the light that came from the half-awakening soul? Wiser women than good, kindly, simple-hearted Miss Hastings might have been puzzled.

They were not long in finding Sea View—a pretty villa a little way out of the town, standing at the foot of a cliff, surrounded by trees and flowers—one of the prettiest spots in Omberleigh. They were shown into the drawing-room, the windows of which commanded a magnificent view of the sea.

Before they had been there many minutes there entered a fair, gentle, gracious lady, whose eyes filled with tears as she greeted Miss Hastings warmly.

"You are like a spirit from the past," she said. "I can see Laura a little child again as I look at you. Nothing could have pleased me so much as seeing you."

Then she looked admiringly at the beautiful girl by her side. Miss Hastings introduced her.

"Miss Darrell," she said, "it seems strange that I should meet you. My husband in his youth knew Sir Oswald well."

Lady St. Lawrence was just what Miss Hastings had described her—a thoroughly high-bred English lady. In figure she was tall and upright; her face had been beautiful in its youth, and was even now comely and fair; the luxuriant brown hair was streaked here and there with silver. She wore a dress of rich brocade, with some becoming arrangement of flowers and lace on her head; she was charming in her lady-like simplicity and gentleness.

Pauline, knowing that the two ladies would have much to talk about, asked permission to amuse herself with some books she saw upon the table.

"They belong to my son," said Lady St. Lawrence, with a smile.

There were Tennyson, Keats, and Byron, and written inside of each, in a bold, clear hand, was the name "Vane St. Lawrence." Pauline lost herself again in the sweet story of Elaine, from which she was aroused at intervals by the repetition of the words—"My son Vane."

She could not help hearing some part of Lady St. Lawrence's confidential communication, and it was to the effect how deeply she deplored the blindness of her son, who might marry his cousin Lillith Davenant, one of the wealthiest heiresses in England. Miss Hastings was all kindly sympathy.

"It would be such an excellent thing for him," continued Lady St. Lawrence; "and Lillith is a very nice girl. But it is useless counseling him; Vane is like his father. Sir Arthur, you know, always would have his own way."

Pauline began to feel interested in this Vane St. Lawrence, who refused to marry the wealthy heiress because he did not love her.

"He must be somewhat like me," she said to herself with a smile.

Then the conversation changed, and Lady St. Lawrence began to speak of her daughter Laura and her children. Pauline returned to Elaine, and soon forgot everything else.

She was aroused by a slight stir. She heard Lady St. Lawrence say:

"My dear Vane, how you startled me!"

Looking up, she saw before her the same face that had engrossed her thoughts and fancy!

She was nearer to it now, and could see more plainly the exquisite refinement of the beautiful mouth, the clear, ardent expression of the bold, frank eyes, the gracious lines of the clustering hair. Her heart seemed almost to stand still—it was as though she had suddenly been brought face to face with a phantom.

He was bending over Lady St. Lawrence, talking eagerly to her—he was greeting Miss Hastings with much warmth and cordiality. Pauline had time to recover herself before Lady St. Lawrence remembered her. She had time to still the wild beating of her heart—to steady her trembling lips—but the flush was still on her beautiful face and the light in her eyes when he came up to her.

Lady St. Lawrence spoke, but the words sounded to Pauline as though they came from afar off; yet they were very simple.

"Miss Darrell," she said, "let me introduce my son to you."

Then she went back to Miss Hastings, eager to renew the conversation interrupted by the entrance of her son.

What did Sir Vane see in those dark eyes that held him captive? What was looking at him through that most beautiful face? What was it that seemed to draw his heart and soul from him, never to become his own again? To any other stranger he would have spoken indifferent words of greeting and welcome; to this dark-eyed girl he could say nothing. When souls have spoken, lips have not much to say.

They were both silent for some minutes; and then Sir Vane tried to recover himself. What had happened to him? What strange, magic influence was upon him? Ten minutes since he had entered that room heart-whole, fancy-free, with laughter on his lips, and no thought of coming fate. Ten minutes had worked wonders of change; he was standing now in a kind of trance, looking into the grand depths of those dark eyes wherein he had lost himself.

They said but few words; the calm and silence that fell over them during that first interval was not to be broken; it was more eloquent than words. He sat down by her side; she still held the book open in her hands. He glanced at it.

"Elaine," he said, "do you like that story?"

She told him "Yes," and, taking the book from her hands, he read the noble words wherein Sir Lancelot tells the Lily Maid how he will dower her when she weds some worthy knight, but that he can do no more for her.

Was it a dream that she should sit there listening to those words from his lips—she had fancied him Sir Lancelot without stain, and herself Elaine? There was a sense of unreality about it; she would not have been surprised at any moment to awake and find herself in the pretty drawing-room at

Marine Terrace—all this beautiful fairy tale a dream—only a dream. The musical voice ceased at last; and it was to her as though some charm had been broken.

"Do you like poetry, Miss Darrell?" inquired Sir Vane.

"Yes," she replied; "it seems to me part of myself. I cannot explain clearly what I mean, but when I hear such grand thoughts read, or when I read them for myself, it is to me as though they were my own."

"I understand," he responded—"indeed I believe that I should understand anything you said. I could almost fancy that I had lived before, and had known you in another life."

Then Lady St. Lawrence said something about Sea View, and they left fairy-land for a more commonplace sphere of existence.

CHAPTER XXXVI
REDEEMED BY LOVE

"If anything can redeem her, it will be love." So Miss Hastings had said of Pauline long months ago, when she had first seen her grand nature warped and soured by disappointment, shadowed by the fierce desire of revenge. Now she was to see the fulfillment of her words.

With a nature like Pauline's, love was no ordinary passion; all the romance, the fervor, the poetry of her heart and soul were aroused. Her love took her out of herself, transformed and transfigured her, softened and beautified her. She was not of those who could love moderately, and, if one attachment was not satisfactory, take refuge in another. For such as her there was but one love, and it would make or mar her life.

Had Sir Vane St. Lawrence been merely a handsome man she would never have cared for him; but his soul and mind had mastered her. He was a noble gentleman, princely in his tastes and culture, generous, pure, gifted with an intellect magnificent in itself, and cultivated to the highest degree of perfection. The innate nobility of his character at once influenced her. She acknowledged its superiority; she bowed her heart and soul before it, proud of the very chains that bound her.

How small and insignificant everything else now appeared! Even the loss of Darrell Court seemed trifling to her. Life had suddenly assumed another aspect. She was in an unknown land; she was happy beyond everything that she had ever conceived or imagined it possible to be. It was a quiet, subdued happiness, one that was dissolving her pride rapidly as the sunshine dissolves snow—happiness that was rounding off the angles of her character, that was taking away scorn and defiance, and bringing sweet and gracious humility, womanly grace and tenderness in their stead.

While Sir Vane was studying her as the most difficult problem he had ever met with, he heard from Miss Hastings the story of her life. He could understand how the innate strength and truth of the girl's character had rebelled against polite insincerities and conventional untruths; he could understand that a soul so gifted, pure, and eager could find no resting-place and no delight; he could understand, too, how the stately old baronet, the gentleman of the old school, had been frightened at his niece's originality, and scared by her uncompromising love of truth.

Miss Hastings, whose favorite theme in Pauline's absence was praise of her, had told both mother and son the story of Sir Oswald's project and its failure—how Pauline would have been mistress of Darrell Court and all her uncle's immense wealth if she would but have compromised matters and have married Aubrey Langton.

"Langton?" questioned Sir Vane. "I know him—that is, I have heard of him; but I cannot remember anything more than that he is a great *roue*, and a man whose word is never to be believed."

"Then my pupil was right in her estimate of his character," said Miss Hastings. "She seemed to guess it by instinct. She always treated him with the utmost contempt and scorn. I have often spoken to her about it."

"You may rely upon it, Miss Hastings, that the instinct of a good woman, in the opinion she forms of men, is never wrong," observed Sir Vane, gravely; and then he turned to Lady St. Lawrence with the sweet smile his face always wore for her.

"Mother," he said, gently, "after hearing of such heroism as that, you must not be angry about Lillith Davenant again."

"That is a very different matter," opposed Lady St. Lawrence; but it seemed to her son very much the same kind of thing.

Before he had known Pauline long he was not ashamed to own to himself that he loved her far better than all the world beside—that life for him, unless she would share it, was all blank and hopeless. She was to him as part of his own soul, the center of his existence; he knew she was beautiful beyond most women, he believed her nobler and truer than most women had ever been. His faith in her was implicit; he loved her as only noble men are capable of loving.

As time passed on his influence over her became unbounded. Quite unconsciously to herself she worshiped him; unconsciously to herself her thoughts, her ideas, all took their coloring from his. She who had delighted in cynicism, whose beautiful lips had uttered such hard and cruel words, now took from him a broader, clearer, kinder view of mankind and human nature. If at times the old habit was too strong for her, and some biting sarcasm would fall from her, some cold cynical sneer, he would reprove her quite fearlessly.

"You are wrong, Miss Darrell—quite wrong," he would say. "The noblest men have not been those who sneered at their fellow-men, but those who have done their best to aid them. There is little nobility in a deriding spirit."

And then her face would flush, her lips quiver, her eyes take the grieved expression of a child who has been hurt.

"Can I help it," she would say, "when I hear what is false?"

"Your ridicule will not remedy it," he would reply. "You must take a broader, more kindly view of matters. You think Mrs. Leigh deceitful, Mrs. Vernon worldly; but, my dear Miss Darrell, do you remember this, that in every woman and man there is something good, something to be admired, some grand or noble quality? It may be half-hidden by faults, but it is there, and for the sake of the good we must tolerate the bad. No one is all bad. Men and women are, after all, created by God; and there is some trace of the Divine image left in every one."

This was a new and startling theory to the girl who had looked down with contempt not unmixed with scorn on her fellow-creatures—judging them by a standard to which few ever attain.

"And you really believe there is something good in every one?" she asked.

"Something not merely good, but noble. My secret conviction is that in every soul there is the germ of something noble, even though circumstances may never call it forth. As you grow older and see more of the world, you will know that I am right."

"I believe you!" she cried, eagerly. "I always believe every word you say!"

Her face flushed at the warmth of her words.

"You do me justice," he said. "I have faults by the million, but want of sincerity is not among them."

So, little by little, love redeemed Pauline, took away her faults, and placed virtues in their stead. It was almost marvelous to note how all sweet, womanly graces came to her, how the proud face cleared and grew tender, how pride died from the dark eyes, and a glorious love-light came in its stead, how she became patient and gentle, considerate and thoughtful, always anxious to avoid giving pain to others. It would have been difficult for any one to recognize the brilliant, willful Pauline Darrell in the loving, quiet, thoughtful girl whom love had transformed into something unlike herself.

There came a new world to her, a new life. Instead of problems difficult to solve, life became full of sweet and gracious harmonies, full of the very warmth and light of Heaven, full of unutterable beauty and happiness; her soul reveled in it, her heart was filled with it.

All the poetry, the romance, had come true—nay, more than true. Her girlish dreams had not shown her such happiness as that which dawned upon her now. She had done what she had always said she should do—recognized her superior, and yielded full reverence to him. If anything had happened to disenchant her, if it had been possible for her to find herself mistaken in him, the sun of the girl's life would have set forever, would have gone down in utter darkness, leaving her without hope.

This beautiful love-idyl did not remain a secret long; perhaps those most interested were the last to see it. Miss Hastings, however, had watched its progress, thankful that her prophecy about her favorite was to come true. Later on Lady St. Lawrence saw it, and, though she could not help mourning over Lillith Davenant's fortune, she owned that Pauline Darrell was the most beautiful, the most noble, the most accomplished girl she had ever met. She had a moderate fortune, too; not much, it was true; yet it was better than nothing.

"And, if dear Vane has made up his mind," said the lady, meekly, "it will, of course, be quite useless for me to interfere."

Sir Vane and Pauline were always together; but hitherto no word of love had been spoken between them. Sir Vane always went to Marine Terrace the first thing in the morning; he liked to see the beautiful face that had all the bloom and freshness of a flower. He always contrived to make such arrangements as would insure that Pauline and he spent the morning together. The afternoon was a privileged time; it was devoted by the elder ladies, who were both invalids, to rest. During that interval Sir Vane read to Pauline, or they sat under the shadow of the great cliffs, talking until the two souls were so firmly knit that they could never be severed again. In the evening they walked on the sands, and the waves sang to them of love that was immortal, of hope that would never die—sang of the sweet story that would never grow old.

CHAPTER XXXVII
PRIDE BROUGHT LOW

Pauline could have passed her life in the happy dream that had come to her; she did not go beyond it—the golden present was enough for her. The full, happy, glorious life that beat in her heart and thrilled in her veins could surely never be more gladsome. She loved and was beloved, and her lover was a king among men—a noble, true-hearted gentleman, the very ideal of that of which she had always dreamed; she did not wish for any change. The sunrise was blessed because it brought him to her; the sunset was as dear, for it gave her time to dream of him. She had a secret longing that this might go on forever; she had a shy fear and almost child-like dread of words that must be spoken, seeing that, let them be said when they would, they must bring a great change into her life.

In this she was unlike Sir Vane; the prize he hoped to win seemed to him so beautiful, so valuable, that he was in hourly dread lest others should step in and try to take it from him—lest by some mischance he should lose that which his whole soul was bent upon winning.

He understood the girlish shyness and sweet fear that had changed the queenly woman into a timid girl; he loved her all the more for it, and he was determined to win her if she was to be won. Perhaps she read that determination in his manner, for of late she had avoided him. She remained with Miss Hastings, and, when that refuge was denied her, she sought Lady St. Lawrence; but nothing could shield her long.

"Miss Darrell," said Sir Vane, one afternoon, "I have a poem that I want to read to you."

She was seated on a low stool at Lady St. Lawrence's feet, her beautiful face flushing at his words, her eyes drooping with shy, sweet pleasure that was almost fear.

"Will you not read it to me now, and here?" she asked.

"No; it must be read by the sea. It is like a song, and the rush of the waves is the accompaniment. Miss Hastings, if you have brought up your pupil with any notion of obedience, enforce it now, please. Tell Miss Darrell to put on her hat and come down to the shore."

Miss Hastings smiled.

"You are too old now, Pauline, to be dictated to in such matters," said Miss Hastings; "but if Sir Vane wishes you to go out, there is no reason why you should not oblige him."

Lady St. Lawrence laid her hand on the beautiful head.

"My son has few pleasures," she said; "give him this one."

Pauline complied. Time had been when anything like a command had instantly raised a spirit of rebellion within her; but in this clearer light that had fallen upon her she saw things so differently; it was as though her soul had eyes and they were just opened.

She rose and put on the pretty, plumed hat which Miss Hastings brought for her; she drew an Indian shawl over her shoulders. She never once looked at Sir Vane.

"Your goodness is not only an act of charity," he said, "but it is also a case in which virtue will be its own reward. You have no notion how beautifully the sun is shining on the sea."

So they went out together, and Lady St. Lawrence looked after them with a sigh.

"She is a most beautiful girl, certainly, and I admire her. If she only had Lillith Davenant's money!"

Sir Vane and Pauline walked in silence down to the shore, and then the former turned to his companion.

"Miss Darrell," he said, "will you tell me why you were not willing to come out with me—why you have avoided me and turned the light of your beautiful face from me?"

Her face flushed, and her heart beat, but she made no answer.

"I have borne my impatience well for the last three days," he said; "now I must speak to you, for I can bear it no longer, Pauline. Oh, do not turn away from me! I love you, and I want you to be my wife—my wife, darling; and I will love you—I will cherish you—I will spend my whole life in working for you. I have no hope so great, so sweet, so dear, as the hope of winning you."

She made him no answer. Yet her silence was more eloquent than words.

"It seems a strange thing to say, but, Pauline, I loved you the first moment I saw you. Do you remember, love? You were sitting with one of my books in your hand, and the instant my eyes fell upon your beautiful face a great calm came over me. I could not describe it; I felt that in that minute my life was completed. My whole heart went out to you, and I knew, whether you ever learned to care for me or not, that you were the only woman in all the world for me."

She listened with a happy smile playing round her beautiful lips, her dark eyes drooping, her flower-like face flushed and turned from his.

"You are my fate—my destiny! Ah! if you love me, Pauline—if you will only love me, I shall not have lived in vain! Your love would incite me to win name and fame—not for myself, but for you. Your love would crown a king—what would it not do for me? Turn your face to me, Pauline? You are not angry? Surely great love wins great love—and there could be no love greater than mine."

Still the beautiful face was averted. There was the sunlight on the sea; the western wind sighed around them. A great fear came over him. Surely, on this most fair and sunny day, his love was not to meet a cruel death. His voice was so full of this fear when he spoke again that she, in surprise, turned and looked at him.

"Pauline," he cried, "you cannot mean to be cruel to me. I am no coward, but I would rather face death than your rejection."

Then it was that their eyes met; and that which he saw in hers was a revelation to him. The next moment he had clasped her to his heart, and was pouring out a torrent of passionate words—such words, so tender, so loving, so full of passion and hope, that her face grew pale as she listened, and the beautiful figure trembled.

"I have frightened you, my darling," he said, suddenly. "Ah! do forgive me. I was half mad with joy. You do not know how I have longed to tell you this, yet feared—I knew not what—you seemed so far above me, sweet. See, you are trembling now! I am as cruel as a man who catches in his hands a white dove that he has tamed, and hurts it by his grasp. Sit down here and rest, while I tell you over and over again, in every fashion, in every way, how I love you."

The sun never shone upon happier lovers than those. The golden doors of Love's paradise were open to them.

"I never knew until now," said Vane, "how beautiful life is. Why, Pauline, love is the very center of it; it is not money or rank—it is love that makes life. Only to think, my darling, that you and I may spend every hour of it together."

She raised her eyes to the fair, calm heavens, and infinite happiness filled her soul to overflowing; a deep, silent prayer ascended unspoken from her heart.

Suddenly she sprang from his side with a startled cry.

"Oh, Vane!" she said, with outstretched hands, "I had forgotten that I am unworthy. I can never marry you!"

He saw such wild despair in her face, such sudden, keen anguish, that he was half startled; and, kneeling by her side, he asked:

"Why, my darling? Tell me why. You, Pauline," he cried—"you not worthy of me! My darling, what fancy is it—what foolish idea—what freak of the imagination? You are the noblest, the truest, the dearest woman in the whole wide world! Pauline, why are you weeping so? My darling, trust me—tell me."

She had shrunk shuddering from him, and had buried her face in her hands; deep, bitter sobs came from her lips; there was the very eloquence of despair in her attitude.

"Pauline," said her lover, "you cannot shake my faith in you; you cannot make me think you have done wrong; but will you try, sweet, to tell me what it is?"

He never forgot the despairing face raised to his, the shadow of such unutterable sorrow in the dark eyes, the quivering of the pale lips, the tears that rained down her face—it was such a change from the radiant, happy girl of but a few minutes ago that he could hardly believe it was the same Pauline.

He bent over her as though he would fain kiss away the fast falling tears; but she shrank from him.

"Do not touch me, Vane!" she cried; "I am not worthy. I had forgotten; in the happiness of loving you, and knowing that I was beloved, I had forgotten it—my own deed has dishonored me! We must part, for I am not worthy of you."

He took both her hands in his own, and his influence over her was so great that even in that hour she obeyed him implicitly, as though she had been a child.

"You must let me judge, Pauline," he said, gently. "You are mine by right of the promise you gave me a few minutes since—the promise to be my wife; that makes you mine—no one can release you from it. By virtue of that promise you must trust me, and tell me what you have done."

He saw that there was a desperate struggle in her mind—a struggle between the pride that bade her rise in rebellion and leave him with her secret untold, and the love that, bringing with it sweet and gracious humility, prompted her to confess all to him. He watched her with loving eyes; as that struggle ended, so would her life take its shape.

He saw the dark eyes grow soft with good thoughts; he saw the silent, proud defiance die out of the beautiful face; the lips quivered, sweet humility seemed to fall over her and infold her.

"I have done a cruel deed, Vane," she said—"an act of vengeance that cuts me off from the roll of noble women, and dishonors me."

Still keeping his hold of the white hand, he said:

"Tell me what it was—I can judge far better than you."

It seemed to her fevered fancy that the song of the waves died away, as though they were listening; that the wind fell with a low sigh, and the birds ceased their song—a silence that was almost terrible fell around her—the blue sky seemed nearer to her.

"Speak to me, Vane!" she cried; "I am frightened!"

He drew her nearer to him.

"It is only fancy, my darling. When one has anything weighty to say, it seems as though earth and sky were listening. Look at me, think of me, and tell me all."

She could never remember how she began her story—how she told him the whole history of her life—of the happy years spent with her father in the Rue d'Orme, when she learned to love art and nature, when she learned to love truth for its own sake, and was brought up amid those kindly, simple-hearted artist friends, with such bitter scorn, such utter contempt of all conventionalities—of her keen and passionate sorrow when her father died, and Sir Oswald took her home to Darrell Court, telling her that her past life was at an end forever, and that even the name she had inherited from her father must be changed for the name of her race—how after a time she had grown to love her home with a keen, passionate love, born of pride in her race and in her name—of the fierce battle that raged always between her stern, uncompromising truth and the worldly polish Sir Oswald would have had her acquire.

She concealed nothing from him, telling him of her faults as well as her trials. She gave him the whole history of Aubrey Langton's wooing, and her contemptuous rejection of his suit.

"I was so proud, Vane," she said, humbly. "Heaven was sure to punish me. I surrounded myself, as it were, with a barrier of pride, scorn, and contempt, and my pride has been brought low."

She told him of Sir Oswald's anger at her refusal to marry Aubrey, of her uncle's threat that he would marry and disinherit her, of her scornful disbelief—there was no incident forgotten; and then she came to the evening when Sir Oswald had opened the box to take out the diamond ring, and had spoken before them all of the roll of bank-notes placed there.

"That night, Vane," she said, "there was a strange unrest upon me. I could not sleep. I have had the same sensation when the air has been overcharged with electricity before a storm; I seemed to hear strange noises, my heart beat, my face was flushed and hot, every nerve seemed to thrill with pain. I opened the window, thinking that the cool night air would drive the fever from my brain.

"As I sat there in the profound silence, I heard, as plainly as I hear myself speaking now, footsteps—quiet, stealthy footsteps—go past my door.

"Let me explain to you that the library, where my uncle kept his cash-box and his papers, is on the ground floor; on the floor above that there are several guest-chambers. Captain Langton slept in one of these. My uncle slept on the third floor, and, in order to reach his room, was obliged to go through the corridor where the rooms of Miss Hastings and myself were.

"I heard those quiet, stealthy footsteps, Vane, and my heart for a few moments beat painfully.

"But the Darrells were never cowards. I went to my door and opened it gently. I could see to the very end of the corridor, for at the end there was a large arched window, and a faint gray light coming from it showed me a stealthy figure creeping silently from Sir Oswald's room; the gray light showed me also a glimmer of steel, and I knew, almost by instinct, that that silent figure carried Sir Oswald's keys in its hands.

"In a moment I had taken my resolve. I pushed my door to, but did not close it; I took off my slippers, lest they should make a sound, and followed the figure down stairs. As I have said before, the Darrells were never cowards; no dread came to me; I was intent upon one thing—the detection of the wrongdoer.

"Not more than a minute passed while I was taking off my shoes, but when I came to the foot of the grand staircase light and figure had both disappeared. I cannot tell what impulse led me to the library—perhaps the remembrance of Sir Oswald's money being there came to me. I crossed the hall and opened the library door.

"Though I had never liked Captain Langton, the scene that was revealed to me came upon me as a shock—one that I shall never forget. There was Captain Langton with my uncle's cash-box before him, and the roll of bank-notes in his hand. He looked up when I entered, and a terrible curse fell from his lips—a frightful curse. His face was fearful to see. The room lay in the shadow of dense darkness, save where the light he carried shone like a faint star. The face it showed me was one I shall never forget; it was drawn, haggard, livid, with bloodless lips and wild, glaring eyes.

"He laid the bank-notes down, and, going to the door, closed it softly, turning the key; and then clutching my arm in a grasp of iron, he hissed rather than said:

"'What fiend has brought you here?'

"He did not frighten me, Vane; I have never known fear. But his eyes were full of murderous hate, and I had an idea that he would have few scruples as to taking my life.

"'So, Captain Aubrey Langton,' I said, slowly, 'you are a thief! You are robbing the old friend who has been so good to you!'

"He dragged me to the table on which the money lay, and then I saw a revolver lying there, too.

"'One word,' he hissed, 'one whisper above your breath, and you shall die!'

"I know my face expressed no fear—nothing but scorn and contempt— for his grew more livid as he watched me.

"'It is all your fault!' he hissed into my ear; 'it is your accursed pride that has driven me to this! Why did you not promise to marry me when my life lay in your hands?'

"I laughed—the idea of a Darrell married to this midnight thief!

"'I told you I was a desperate man,' he went on. 'I pleaded with you, I prayed to you, I laid my life at your feet, and you trampled on it with scorn. I told you of my debts, my difficulties, and you laughed at them. If I could have gone back to London betrothed to you, every city usurer would have been willing to lend me money. I am driven to this, for I cannot go back to face ruin. You have driven me to it; you are the thief, though my hands take the money. Your thrice-accursed pride has ruined me!'

"'I shall go to Sir Oswald,' I said, 'and wake him. You shall not rob him!'

"'Yes,' he returned, 'I shall. I defy you, I dare you; you shall tell no one.'

"He took the revolver from the table and held it to my head; I felt the cold steel touch my forehead.

"'Now,' he said, 'your life is in your own hands; you must take an oath not to betray me, or I will fire.'

"'I am not afraid to die; I would rather die than hide such sin as yours. You cannot frighten me; I shall call for assistance.'

"'Wait a moment,' he said, still keeping that cold steel to my forehead, and still keeping his murderous eyes on my face; 'listen to what I shall do. The moment you cry out I shall fire, and you will fall down dead—I told you I was a desperate man. Before any one has time to come I shall place the bank-notes in your hand, and afterward I shall tell Sir Oswald that, hearing a noise in the library, and knowing money was kept there, I hastened down, and finding a thief, I fired, not knowing who it was—and you, being dead, cannot contradict me.'

"'You dare not be so wicked!' I cried.

"'I dare anything—I am a desperate man. I will do it, and the whole world will believe me; they will hold you a thief, but they will believe me honest.'

"And, Vane, I knew that what he said was true; I knew that if I chose death I should die in vain—that I should be branded as a thief, who had been shot in the very act of stealing.

"'I will give you two minutes,' he said, 'and then, unless you take an oath not to betray me, I will fire.'

"I was willing to lose my life, Vane," she continued, "but I could not bear that all the world should brand me as a thief—I could not bear that a Darrell should be reckoned among the lowest of criminals. I vow to you it was no coward fear for my life, no weak dread of death that forced the oath from my lips, but it was a shrinking from being found dead there with Sir Oswald's money in my hand—a shrinking from the thought that they would come to look upon my face and say to each other, 'Who would have thought, with all her pride, that she was a thief?' It was that word 'thief,' burning my brain, that conquered.

"'You have one minute more,' said the hissing whisper, 'and then, unless you take the oath——'

"'I will take it,' I replied; 'I do so, not to save my life, but my fair name.'

"'It is well for you,' he returned; and then he forced me to kneel, while he dictated to me the words of an oath so binding and so fast that I dared not break it.

"Shuddering, sick at heart, wishing I had risked all and cried out for help, I repeated it, and then he laid the revolver down.

"'You will not break that oath,' he said. 'The Darrells invariably keep their word.'

"Then, coolly as though I had not been present, he put the bank-notes into his pocket, and turned to me with a sneer.

"'You will wonder how I managed this,' he said. 'I am a clever man, although you may not believe it. I drugged Sir Oswald's wine, and while he slept soundly I took the keys from under his pillow. I will put them back again. You seem so horrified that you had better accompany me and see that I do no harm to the old man.'

"He put away the box and extinguished the light. As we stood together in the dense gloom, I felt his breath hot upon my face.

"'There is no curse a man can invoke upon the woman who has ruined him,' he said, 'that I do not give to you; but, remember, I do not glory in my crime—I am ashamed of it.'

"In the darkness I groped my way to the door, and opened it; in the darkness we passed through the hall where the armor used by warriors of old hung, and in the darkness we went up the broad staircase. I stood at the door of Sir Oswald's room while Captain Langton replaced the keys, and then, without a word, I went to my own chamber.

"Vane, I can never tell you of the storm, the tempest of hate that raged within me. I could have killed myself for having taken the oath. I could have killed Captain Langton for having extorted it. But there was no help for it then. Do you think I did wrong in taking it?"

"No, my darling," he replied, "I do not. Few girls would have been so brave. You are a heroine, Pauline."

"Hush!" she said, interrupting him. "You have not heard all. I do not blame myself for acting as I did. I debated for some time whether I ought to keep the oath or not. Every good impulse of gratitude prompted me to break it; yet again it seemed to me a cowardly thing to purchase my life by a lie. Time passed on—the wonder all died away. I said to myself that, if ever any one were falsely accused, I would speak out; but such an event never happened; and not very long after, as you know, Sir Oswald died. I did not like living under the shadow of that secret—it robbed my life of all brightness. Captain Langton came again. No words of mine can tell the contempt in which I held him, the contempt with which I treated him; every one noticed it, but he did not dare to complain. He did dare, however, to offer me his hateful love again, and, when I repulsed him in such a fashion as even he could not overlook, he turned all his attention to Lady Darrell. I am a wicked girl, Vane—now that the light of your love has revealed so much to me, I can see how wicked. I have told you that I had sworn to myself to be revenged on Lady Darrell for coming between me and my inheritance. I have seen more of the world since then, but at that time it seemed to me an unparalleled thing that a young girl like her should marry an old man like Sir Oswald entirely for his money. I told her if she did so I would be revenged. I know it was wrong," Pauline continued, humbly; "at the time I thought it brave and heroic, now I know it was wrong, and weak, and wicked—your love has taught me that."

"It was an error that sprang from pride," he said, gently; "there is nothing to part us."

"You have not heard all. Vane, I knew Captain Langton to be a thief—to be a man who would not scruple at murder if need required. I knew that all the love he could ever give to any one he had given to me, yet I——"

She paused, and the sad face raised humbly to his grew crimson with a burning blush.

"Oh, Vane, how can I tell you the shameful truth? Knowing what he was, knowing that he was going to marry Lady Darrell, I yet withheld the truth. That was my revenge. I knew he was a thief, a cruel, wicked slanderer, a thoroughly bad man, yet, when one word from me would have saved her from accepting his proposal, I, for my vengeance sake, refused to speak that word."

Her voice died away in a low whisper; the very sound of her words seemed to frighten her. Vane St. Lawrence's face grew pale and stern.

"It was unworthy of you, Pauline," he said, unhesitatingly. "It was a cruel revenge."

"I know it," she admitted. "No words can add to the keen sense of my dishonor."

"Tell me how it was," he said, more gently.

"I think," continued Pauline, "that she had always liked Captain Langton. I remember that I used to think so before she married my uncle. But she had noticed my contempt for him. It shook her faith in him, and made her doubt him. She came to me one day, Vane, with that doubt in her face and in her words. She asked me to tell her if I knew anything against him—if there was any reason why she should doubt him. She asked me then, before she allowed herself to love him; one word from me then would have saved her, and that word, for my vengeance sake, I would not speak."

"It should have been spoken," observed Sir Vane, gravely.

"I know it. Captain Langton has no honor, no conscience. He does not even like Lady Darrell; he will marry her solely that he may have Darrell Court. He will afterward maltreat her, and hold her life as nothing; he will squander the Darrell property. Vane, as truly as the bright heaven shines above me, I believe him to have no redeeming quality."

There was silence for some minutes, and then Sir Vane asked:

"Tell me, Pauline—do you think that Lady Darrell would marry him if she knew what you have just told me?"

"I am sure she would not. She is very worldly, and only lives what one may call a life of appearances; she would not marry him if she knew him to be a thief—she would shrink from him. Elegant, polished, amiable women like Lady Darrell are frightened at crime."

"That one word ought to have been spoken, Pauline, out of sheer womanly pity and sheer womanly grace. How could you refuse to speak when she came to you with a prayer on her lips?"

"The pride and thirst for vengeance were too strong for me," she replied.

"And to these you have sacrificed the life and happiness of a woman who has never really injured you. Lady Darrell and Captain Langton are not yet married—are they, Pauline?"

"No, they are to be married in the spring," she answered.

"Then listen to me, my darling. This marriage must never take place. Your silence is wicked—you cannot honorably and conscientiously stand by and see Lady Darrell throw herself away on a thief. You have done a grievous wrong, Pauline. You must make a noble atonement."

Something like a gleam of hope came into her eyes.

"Can I atone?" she asked. "I will do so if I know how, even at the price of my life."

"I tell you, frankly," he said, "that you have done grievously wrong. When that poor lady came to you in her doubt and perplexity, you ought to have told her at least as much of the truth as would have prevented the marriage. But, my darling, this shall not part us. If I teach you how to atone will you atone?"

She crossed her hands as one praying.

"I will do anything you tell me, Vane."

"You must go to Darrell Court, and you must make to Lady Darrell the same ample avowal you have made to me; tell her the same story—how you vowed vengeance against her, and how you carried that vengeance out; and then see what comes of it."

"But suppose she will not believe me—what then?"

"You will have done your best—you will at least have made atonement for your secrecy. If, with her eyes open, Lady Darrell marries Captain Langton after that, you will have nothing to blame yourself for. It will be hard for you, my darling, but it is the brave, right, true thing to do."

"And you do not hate me, Vane?"

"No; I love you even better than I did. The woman brave enough to own her faults and desirous to atone for them deserves all the love a man can give her. Pauline, when you have done this, my darling, may I ask you when you will be my wife?"

She sobbed out that she was unworthy—all unworthy; but he would not even hear the words.

"None the less dear are you for having told me your faults. There is only one word now, my darling, to keep in view; and that is, 'atonement.'"

She looked up at him with happy, glistening eyes.

"Vane," she said, "I will go to Darrell Court to-morrow. I shall never rest now until I have done what you wish me to do."

So far had love redeemed her that she was ready to undo all the wrong she had done, at any cost to her pride.

But love was to work even greater wonders for her yet.

CHAPTER XXXVIII
PAULINE AND LADY DARRELL

Pauline communicated her resolution of going to Darrell Court to Miss Hastings, and that lady looked up in surprise almost too great for words.

"You are going to Darrell Court to-morrow!" she exclaimed. "It cannot be, Pauline; you must not travel alone. If you go, I must go with you."

But Pauline threw one arm caressingly round her friend's neck.

"Do not try to stop me," she said, pleadingly, "and let me go alone. I did a great wrong at Darrell Court, and I must return to set it right. Only alone can I do that."

"Pauline," asked Miss Hastings, gravely, "do you wish to atone for your revenge?"

"I do," she replied, simply. "You must let me go alone; and when I come back I shall have something to tell you—something that I know will please you very much."

Miss Hastings kissed the beautiful face.

"It is as I thought," she said to herself—"in her case love has worked wonders—it has redeemed her."

Lady Darrell sat alone in her dressing-room; the autumn day was drawing to a close. Greatly to her delight and surprise, Captain Langton had unexpectedly appeared that morning. He knew that in the absence of Miss Hastings he could not stop at Darrell Court; but he was paying a visit, he told Lady Darrell, to Sir Peter Glynn, and hoped to see her every day. He had declined dining at the Court, but promised to spend some part of the evening there.

Lady Darrell had ordered an early dinner, and sat in her dressing-room awaiting her maid. Of course she was going to dress for the captain—to set off her delicate beauty to the greatest advantage. A superb costume of pale pink brocade, with rich trimmings of white lace, was ready for her. A suit of pearls and opals lay in their open cases. The room presented a picturesque appearance of unbounded and splendid confusion—lace, jewelry, fans, slippers, all kinds of valuable and pretty ornaments were there; but nothing in that room was one half so fair as the beautiful woman who sat with a pleased smile upon her face.

Yet there was something like a sigh on her lips. Did he love her? Of her own feelings she had no doubt. She loved him with her whole heart—as she had never imagined herself capable of loving any one. But did he love her? There was somewhat of coldness and indifference in his manner— something she could not understand. He had greeted her carelessly—he had bidden her a careless farewell, she said to herself. Yet he must love her; for the face reflected in the mirror was a very fair one.

Then she remembered Pauline, and the old wonder came over her why Pauline had always such great, such unbounded contempt for him.

Her maid came in, and Lady Darrell put on the pink brocade with its white lace trimmings. The maid, in ecstasies, cried out that it was superb— that "my lady" had "never looked so beautiful."

Lady Darrell took up the pearl necklace and held it against the pink brocade to note the contrast. While she held it in her hands one of the servants gave a hurried rap at the door. She came to announce that Miss Darrell had arrived suddenly, and wished to see Lady Darrell at once.

"Miss Darrell! Then something must be the matter with Miss Hastings. Ask her to come to me at once."

In a few moments Pauline was standing in that brilliant room, looking pale and anxious.

"No," she said, in answer to Lady Darrell's eager question; "there is nothing the matter with Miss Hastings. I wanted to see you; I want to see you alone. Can you spare a few minutes?"

Lady Darrell dismissed her maid, and then turned to Pauline.

"What is it?" she asked. "What has brought you here so suddenly?"

Without one word, Pauline went to the door and locked it, and then she went back to Lady Darrell, who was watching her in wonder.

"I have done you a great wrong," she said, humbly, "and I have come to atone for it."

Lady Darrell drew back, trembling with strange, vague fear.

"Oh, Pauline, Pauline, what have you done?"

Pauline threw aside her traveling cloak and took off her hat; and then she came to Lady Darrell.

"Let me tell you my story, kneeling here," she said; and she knelt down before Lady Darrell, looking as she spoke straight into her face. "Let me tell you before I begin it," she added, "that I have no excuse to offer for myself—none. I can only thank Heaven that I have seen my fault before—for your sake—it is too late."

Slowly, gravely, sometimes with bitter tears and with sobs that came from the depths of her heart, Pauline told her story—how the captain had loved her, how ill he had taken her repulse, how she had discovered his vile worthlessness, but for the sake of her revenge had said nothing.

Lady Darrell listened as to her death-knell.

"Is this true, Pauline?" she cried. "You vowed vengeance against me—is this your vengeance, to try to part me from the man I love, and to take from me the only chance of happiness that my wretched life holds?"

Her fair face had grown deadly pale; all the light and the happiness had fled from it; the pearls lay unheeded, the blue eyes grew dim with tears.

"Is it possible, Pauline?" she cried again. "Have I given my love to one dishonored? I cannot believe it—I will not believe it! It is part of your vengeance against me. What have I done that you should hate me so?"

The dark eyes and the beautiful face were raised to hers.

"Dear Lady Darrell," said the girl, "I have never spoken a loving word to you before; but I tell you now that, if I could give my life to save you from this sorrow, I would do so."

"Aubrey Langton a thief!" cried Lady Darrell. "It is not true—I will swear that it is not true! I love him, and you want to take him from me. How could you dare to invent such a falsehood of him, a soldier and a gentleman? You are cruel and wicked."

Yet through all her passionate denials, through all her bitter anger, there ran a shudder of deadly fear—a doubt that chilled her with the coldness of death—a voice that would be heard, crying out that here was no wrong, no falsehood, but the bare, unvarnished truth. She cast it from her—she trampled it under foot; and the girl kneeling at her feet suffered as much as she did herself while she watched that struggle.

"You say that he would have murdered you—that he held a pistol to your forehead, and made you take that oath—he, Aubrey Langton, did that?"

"He did!" said Pauline. "Would to Heaven I had told you before."

"Would to Heaven you had!" she cried. "It is too late now. I love him—I love him, and I cannot lose him. You might have saved me from this, and you would not. Oh, cruel and false!"

"Dearest Lady Darrell," said the girl, "I would wash out my fault with my heart's blood if I could. There is no humiliation that I would not undergo, no pain that I would not suffer, to save you."

"You might have saved me. I had a doubt, and I went to you, Pauline, humbly, not proudly. I prayed you to reveal the truth, and you treated me with scorn. Can it be that one woman could be so cruel to another? If you had but spoken half the truth you have now told me, I should have believed you, and have gone away; I should have crushed down the love that was rising in my heart, and in time I should have forgotten it. Now it is too late. I love him, and I cannot lose him—dear Heaven, I cannot lose him!"

She flung up her arms with a wild cry of despair. None ever suffered more than did Pauline Darrell then.

"Oh, my sin," she moaned, "my grievous sin!"

She tried to soothe the unhappy woman, but Lady Darrell turned from her with all the energy of despair.

"I cannot believe you," she cried; "it is an infamous plot to destroy my happiness and to destroy me. Hark! There is Aubrey Langton's voice; come with me and say before him what you have said to me."

CHAPTER XXXIX
FACE TO FACE

Captain Langton looked up in surprise not altogether unfounded, the sight that met his eyes was so unusual.

Before him stood Lady Darrell, her face white as death, her lips quivering with excitement, her superb dress of pink brocade all disarranged, her golden hair falling over her beautiful shoulders—a sight not to be forgotten; she held Pauline by the hand, and in all her life Lady Darrell had never looked so agitated as now.

"Captain Langton," said Lady Darrell, "will you come here? I want you most particularly."

It was by pure chance that she opened the library door—it was the one nearest to her.

"Will you follow me?" she said.

He looked from one to the other with somewhat of confusion in his face.

"Miss Darrell!" he cried. "Why, I thought you were at Omberleigh!"

Pauline made no reply.

Lady Darrell held the library door open while they entered, and then she closed it, and turned the key.

Captain Langton looked at her in wonder.

"Elinor," he said, "what does this mean? Are you going to play a tragedy or a farce?"

"That will depend upon you," she answered; "I am glad and thankful to have brought you and Miss Darrell face to face. Now I shall know the truth."

The surprise on his face deepened into an angry scowl.

"What do you mean?" he demanded, sharply. "I do not understand."

It was a scene never to be forgotten. The library was dim with the shadows of the autumn evening, and in the gloom Lady Darrell's pale pink dress, golden hair, and white arms bare to the shoulder, seemed to attract all the light; her face was changed from its great agitation—the calm, fair beauty, the gentle, caressing manner were gone.

Near her stood Pauline, whose countenance was softened with compassion and pity unutterable, the dark eyes shining as through a mist of tears.

Before them, as a criminal before his judges, stood Aubrey Langton, with an angry scowl on his handsome face, and yet something like fear in his eyes.

"What is it?" he cried, impatiently. "I cannot understand this at all."

Lady Darrell turned her pale face to him.

"Captain Langton," she said, gravely, "Miss Darrell brings a terrible accusation against you. She tells me that you stole the roll of notes that Sir Oswald missed, and that at the price of her life you extorted an oath from her not to betray you; is it true?"

She looked at him bravely, fearlessly.

"It is a lie!" he said.

Lady Darrell continued:

"Here, in this room, where we are standing now, she tells me that the scene took place, and that, finding she had discovered you in the very act of theft, you held a loaded pistol to her head until she took the oath you dictated. Is it true or false?"

"It is a lie!" he repeated; but his lips were growing white, and great drops stood upon his brow.

"She tells me," resumed Lady Darrell, "that you loved her, and that you care only for Darrell Court, not for me. Is it true?"

"It is all false," he said, hoarsely—"false from beginning to end! She hates you, she hates me, and this foul slander has only been invented to part us!"

Lady Darrell looked from one to the other.

"Now Heaven help me!" she cried. "Which am I to believe?"

Grave and composed, with a certain majesty of truth that could never be mistaken, Pauline raised her right hand.

"Lady Darrell," she said, "I swear to you, in the presence of Heaven, that I have spoken nothing but the truth."

"And I swear it is false!" cried Aubrey Langton.

But appearances were against him; Lady Darrell saw that he trembled, that his lips worked almost convulsively, and that great drops stood upon his brow.

Pauline looked at him; those dark eyes that had in them no shadow save of infinite pity and sorrow seemed to penetrate his soul, and he shrank from the glance.

"Elinor," he cried, "you believe me, surely? Miss Darrell has always hated you, and this is her revenge."

"Lady Darrell," said the girl, "I am ashamed of my hatred and ashamed of my desire for vengeance. There is no humiliation to which I would not submit to atone for my faults, but every word I have said to you is true."

Once more with troubled eyes Lady Darrell looked from one to the other; once more she murmured:

"Heaven help me! Which am I to believe?"

Then Captain Langton, with a light laugh, said:

"Is the farce ended, Lady Darrell? You see it is no tragedy after all."

Pauline turned to him, and in the light of that noble face his own grew mean and weak.

"Captain Langton," she said, "I appeal to whatever there is of good and just in you. Own to the truth. You need not be afraid of it—Lady Darrell will not injure you. She will think better of you if you confess than if you deny. Tell her that you were led into error, and trust to her kindness for pardon."

"She speaks well," observed Lady Darrell, slowly. "If you are guilty, it is better to tell me so."

He laughed again, but the laugh was not pleasant to hear. Pauline continued:

"Let the evil rest where it is, Captain Langton; do not make it any greater. In your heart you know that you have no love for this lady—it is her fortune that attracts you. If you marry her, it will only be to make her unhappy for life. Admit your fault and leave her in peace."

"You are a remarkably free-spoken young lady, Miss Darrell—you have quite an oratorical flow of words. It is fortunate that Lady Darrell knows you, or she might be tempted to believe you. Elinor, I rest my claim on this—since you have known Miss Darrell, have you ever received one act of kindness from her, one kind word even?"

Lady Darrell was obliged to answer:

"No."

"Then I leave it," he said, "to your sense of justice which of us you are to believe now—her who, to anger you, swears to my guilt, or me, who swears to my innocence? Elinor, my love, you cannot doubt me."

Pauline saw her eyes soften with unutterable tenderness—he saw a faint flush rise on the fair face. Almost involuntarily Lady Darrell drew near to him.

"I cannot bear to doubt you, Aubrey," she said. "Oh, speak the truth to me, for my love's sake!"

"I do speak the truth. Come with me; leave Miss Darrell for a while. Walk with me across the lawn, and I will tell you what respect for Miss Darrell prevents my saying here."

Lady Darrell turned to Pauline.

"I must hear what he has to say—it is only just."

"I will wait for you," she replied.

The captain was always attentive; he went out into the hall and returned with a shawl that he found there.

"You cannot go out with those beautiful arms uncovered, Elinor," he said, gently.

He placed the shawl around her, trying to hide the coward, trembling fear.

"As though I did not love you," he said, reproachfully. "Show me another woman only half so fair."

Pauline made one more effort.

"Lady Darrell," she cried, with outstretched hands, "you will not decide hastily—you will take time to judge?"

But as they passed out together, something in the delicate face told her that her love for Aubrey Langton was the strongest element in her nature.

"Lady Darrell," she cried again, "do not listen to him! I swear I have told you the truth—Heaven will judge between him and me if I have not!"

"You must have studied tragedy at the Porte St. Martin," said Aubrey Langton, with a forced laugh; "Lady Darrell knows which to believe."

She watched them walk across the lawn, Captain Langton pleading earnestly, Lady Darrell's face softening as she listened.

"I am too late!" cried the girl, in an agony of self-reproach. "All my humiliation is in vain; she will believe him and not me. I cannot save her now, but one word spoken in time might have done so."

Oh, the bitterness of the self-reproach that tortured her—the anguish of knowing that she could have prevented Lady Darrell's wrecking her whole life, yet had not done so! It was no wonder that she buried her face in her hands, weeping and praying as she had never wept and prayed in her life before.

"Elinor, look at me," said Captain Langton; "do I look like a thief and a would-be murderer?"

Out of Pauline's presence the handsome face had regained its usual careless, debonair expression.

She raised her eyes, and he saw in them the lingering doubt, the lingering fear.

"If all the world had turned against me," he said, "and had refused to believe in me, you, Elinor, my promised wife, ought to have had more faith."

She made no reply. There had been something in the energy of Pauline's manner that carried conviction with it; and the weak heart, the weak nature that had always relied upon others, could form no decision unaided.

"For argument sake, let us reverse the case. Say that some disappointed lover of yours came to tell to me that you had been discovered stealing; should I not have laughed? Why, Elinor, you must be blind not to see the truth; a child might discern it. The fact is that long ago I was foolish enough to believe myself in love with Miss Darrell; and she—well, honestly speaking, she is jealous. A gentleman does not like to refer to such things, but that is the simple truth. She is jealous, and would part us if she could; but she shall not. My beautiful Elinor is all my own, and no half-crazed, jealous girl shall come between us."

"Is it so, Aubrey?" asked Lady Darrell.

"My dearest Elinor, that is the whole secret of Miss Darrell's strange conduct to me. She is jealous—and you know, I should imagine, what jealous women are like."

She tried to believe him, but, when she recalled the noble face, with its pure light of truth and pity, she doubted again. But Captain Langton pleaded, prayed, invented such ridiculous stories of Pauline, made such fervent protestations of love, lavished such tender words upon her, that the weak heart turned to him again, and again its doubtings were cast aside.

"How we shall laugh over this in the happy after years!" he said. "It is really like a drama. Oh, Elinor, I am so thankful that I was here to save you! And now, my darling, you are trembling with cold. My fair, golden-haired Elinor, what must you think of that cruel girl? How could she do it? No; I will not go in again to-night—I should not be able to keep my temper. Your grand tragedy heroine will be gone to-morrow."

They stood together under the shadow of the balcony, and he drew her nearer to him.

"Elinor," he said, "I shall never rest again until you are my wife. This plot has failed; Miss Darrell will plot again to part us. I cannot wait until the spring—you must be my wife before then. To-morrow morning I shall ride over to talk to you about it."

She clasped her arms round his neck, and raised her sweet face to his.

"Aubrey," she said, wistfully, "you are not deceiving me?"

"No, my darling, I am not."

He bent down and kissed her lips. She looked at him again, pleadingly, wistfully.

"Heaven will judge between us, Aubrey," she said, solemnly. "I have a sure conviction that I shall know the truth."

"I hope Heaven will assist you," he returned, lightly; "I am quite sure the decision will be in my favor."

And those words, so wickedly, so blasphemously false, were the last he ever spoke to her.

CHAPTER XL
DYING IN SIN

Captain Langton left Lady Darrell at the door of the porch, and went round to the stables. He was a man as utterly devoid of principle as any man could well be, yet the untruths he had told, the false testimony he had given, the false oaths he had taken, had shaken his nerves.

"I should not care to go through such a scene as that again," he said — "to stand before two women as before my judges."

He found his hands unsteady and his limbs trembling; the horse he had to ride was a spirited one. The captain half staggered as he placed his hand on the saddle.

"I am not very well," he said to one of the grooms; "go to the house and tell Frampton, the butler, to bring some brandy here."

In a few minutes the butler appeared with a tray, on which stood bottle and glass.

"This is some very old brandy, sir," he said, "and very strong."

But Captain Langton did not appear to heed him; he poured out half a tumblerful and drank it, while the butler looked on in amazement.

"It is very strong, sir," he repeated.

"I know what I am doing," returned the captain, with an oath.

He was dizzy with fear and with his after-success; he shuddered again as he mounted his horse, and the memory of Pauline's face and Pauline's words came over him. Then he galloped off, and Frampton, turning to the groom, with a scared face, said:

"If he gets home safely after taking so much of that brandy, and with that horse, I will never venture to say what I think again."

Lady Darrell returned to the library, where she had left Pauline. They looked at each other in silence, and then Lady Darrell said:

"I—I believe in him, Pauline; he cannot be what you say."

Miss Darrell rose and went up to her; she placed her in a chair, and knelt at her feet.

"You do not believe what I have told you?" she questioned, gently.

"I cannot; my love and my faith are all his."

"I have done my best," said Pauline, sorrowfully, "and I can do no more. While I live I shall never forgive myself that I did not speak sooner, Lady Darrell. Elinor, I shall kneel here until you promise to forgive me."

Then Lady Darrell looked at the beautiful face, with its expression of humility.

"Pauline," she said, suddenly, "I hardly recognize you. What has come to you? What has changed you?"

Her face crimson with hot blushes, Pauline answered her.

"It is to me," she said, "as though a vail had fallen from before my eyes. I can see my sin in all its enormity. I can see to what my silence has led, and, though you may not believe me, I shall never rest until you say that you have forgiven me."

Lady Darrell was not a woman given to strong emotion of any kind; the deepest passion of her life was her love for Aubrey Langton; but even she could give some faint guess as to what it had cost the proud, willful Pauline to undergo this humiliation.

"I do forgive you," she said. "No matter how deeply you have disliked me, or in what way you have plotted against me, I cannot refuse you. I forgive you, Pauline."

Miss Darrell held up her face.

"Will you kiss me?" she asked. "I have never made that request in all my life before, but I make it now."

Lady Darrell bent down and kissed her, while the gloom of the evening fell round them and deepened into night.

"If I only knew what to believe!" Lady Darrell remarked. "First my heart turns to him, Pauline, and then it turns to you. Yet both cannot be right—one must be most wicked and most false. You have truth in your face—he had truth on his lips when he was talking to me. Oh, if I knew—if I only knew!"

And when she had repeated this many times, Pauline said to her:

"Leave it to Heaven; he has agreed that Heaven shall judge between us, and it will. Whoever has told the lie shall perish in it."

So some hours passed, and the change that had come over Lady Darrell was almost pitiful to see. Her fair face was all drawn and haggard, the brightness had all left it. It was as though years of most bitter sorrow had passed over her. They had spoken to her of taking some refreshment, but she had sent it away. She could do nothing but pace up and down with wearied step, moaning that she only wanted to know which was right, which to believe, while Pauline sat by her in unwearied patience. Suddenly Lady Darrell turned to her.

"What is the matter with me?" she asked. "I cannot understand myself; the air seems full of whispers and portents—it is as though I were here awaiting some great event. What am I waiting for?"

They were terrible words, for the answer to them was a great commotion in the hall—the sound of hurried footsteps—of many voices. Lady Darrell stood still in dismay.

"What is it?" she cried. "Oh, Pauline, I am full of fear—I am sorely full of fear!"

It was Frampton who opened the door suddenly, and stood before them with a white, scared face.

"Oh, my lady—my lady!" he gasped.

"Tell her quickly," cried Pauline; "do you not see that suspense is dangerous?"

"One of the Court servants," said the butler, at once, in response, "returning from Audleigh Royal, has found the body of Captain Langton lying in the high-road, where his horse had thrown him, dragged him, and left him—dead!"

"Heaven be merciful to him!" cried Pauline Darrell. "He has died in his sin."

But Lady Darrell spoke no words. Perhaps she thought to herself that Heaven had indeed judged between them. She said nothing—she trembled—a gasping cry came from her, and she fell face forward on the floor.

They raised her and carried her up stairs. Pauline never left her; through the long night-watches and the long days she kept her place by her side, while life and death fought fiercely for her. She would awake from her stupor at times, only to ask about Aubrey—if it could be true that he was dead—and then seemed thankful that she could understand no more.

They did not think at first that she could recover. Afterward Doctor Helmstone told her that she owed her life to Pauline Darrell's unchanging love and care.

CHAPTER XLI
THE WORK OF ATONEMENT

The little town of Audleigh Royal had never been so excited. It was such a terrible accident. Captain Langton, the guest of Sir Peter Glynn, so soon to be master of Darrell Court—a man so handsome, so accomplished, and so universal a favorite—to be killed in the gloom of an autumn night, on the high-road! Society was grieved and shocked.

"That beautiful young lady at the Hall, who loved him so dearly, was," people whispered to each other, "at death's door—so deep was her grief."

An inquest was held at the "Darrell Arms;" and all the revelations ever made as to the cause of Captain Langton's death were made then. The butler and the groom at Darrell Court swore to having felt some little alarm at seeing the deceased drink more than half a tumblerful of brandy. The butler's prophecy that he would never reach home in safety was repeated. One of the men said that the captain looked pale and scared, as though he had seen a ghost; another told how madly he had galloped away; so that no other conclusion could be come to but this—that he had ridden recklessly, lost all control over the horse, and had been thrown. There was proof that the animal had dragged him along the road for some little distance; and it was supposed the fatal wound had been inflicted when his head was dashed against the mile-stone close to which he had been found.

It was very shocking, very terrible. Society was distressed. The body lay at the "Darrell Arms" until all arrangements had been made for the funeral. Such a funeral had never been seen in Audleigh Royal. Rich and poor, every one attended.

Captain Langton was buried in the pretty little cemetery at Audleigh; and people, as they stood round the grave, whispered to each other that, although the horse that killed him had cost over a hundred pounds, Sir Peter Glynn had ordered it to be shot.

Then, when the autumn had faded into winter, the accident was forgotten. Something else happened which drove it from people's minds, and the tragedy of Audleigh Royal became a thing of the past.

Pauline did not return to Omberleigh. Miss Hastings was dreadfully shocked when she received a letter telling her of Captain Langton's death and of Lady Darrell's serious illness. No persuasions could induce her to remain longer away. She returned that same day to the Court, and insisted upon taking her share in the nursing of Lady Darrell.

Lady Hampton looked upon the captain's accident as the direct interposition of Providence. Of course such a death was very shocking, very terrible; but certainly it had never been a match she approved; and, after all, say what one would, everything had happened for the best.

Lady Hampton went over to Darrell Court, and assisted in attending to the invalid; but her thoughts ran more on Lord Aynsley, and the chances of his renewing his offer, than on anything else. Elinor would soon recover, there was no fear; the shock to her nerves had been great, but people never died of nervousness; and, when she did get well, Lady Hampton intended to propose a season in London.

But Lady Darrell did not get well as soon as Lady Hampton had anticipated. Indeed, more than one clever doctor, on leaving her presence, shook his head gravely, and said it was doubtful whether Lady Darrell would ever recover at all; the shock to her nerves had been terrible.

But there was something to be said also of a blighted life and a broken heart.

Autumn had drifted into winter; and one morning Lady Darrell, who had been sleeping more soundly than usual, suddenly turned to Pauline, who seldom left her.

"Pauline," she whispered, "you have not told any one, have you?"

"Told what?" she inquired.

"About poor Aubrey's faults:-I know now that he was guilty. Strange, solemn thoughts, strange revelations, come to us, are made to us in sickness, when we lie, where I have been lying, in the valley of the shadow of death. I know that he was guilty, and that he died in his sin. I know it now, Pauline."

Miss Darrell bent over her and kissed the white brow.

"Listen to me, dear," continued the weak voice. "Let this secret die with us—let there be a bond between us never to reveal it. You will never tell any one about it, will you, Pauline?"

"No," she replied, "never. I should never have told you but that I hoped to save you from a dreadful fate—and it would have been a dreadful fate for you to have married him; he would have broken your heart."

"It is broken now," she said, gently. "Yet it comforts me to know that no reproach will be heaped on Aubrey's memory."

"You will get better," observed Pauline, hopefully, "and then there will be happier days in store for you."

"There will be no happy days for me," returned Lady Darrell, sorrowfully. "You see, Pauline, I loved him very dearly—more dearly than I knew. I had never loved any one very much until I saw him. I could more easily have checked a raging fire than have restrained my love after I had once given it. My life had in some way passed into his, and now I do not care to live."

"But you have so much to live for," said Pauline.

"Not now. I do not care for aught about me. I have tried to remember Darrell Court and all my wealth and grandeur, but they give me no pleasure—the shadow of death lies over all."

And it was all in vain that Pauline tried to rouse her; Lady Darrell, after her unhappy love, never cared to be roused again. Lady Hampton would not think seriously of her illness—it would pass away in time, she said; but Miss Hastings shook her head gravely, and feared the worst.

The time came when Pauline told some part of her story to the governess. She did not mention Aubrey's crime—that secret she kept until death—but she gave a sketch of what had passed between her and Lady Darrell.

"Did I do right?" she asked, with that sweet humility which had vanquished all pride in her.

"You acted worthily," replied Miss Hastings, while she marveled at the transformation which love had wrought in that once proud, willful girl.

Time passed on, and by the wish of Miss Hastings a celebrated physician was sent for from London, for Lady Darrell grew no better. His opinion sounded somewhat like a death-warrant.

"She may recover sufficiently to quit her room and to linger on in life—how long is uncertain; but the shock to her nerves she will never fully recover from—while she lives she will be a victim to nervousness. But I do not think she will live long. Let her have as much cheerful society as possible, without fatigue; nothing more can be done for her."

And with that they were obliged to be content. Lady Hampton would not admit that the London physician was correct.

"Nerves are all nonsense," she said, brusquely. "How many nervous shocks have I been through, with husband dead and children dead? Elinor's only danger is her mother's complaint. She died of consumption quite young."

It was found, however, despite Lady Hampton's disbelief, that the London physician had spoken truthfully. Lady Darrell rose from her sick bed, but she was but the shadow of herself, and a victim to a terrible nervous disorder.

Miss Hastings watched over her with great anxiety, but Pauline was like a second self to the unhappy lady. They were speaking of her one day, and Miss Hastings said:

"An illness like Lady Darrell's is so uncertain, Pauline; you must not occupy yourself with her so entirely, or you will lose your own health."

But Pauline looked up with a smile—perhaps the gravest, the sweetest and most tender her face had ever worn.

"I shall never leave her," she returned.

"Never leave her?" questioned Miss Hastings.

"No. I shall stay with her to comfort her while life lasts, and that will be my atonement."

CHAPTER XLII
LOVE AND SORROW

The beautiful golden summer came round, and Darrell Court looked picturesque and lovely with its richness of foliage and flush of flowers. The great magnolia trees were all in bloom—the air was full of their delicate, subtle perfume; the chestnuts were in bloom, the limes all in blossom. Sweet summer had scattered her treasures with no niggard hand; and Lady Darrell had lived to see the earth rejoice once more.

Under the limes, where the shadows of the graceful, tremulous, scented leaves fell on the grass—the limes that were never still, but always responding to some half-hidden whisper of the wind—stood Pauline Darrell and her lover, Sir Vane St. Lawrence. They had met but once since their hurried parting at Omberleigh. Vane had been to Darrell Court—for their engagement was no secret now. They wrote to each other constantly.

On this fair June day Sir Vane had come to the Court with news that stirred the depths of the girl's heart as a fierce wind stirs the ripples on a lake.

As the sunlight fell through the green leaves and rested on her, the change in her was wonderful to see. The beautiful, noble face had lost all its pride, all its defiance; the play of the lips was tremulous, sensitive, and gentle; the light in the dark eyes was of love and kindness. Time had added to her loveliness; the grand, statuesque figure had developed more perfectly; the graceful attitudes, the unconscious harmony, the indefinable grace and fascination were more apparent than ever. But she no longer carried her grand beauty as a protest, but made it rather the crown of a pure and perfect womanhood.

Something dimmed the brightness of her face, for Sir Vane had come to her with strange news and a strange prayer. His arm was clasped round her as they walked under the shadow of the limes where lovers' footsteps had so often strayed.

"Yes, Pauline, it has come so unexpectedly at last," spoke Sir Vane. "Ever since Graveton has been in office, my dear mother has been unwearied in asking for an appointment for me. You know the story of our impoverished fortunes, and how anxious my dear mother is to retrieve them."

Her hand seemed to tighten its clasp on his, as she answered:

"Yes, I know."

"Now an opportunity has come. Graveton, in answer to my mother's continued requests, has found for me a most lucrative office; but, alas, my love, it is in India, and I must shortly set out."

"In India!" repeated Pauline; "and you must set out shortly, Vane? How soon?"

"In a fortnight from now," he answered. "It is an office that requires filling up at once, Pauline. I have come to ask if you will accompany me? Will you pardon the short notice, and let me take my wife with me to that far-off land? Do not let me go alone into exile—come with me, darling."

The color and light died out of her beautiful face, her lips quivered, and her eyes grew dim as with unshed tears.

"I cannot," she replied; and there was a silence between them that seemed full of pain.

"You cannot, Pauline!" he cried, and the sadness and disappointment in his voice made her lips quiver again. "Surely you will not allow any feminine nonsense about dress and preparations, any scruple about the shortness of time, to come between us? My mother bade me say that if you will consent she will busy herself night and day to help us to prepare. She bade me add her prayer to mine. Oh, Pauline, why do you say you cannot accompany me?"

The first shock had passed for her, and she raised her noble face to his.

"From no nonsense, Vane," she said. "You should know me better, dear, than that. Nothing can part us but one thing. Were it not for that, I would go with you to the very end of the world—I would work for you and with you."

"But what is it, Pauline?" he asked. "What is it, my darling?"

She clung to him more closely still.

"I cannot leave her, Vane—I cannot leave Lady Darrell. She is dying slowly—hour by hour, day by day—and I cannot leave her."

"But, my darling Pauline, there are others beside you to attend to the lady—Lady Hampton and Miss Hastings. Why should you give up your life thus?"

"Why?" she repeated. "You know why, Vane. It is the only atonement I can offer her. Heaven knows how gladly, how happily, I would this moment place my hand in yours and accompany you; my heart longs to do so. You are all I have in the world, and how I love you you know, Vane. But it seems to me that I owe Lady Darrell this reparation, and at the price of my whole life's happiness I must make it."

He drew her nearer to him, and kissed the trembling lips.

"She has suffered so much, Vane, through me—all through me. If I had but foregone my cruel vengeance, and when she came to me with doubt in her heart if I had but spoken one word, the chances are that by this time she would have been Lady Aynsley, and I should have been free to accompany you, my beloved; but I must suffer for my sin. I ought to suffer, and I ought to atone to her."

"Your life, my darling," he said, "your beautiful bright life, your love, your happiness, will all be sacrificed."

"They must be. You see, Vane, she clings to me in her sorrow. His name—Aubrey Langton's name—never passes her lips to any one else but me. She talks of him the night and the day through—it is the only comfort she has; and then she likes me to be with her, to talk to her, and soothe her, and she tires so soon of any one else. I cannot leave her, Vane—it would shorten her life, I am sure."

He made no answer. She looked up at him with tearful eyes.

"Speak to me, Vane. It is hard, I know—but tell me that I am right."

"You are cruelly right," he replied. "Oh, my darling, it is very hard! Yet you make her a noble atonement for the wrong you have done—a noble reparation. My darling, is this how your vow of vengeance has ended—in the greatest sacrifice a woman could make."

"Your love has saved me," she said, gently—"has shown me what is right and what is wrong—has cleared the mist from my eyes. But for that— oh, Vane, I hate to think what I should have been!"

"I wish it were possible to give up the appointment," he remarked, musingly.

"I would not have you do it, Vane. Think of Lady St. Lawrence—how she has worked for it. Remember, it is your only chance of ever being what she wishes to see you. You must not give it up."

"But how can I leave you, Pauline?"

"If you remain in England, it will make but little difference," she said. "I can never leave Lady Darrell while she lives."

"But, Pauline, it may be four, five, or six years before I return, and all that time I shall never see you."

She wrung her hands, but no murmur passed her lips, save that it was her fault—all her fault—the price of her sin.

"Vane," she said, "you must not tell Lady Darrell what you came to ask me. She must know that you are here only to say good-by. I would rather keep her in ignorance; she will be the happier for not knowing."

Was ever anything seen like that love and that sorrow—the love of two noble souls, two noble hearts, and the sorrow that parting more bitter than death brought upon them? Even Miss Hastings did not know until long after Sir Vane was gone of the sacrifice Pauline had made in the brave endeavor to atone for her sin.

She never forgot the agony of that parting—how Sir Vane stood before them, pale, worn, and sad, impressing one thing on them all—care for his darling. Even to Lady Darrell, the frail, delicate invalid, whose feeble stock of strength seemed to be derived from Pauline, he gave many charges.

"It will be so long before I see her again," he said; "but you will keep her safely for me."

"I almost wonder," said Lady Darrell, "why you do not ask Pauline to accompany you, Sir Vane. For my own sake, I am most selfishly glad that you have not done so—I should soon die without her."

They looked at each other, the two who were giving up so much for her, but spoke no word.

Sir Vane was obliged to return to London that same day. He spoke of seeing Pauline again, but she objected—it would only be a renewal of most bitter and hopeless sorrow. So they bade each other farewell under the lime trees. The bitter yet sweet memory of it lasted them for life.

Miss Hastings understood somewhat of the pain it would cause, but with her gentle consideration, she thought it best to leave Pauline for a time. Hours afterward she went in search of her, and found her under the limes, weeping and moaning for the atonement she had made for her sin.

CHAPTER XLIII
LADY DARRELL'S WILL

Two years passed away, and Sir Vane St. Lawrence's circumstances were rapidly improving; his letters were constant and cheerful—he spoke always of the time when he should come home and claim Pauline for his wife. She only sighed as she read the hopeful words, for she had resolved that duty should be her watchword while Lady Darrell lived—even should that frail, feeble life last for fifty years, she would never leave her.

There came to her chill doubts and fears, dim, vague forebodings that she should never see Vane again—that their last parting was for ever; not that she doubted him, but that it seemed hopeless to think he would wait until her hair was gray, and the light of her youth had left her.

Never mind—she had done her duty; she had sinned, but she had made the noblest atonement possible for her sin.

Two years had passed, and the summer was drawing to a close. To those who loved and tended her it seemed that Lady Darrell's life was closing with it. Even Lady Hampton had ceased to speak hopefully, and Darrell Court was gloomy with the shadow of the angel of death.

There came an evening when earth was very lovely—when the gold of the setting sun, the breath of the western wind, the fragrance of the flowers, the ripple of the fountains, the song of the birds, were all beautiful beyond words to tell; and Lady Darrell, who had lain watching the smiling summer heavens, said:

"I should like once more to see the sun set, Pauline. I should like to sit at the window, and watch the moon rise."

"So you shall," responded Pauline. "You are a fairy queen. You have but to wish, and the wish is granted."

Lady Darrell smiled—no one ever made her smile except Pauline; but the fulfillment of the wish was not so easy after all. Lady Hampton's foreboding was realized. Lady Darrell might have recovered from her long, serious illness but that her mother's complaint, the deadly inheritance of consumption, had seized upon her, and was gradually destroying her.

It was no easy matter now to dress the wasted figure; but Pauline seemed to have the strength, the energy of twenty nurses. She was always willing, always cheerful, always ready; night and day seemed alike to her; she would look at her hands, and say:

"Oh! Elinor, I wish I could give you one-half my strength—one-half my life!"

"Do you? Pauline, if you could give me half your life, would you do so?"

"As willingly as I am now speaking to you," she would answer.

They dressed the poor lady, whose delicate beauty had faded like some summer flower. She sat at the window in a soft nest of cushions which Pauline had prepared for her, her wasted hands folded, her worn face brightened with the summer sunshine. She was very silent and thoughtful for some time, and then Pauline, fearing that she was dull, knelt in the fashion that was usual to her at Lady Darrell's feet, and held the wasted hands in hers.

"What are you thinking about, Elinor?" Pauline asked. "Something as bright as the sunshine?"

Lady Darrell smiled.

"I was just fancying to myself that every blossom of that white magnolia seemed like a finger beckoning me away," she said; "and I was thinking also how full of mistakes life is, and how plainly they can be seen when we come to die."

Pauline kissed the thin fingers. Lady Darrell went on.

"I can see my own great mistake, Pauline. I should not have married Sir Oswald. I had no love for him—not the least in the world; I married him only for position and fortune. I should have taken your warning, and not have come between your uncle and you. His resentment would have died away, for I am quite sure that in his heart he loved you; he would have forgiven you, and I should have had a happier, longer life. That was my mistake—my one great mistake. Another was that I had a certain kind of doubt about poor Aubrey. I cannot explain it; but I know that I doubted him even when I loved him, and I should have waited some time before placing the whole happiness of my life in his hands. Yet it seems hard to pay for those mistakes with my life, does it not?"

And Pauline, to whom all sweet and womanly tenderness seemed to come by instinct, soothed Lady Darrell with loving words until she smiled again.

"Pauline," she said, suddenly, "I wish to communicate something to you. I wish to tell you that I have made my will, and have left Darrell Court to you, together with all the fortune Sir Oswald left me. I took your inheritance from you once, dear; now I restore it to you. I have left my aunt, Lady Hampton, a thousand a year; you will not mind that—it comes back to you at her death."

"I do not deserve your kindness," said Pauline, gravely.

"Yes, you do; and you will do better with your uncle's wealth than I have done. I have only been dead in life. My heart was broken—and I have had no strength, no energy. I have done literally nothing; but you will act differently, Pauline—you are a true Darrell, and you will keep up the true traditions of your race. In my poor, feeble hands they have all fallen through. If Sir Vane returns, you will marry him; and, oh! my darling, I wish you a happy life. As for me, I shall never see the sun set again."

The feeble voice died away in a tempest of tears; and Pauline, frightened, made haste to speak of something else to change the current of her thoughts.

But Lady Darrell was right. She never saw the sun set or the moon rise again—the frail life ended gently as a child falls asleep. She died the next day, when the sun was shining its brightest at noon; and her death was so calm that they thought it sleep.

She was buried, not in the Darrell vault, but, by Pauline's desire, in the pretty cemetery at Audleigh Royal. Her death proved no shock, for every one had expected it. Universal sympathy and kindness followed her to her grave. The short life was ended, and its annals were written in sand.

Lady Hampton had given way; her old dislike of Pauline had changed into deep admiration of her sweet, womanly virtues, her graceful humility.

"If any one had ever told me," she said, "that Pauline Darrell would have turned out as she has, I could not have believed it. The way in which she devoted herself to my niece was wonderful. I can only say that in my opinion she deserves Darrell Court."

The legacy made Lady Hampton very happy; it increased her income so handsomely that she resolved to live no longer at the Elms, but to return to London, where the happiest part of her life had been spent.

"I shall come to Darrell Court occasionally," she said, "so that you may not quite forget me;" and Pauline was surprised to find that she felt nothing save regret at parting with one whom she had disliked with all the injustice of youth.

A few months afterward came a still greater surprise. The lover from whom Miss Hastings had been parted in her early youth—who had left England for Russia long years ago, and whom she had believed dead—returned to England, and never rested until he had found his lost love.

In vain the gentle, kind-hearted lady protested that she was too old to marry—that she had given up all thoughts of love. Mr. Bereton would not hear of it, and Pauline added her entreaties to his.

"But I cannot leave you, my dear," said Miss Hastings. "You cannot live all by yourself."

"I shall most probably have to spend my life alone," she replied, "and I will not have your happiness sacrificed to mine."

Between her lover and her pupil Miss Hastings found all resistance hopeless. Pauline took a positive delight and pleasure in the preparations for the marriage, and, in spite of all that Miss Hastings could say to the contrary, she insisted upon settling a very handsome income upon her.

There was a tone of sadness in all that Pauline said with reference to her future which struck Miss Hastings with wonder.

"You never speak of your own marriage," she said, "or your own future—why is it, Pauline?"

The beautiful face was overshadowed for a moment, and then she replied:

"It is because I have no hope. I had a presentiment when Vane went away, that I should not see him again. There are some strange thoughts always haunting me. If I reap as I have sowed, what then?"

"My dear child, no one could do more than you have done. You repented of your fault, and atoned for it in the best way you were able."

But the lovely face only grew more sad.

"I was so willful, so proud, so scornful. I did not deserve a happy life. I am trying to forget all the romance and the love, all the poetry of my youth, and to live only for my duty."

"But Sir Vane will come back," said Miss Hastings.

"I do not know—all hope seemed to die in my heart when he went away. But let us talk of you and your future without reference to mine."

Miss Hastings was married, and after she had gone away Pauline Darrell was left alone with her inheritance at last.

CHAPTER XLIV
SHADOW OF ABSENT LOVE

Six years had passed since the marriage of the governess left Miss Darrell alone. She heard as constantly as ever from Sir Vane; he had made money rapidly. It was no longer the desire to make a fortune which kept him away, but the fact that in the part of the country where he was great danger existed, and that, having been placed there in a situation of trust, he could not well leave it; so of late a hopeless tone had crept into his letters. He made no reference to coming home; and Pauline, so quick, so sensitive, saw in this reticence the shadow of her own presentiment.

Six years had changed Pauline Darrell from a beautiful girl to a magnificent woman; her beauty was of that grand and queenly kind that of itself is a noble dowry. The years had but added to it. They had given a more statuesque grace to the perfect figure; they had added tenderness, thought, and spirituality to the face; they had given to her beauty a charm that it had never worn in her younger days.

Miss Darrell, of Darrell Court, had made for herself a wonderful reputation. There was no estate in England so well managed as hers. From one end to the other the Darrell domain was, people said, a garden. Pauline had done away with the old cottages and ill-drained farm-houses, and in their stead pretty and commodious buildings had been erected. She had fought a long and fierce battle with ignorance and prejudice, and she had won.

She had established schools where children were taught, first to be good Christians, and then good citizens, and where useful knowledge was made much of. She had erected almshouses for the poor, and a church where rich and poor, old and young, could worship God together. The people about her rose up and called her blessed; tenants, dependents, servants, all had but one word for her, and that was of highest praise. To do good seemed the object of her life, and she had succeeded so far.

No young queen was ever more popular or more beloved than this lady with her sweet, grave smile, her tender, womanly ways, her unconscious grandeur of life. She made no stir, no demonstration, though she was the head of a grand old race, the representative of an old honored family, the holder of a great inheritance; she simply did her duty as nobly as she knew how to do it. There was no thought of self left in her, her whole energies were directed for the good of others. If Sir Oswald could have known how the home he loved was cared for, he would have been proud of his successor. The hall itself, the park, the grounds, were all in perfect order. People wondered how it was all arranged by this lady, who never seemed hurried nor talked of the work she did.

Pauline occupied herself incessantly, for the bright hopes of girlhood, she felt, were hers no longer; she had admitted that the romance, the passion, the poetry of her youth were unforgotten, but she tried to think them dead. People wondered at her gravity. She had many admirers, but she never showed the least partiality for any of them. There seemed to be some shadow over her, and only those who knew her story knew what it was—that it was the shadow of her absent love.

She was standing one day in the library alone, the same library where so much of what had been eventful in her life had happened. The morning had been a busy one; tenants, agents, business people of all kinds had been there, and Pauline felt tired.

Darrell Court, the grand inheritance she had loved and in some measure longed for, was hers; she was richer than she had ever dreamed of being, and, as she looked round on the treasures collected in the library, she thought to herself with a sigh, "Of what avail are they, save to make others happy?" She would have given them all to be by Vane's side, no matter how great their poverty, no matter what they had to undergo together; but now it seemed that this bright young love of hers was to wither away, to be heard of no more.

So from the beautiful lips came a deep sigh; she was tired, wearied with the work and incessant care that the management of her estates entailed. She did not own it even to herself, but she longed for the presence of the only being whom she loved.

She was bending over some beautiful japonicas—for, no matter how depressed she might be, she always found solace in flowers—when she heard the sound of a horse's rapid trot.

"Farmer Bowman back again," she said to herself, with a smile; "but I must not give way to him."

She was so certain that it was her tiresome tenant that she did not even turn her head when the door opened and some one entered the room— some one who did not speak, but who went up to her with a beating heart, laid one hand on her bowed head, and said:

"Pauline, my darling, you have no word of welcome for me?"

It was Vane. With a glad cry of welcome—a cry such as a lost child gives when it reaches its mother's arms—the cry of a long-cherished, trusting love—she turned and was clasped in his arms, her haven of rest, her safe refuge, her earthly paradise, attained at last.

"At last!" she murmured.

But he spoke no word to her. His eyes were noting her increased beauty. He kissed the sweet lips, the lovely face.

"My darling," he said, "I left you a beautiful girl, but I find you a woman beautiful beyond all comparison. It has seemed to me an age since I left you, and now I am never to go away again. Pauline, you will be kind to me for the sake of my long, true, deep love? You will be my wife as soon as I can make arrangements—will you not?"

There was no coquetry, no affectation about her; the light deepened on her noble face, her lips quivered, and then she told him:

"Yes, whenever you wish."

They conversed that evening until the sun had set. He told her all his experience since he had left her, and she found that he had passed through London without even waiting to see Lady St. Lawrence, so great had been his longing to see her.

But the next day Lady St. Lawrence came down, and by Sir Vane's wish preparations for the marriage were begun at once. Pauline preferred to be married at Audleigh Royal and among her own people.

They tell now of that glorious wedding—of the sun that seemed to shine more brightly than it had ever shone before—of the rejoicings and festivities such as might have attended the bridal of an empress—of the tears and blessings of the poor—of the good wishes that would have made earth Heaven had they been realized. There never was such a wedding before.

Every other topic failed before the one that seemed inexhaustible—the wonderful beauty of the bride. She was worthy of the crown of orange-blossoms, and she wore them with a grace all her own. Then, after the wedding, Sir Vane and Pauline went to Omberleigh. That was the latter's fancy, and, standing that evening where she had seen Vane first, she blessed him and thanked him with grateful tears that he had redeemed her by his great love.

There was a paragraph in a recent issue of the *Times* announcing that Oswald St. Lawrence, second son of Sir Vane and Lady St. Lawrence, had, by letters-patent, assumed the name of Darrell. So that the old baronet's prayer is granted, and the race of Darrell—honored and respected, beloved and esteemed—is not to be without a representative.